The past was a constant threat . . .

Camille kept sneaking furtive looks into the audience. Instinct told her she wasn't imagining things. Something was definitely wrong.

Had the crime finally been traced to her after all this time? She wondered if she could be extradited to France.

"Who would like to find a little extra money in his or her pocket?" she asked, forcing herself to continue with her magic act.

There was a chorused "Me!" in response.

"Then getting a volunteer for my next . . ." Her voice faded as a man walked up onto the stage.

Justin St. Cyr! It had been years since Camille had seen him, but she recognized the master magician immediately.

What the hell was Justin doing here? How had he found her? Could he possibly know . . .?

ABOUT THE AUTHOR

Patricia Rosemoor began creating romantic
fantasies while in grade school, never
guessing she would someday share her stories
with more than her best friends. A native
Chicagoan, she supervises the television
production facility of a suburban community
college. Patricia finds time to write because
her husband helps with the research, her four
cats assist with the computer work and her
dog against unwanted interruptions. She also
writes with a partner as Lynn Patrick.

Books by Patricia Rosemoor

HARLEQUIN INTRIGUE
38–DOUBLE IMAGES

These books may be available at your local bookseller.

Don't miss any of our special offers. Write to us at the
following address for information on our newest releases.

Harlequin Reader Service
901 Fuhrmann Blvd., P.O. Box 1397, Buffalo, NY 14240
Canadian address: P.O. Box 603,
Fort Erie, Ont. L2A 5X3

DANGEROUS ILLUSIONS
PATRICIA ROSEMOOR

Harlequin Books

TORONTO • NEW YORK • LONDON
AMSTERDAM • PARIS • SYDNEY • HAMBURG
STOCKHOLM • ATHENS • TOKYO • MILAN

I'd like to express my gratitude
to Roy Dubé for his macabre inspiration;
to members of the Chicago North Chapter
of Romance Writers of America
for their prophetic support;
and to Linda Sweeney
for her spellbinding patience.

Harlequin Intrigue edition published December 1986

ISBN 0-373-22055-3

Prologue

It was a silent midnight, eerily forbidding. A conjurer's moon shone over the small college town, silvering a creeping fog that rose from the damp ground. Translucent fingers of mist curled and twisted along the deserted streets, greedily devouring all that stood before them.

A good cover—not that he'd be seen or heard if he didn't want to be.

Standing under a gnarled and ancient tree, Justin St. Cyr took a Gauloises from his monogrammed gold cigarette case. At the snap of his fingers, a flame flared. A simple trick, but a satisfying one. He lit the French cigarette and inhaled deeply.

Then he aimed his cool gray-blue gaze at the decrepit steamboat-gothic house. Though he could no longer make it out, covered as it was by the fog, he knew the exact placement of the rusty metal sign declaring rooms for rent. What he could still see of the house was dark in silhouette except for a single faint glow emanating from its peak.

A human form passed briefly between the light source and the attic window. An upraised arm brushed long hair, sending burnished strands flying.

Closer, so I can see you.

But the feminine form moved on to some other task, an
Justin dragged on his Gauloises, taking a perverse pleasur
from the harsh cigarette smoke filling his throat.

It had taken him long enough to find her.

Camille Bayard.

The name echoed through his mind, bringing with i
memories and a wry satisfaction mixed with regret. But de
termined to ignore what he owed Max, Justin steeled him
self against the memory of a debt nearly two decades old
He could allow himself no guilt. And he must forget what
he'd once felt for her. He was prepared to do whatever was
necessary.

It wouldn't be very difficult, not if she'd come to this—
working small towns and renting cheap attic rooms in seedy
boardinghouses. She'd hidden herself well. He'd been
looking for her for nearly six months.

He focused his attention on the attic window just as she
appeared behind it and pressed her palms flat against the
glass. Justin crushed the orange glow of his cigarette against
the tree. She stared out into the night as if she were aware of
him watching her, but he knew she'd never spot him.
Though she was three stories above and it was impossible to
see her expression, Justin sensed her unease. He knew that
her straight brows would be flattened over cautious green
eyes, her full mouth pulled down into a frown.

Staring hard, he realized that little covered her tempting
woman's body. A light from behind, perhaps from her
nightstand, made the thin nightgown transparent, revealing the feminine shape beneath. Her body was long and
lean, yet elegantly voluptuous.

At the same time as the greedy fog swallowed her image,
Justin made a frustrating discovery that both angered him

and filled him with unease. In spite of everything he knew—
and of the way he planned to use her—he wanted Camille
Bayard in a very elemental way.

Chapter One

Justin St. Cyr slipped through the doors of the small university theater. The lights dimmed and went dark, yet the raucous din of youthful voices hardly diminished. Homing in on an unoccupied seat on the aisle a few rows ahead, Justin slipped into it.

Music, low and pulsing, backed an omniscient voice that invoked absolute silence from the audience.

"Magic!" The whispered word echoed through the darkness. "The art of legerdemain!" Stronger now, the voice wove its way through Justin's defenses. "Enter the world of illusion." It was her voice, processed and amplified. He shifted in his seat. "Prepare to be perplexed...confused...and amused." The last word ended on a sultry, lingering laugh that crawled right up his spine.

A drumroll and then a male voice: "The Krannert Center for the Performing Arts is proud to present—Clever Cammi!"

A spattering of applause escalated enthusiastically when a small flashpot went off in an explosion of light and smoke. Then the stage lights came up. But instead of the expected magician in front of the black curtain, the audience was staring at a sleek black cat in a sequined cape, serenely licking a paw.

"No, no, no!" The indignant voice was followed by a omanly body in a loose, spangled black tuxedo. Laughter)ined the applause. "When are you going to get it right, elvet? *I* go on first."

Apparently unconcerned, the cat continued to groom erself.

"Come on, now. Don't embarrass me," Camille said in loud stage whisper, waving her hands awkwardly. "Back o your cage. Shoo!"

"Use your magic!" came a shout from the audience.

"Make her disappear!"

"You want me to make her vanish?" Camille looked loubtfully from the audience to Velvet. "She's so stubborn suppose it's the only way." Digging into one of her volu- ninous pockets, she drew out a black silk scarf, shook it, :urned it both ways so that the audience could see it, then held it in front of her furry partner, making it into a cur- :ain. "This won't hurt a bit, Velvet." Dropping into a stage whisper again, she told the cat, "Fancy Feast for your late- night snack. I promise."

The audience tittered.

Watching her go through the necessary hocus-pocus mo- tions of her routine with the scarf, Justin couldn't equate what he'd recently learned about Camille Bayard with this slightly awkward woman in the over-large tuxedo, auburn hair pulled to the side in a wild new wave style. But he had to remember that as a magician, Clever Cammi was first and foremost a practiced actress.

The scarf once more held in position in front of the cat, Camille proudly announced, "Ta-da!" and pulled it away.

A stuffed replica of the black cat lay on the stage.

Camille widened her green eyes. "Oh, Velvet, I'm so-o sorry! What did I do wrong?" She picked up the plush cat and headed for the wings, where a young man was waiting

to take it from her. "Will you ever forgive me? I'll make
up to you, I promise."

Justin couldn't help smiling. Same old Cammi, sar
charming style of presentation. Always underplaying, u
ing humor, touching the hearts of her audience. Shifti
impatiently, he told himself not to be a fool. He couldn
afford to remember the way she'd touched his heart once

He had to think of Genevieve.

Pushing the sleeves of her jacket to her elbows as she r
turned to center stage, Camille Bayard searched the dark
ened audience. She knew she couldn't see past the first fe
rows, but there it was again—the feeling of being watche
for more than her performance. The night before, she'
stared out into the fog like a fool. Was her imagination f
nally getting to her after six months of isolation fror
everything and everyone she'd ever known? Or were gui
and fear preying on her as they had time and time again?

"Magic is an old art," she told her audience, "dating a
far back as the Egyptians. One ancient entertainer cut of
and restored the heads of a goose and a pelican withou
doing any harm to either bird." Camille paused signifi
cantly, wrinkled her forehead and shook her head sadly. "
tried that with Velvet's mother, poor thing." Hearing
muffled groan, she added, "Maybe I should stick to inani
mate objects."

The audience laughed, exactly as she'd hoped they would
From another of her roomy pockets Cammi produced tw
thin ropes. Then she searched inside her jacket. "You car
never find a magic wand when you need one," she mum
bled.

"Over here!" came a loud whisper from the side of the
stage.

Camille caught the silver stick the stagehand threw to her,
then draped both ropes over it. "Using double ropes in

magic is another centuries-old favorite." She kept up the patter, distracting the audience while she tied a careful knot that would allow the ropes to be pulled apart easily. "I need two volunteers wearing bracelets, watches or rings."

Even in the midst of the simple trick with two eager college students to hold her attention, Camille kept sneaking furtive looks into the audience. Instinct told her she wasn't imagining things. The prickling short hairs on the back of her neck confirmed it. Had the crime finally been traced to her after all this time? Perhaps Richard had been caught, and that was why she hadn't been able to locate him. Wondering if she could be extradited and sent back to France, Camille tied a knot over the watches that the volunteers had placed in the center of her joined ropes.

She gave each student an end, mumbled some mysterious words and said, "Pull." The volunteers pulled, and the two ropes separated, spilling the watches into her hands. "I like this part of the show best," Camille confided to the audience. "I haven't had to buy a new watch in years!"

Then, generously handing the items back to the students, she did some more of the close-up magic that had always been her specialty. Even when she was a child, her fingers had been so nimble that Max had often worried aloud that she might decide to become a pickpocket. But Camille had always assured her father that she'd grow up to be a famous magician just like him, The Magnificent Maxwell.

Yet this was a far cry from the kind of performance either of them was used to giving. She'd modified her act for simplicity's sake ever since she began traveling alone. She could only hope that the few secrets she had to share with a new assistant at each stop would never be revealed to the audience. The cups-and-dice routine went off without a hitch, as did her card tricks.

But when she came to her favorite close-up props, th coins, Camille hesitated, her pulse accelerating as if it wer warning her to change her routine. What was wrong with her? She forced herself to continue.

"Who would like to find a little extra money in his or he pocket?"

There was a chorused "Me!" in response.

"Then getting a volunteer for my next . . ."

Her voice faded as a man walked down the aisle and straight up onto the stage. Justin St. Cyr! Though it had been years since she'd seen him, she recognized the master magician immediately. Adrenaline rushed through Camille, making her heart pound in fear. What the hell was Justin doing here? How had he found her? Could he possibly know?

"Your volunteer, Clever Cammi," Justin said, bowing from the waist.

Camille forced a smile to her lips and turned toward the audience. "He's so eager, he must be more needy than he looks."

And he looked fabulous, every bit as tall, dark and handsome as when she'd thought herself in love with him half a lifetime ago. Happiness added to apprehension, making her heart pound more strongly.

"I'm ready when you are."

"First I have to find an appropriate container." She patted her pockets and slipped a hand inside her jacket, all the while setting up the mechanism and palming the first coin. Finally she pulled out a flat round disk and snapped it open. "A top hat." She showed it to the audience, turning it upside down and shaking it. "Empty. Empty. Empty."

"If you fill that entire hat, I could afford to take you to dinner tonight," Justin said.

Trying to fight the tension she felt at his presence, Camille improvised. "I don't think it'll take that much money. I eat like a rabbit." Then, wiggling her straight brows at a sober-faced student in the first row, she explained, "Magician—rabbit. Get it?"

The kid barely smiled until Justin told him, "She'd be a cheap date. I could take her out to the produce section of the local supermarket."

In response, Camille crossed her arms and tapped a foot in a show of annoyance. "Just remember this is *my* show, mister. *I* get the last laugh."

Though his mustache twitched, Justin seemed to take the hint that he should behave himself. Proceeding with the act, Camille plucked a coin from the dark hair slicked back from his face. She dropped it into the hat. While pretending to find more coins at various points on his tall muscular body, she grew aware of his pale gray-blue eyes, which could easily hypnotize her into forgetting what she was doing.

Or into forgetting to wonder why he'd taken the trouble to find her, she realized. Suddenly the most awful thought occurred to her. Afraid something had happened to her father, she tensed with her hand still inside Justin's trouser pocket. Startled eyes opened wide, Camille mouthed the word "Max!" At the tiny shake of Justin's head, she took a deep breath and relaxed, quickly withdrawing her invading hand. Justin seemed as relieved as she.

But if nothing was wrong with her father, why was Justin here?

Refusing to be distracted by whys and whats any further, Camille decided to save her questions for later and concentrate on her performance. Whatever would happen would happen. She had neither the power to stop the past from catching up with her nor the magic that would let her go back in time and change what she'd done in Paris.

"This is going kind of slow," Camille said, jiggling the top hat so that the audience could hear the jingle of coins. "Maybe I'd better figure out a way to collect that money faster. I know! A doubling spell!"

Hoping that he didn't notice the slight tremor of her hand, Camille reached deep into one of Justin's jacket pockets and pretended to find a silk scarf, which she used to cover the top hat. Retrieving her magic wand, she tapped the hat a few times while uttering some mumbo jumbo. Then she pulled the scarf away with a grand flourish and smugly looked out over the audience.

"Your money's been doubled, right? Show them."

"I can't. Sorry."

"What do you mean?" she asked crossly, taking the hat from Justin as though she had to see for herself. "Huh?" Eyes widely innocent, she turned the hat to show the audience its interior. "Empty. Some days absolutely nothing goes right."

THE REST OF THE PERFORMANCE had progressed just as smoothly. It had ended with Camille's transposing the stuffed cat from one cage to another. Of course, when she had uncovered the second cage again, the warm-blooded Velvet was revealed there, alive and well and properly indignant.

The audience had cheered them both.

Now, with the real feline tucked under her arm, Camille headed for her dressing room, a mixture of eagerness and dread alternately quickening and slowing her pace.

Justin St. Cyr.

The man who'd followed in her father's footsteps. Who'd begun his apprenticeship with The Magnificent Maxwell in Paris while Camille had been in California in her divorced mother's custody. Who'd been the object of her adoration

or the eleven months and nine days that he and she and
Max had worked together. Justin, the measure against
whom she'd judged every other man until she'd met Richard. The same Justin who'd gone on to international fame,
known simply as St. Cyr, and who'd become the heart-
throb of women around the world before he'd suddenly
given it all up a few months ago.

Justin St. Cyr here, in a town surrounded by cornfields.
Why?

Before she'd even opened her dressing room door, Camille knew he was waiting inside. No sense in postponing the
inevitable. She turned the handle and bustled through the
doorway, setting Velvet down on the counter amid the mess
of stage makeup and hair ornaments.

"Hello, Justin." Camille met his eyes via the mirror as the
door swung shut, revealing him seated in an upholstered
chair behind her. "Or are you nothing more than an elaborate illusion?"

Justin smiled at her attempt at humor, but there was an
edge to his voice that worried her. "I assure you, Clever
Cammi, that I am no illusion."

Lowering herself to the stool in front of the makeup mirror, she loosened her frizzed-out hair, throwing pins down
onto the counter. Velvet pounced on one and amused herself by whacking the bobby pin around between her paws.

"Justin, it *is* good to see you after all these years." Distractedly Camille picked up a brush. "But . . . why are you
here?"

"To transpose you away from this humdrum little town."

The words sounded innocent enough, but somehow the
smile that played across his lips seemed false.

With her brush poised in the air, she tightened her grip on
it. "And where will I reappear?"

"New York. I'm opening a new club called Illusions nex month. It'll offer dinner, disco and magic to the late nigh crowd."

New York, not Paris. She shouldn't have been so foolis as to suspect Justin. Undoubtedly he didn't even kno about Edouard Roget. And even if he did, his loyalty woul be to Max—and therefore to her—wouldn't it?

Camille hoped the relief in her voice wasn't too evident t Justin as she said, "So you want me to perform for you.' She began brushing the knots out of her hair.

"Not for me, with me. A partnership. It'll be exciting Fresh. Daring."

Dangerous, she added silently, putting down the brush. It would be dangerous to expose herself like that. She had just spent six months burying herself so that she couldn't be found. But she had been found. By him.

Oh, she was tempted. Playing small cities and college towns had been fun for a while—a change of pace, a challenge to her ingenuity—but she was tired of it. She hated the cheap motels and boardinghouses she'd been staying in. Hated not being able to afford better. Hated being so lonely. She longed for bright lights, immense stages, incredible illusions and all the social contacts and fripperies that went with them. But why was he offering it all to her?

"Why me, Justin?"

"Because you're good. I like your style. I remember Paris."

Paris. His tone seemed to change as he said the word. "What is it you remember about Paris?" she asked lightly, trying not to sound as tense as she felt.

"Max. You. The fun we had. Those are some of my finest memories, Clever Cammi. But don't think I'm making the offer out of a sense of obligation. I saw the televised benefit show you appeared in last year and I was quite impressed with the way you managed to captivate your audience." When she remained silent and thoughtful, he pressed her for an answer. "What do you think? Are you interested in becoming my partner?"

Camille stared at Justin's mirror image and wondered how he saw her at this moment. Did he remember the silly fourteen-year-old girl who'd declared her love and begged to go with him when he was ready to leave Paris and start his own act in New York? Did he remember he'd told her he loved her—like a sister? She had always been been grateful he hadn't laughed at her.

She would have been thrilled, deliriously happy to have been given the opportunity to work with him when she was still in her teens or early twenties. But now? She didn't know this man, who must have changed just as she had changed. Too many things had happened in the past few years to allow her to commit herself rashly.

"I'm not sure that a partnership does interest me," she told Justin honestly. "Besides which, I read that you retired several months ago."

"I did and I found I couldn't stand the inactivity. I quit because my heart wasn't in my escapes anymore. To continue would have been suicide. And then I thought I was getting too old to cavort around a stage, anyway." Justin gave her a rueful smile.

"Thirty-eight isn't so old." A little surprised that she remembered he was exactly eight and a half years older than she, Camille quickly added, "I was shocked when I read the announcement in the newspaper. I predicted you'd be bored to tears in less than a month."

"I was." The change of inflection in his voice was subtle, but she heard it when he asked, "And what about you? This is a far cry from your European tour. Why did you leave?"

"To get away from Richard Montgomery," she lied.

Or was it a lie? It was Richard's fault that she was criminal now. Always looking over her shoulder. Alway waiting to be arrested. Justin was staring at her so strangel that she was afraid he could guess what she was thinking.

"By the way, how *is* your husband these days?"

"Ex-husband."

Camille had no idea why she had ever put Richard ir Justin's league. Probably because he'd been so good-looking, so charming, so generous and so seemingly sup-portive of her career. Unfortunately, Richard Montgomery had also been very, very dishonest, while Camille had sim-ply been naive. She hadn't known how he really made his living until after they'd been married for more than a year.

"I don't know how or where Richard spends his days," Camille said when she realized Justin was still waiting for her to answer. She turned away from the mirror to look at him directly. "The last time I saw him was about six months ago, right before the divorce was finalized. That's when I left Paris to come back to the States."

"I heard Richard didn't want the divorce, that he was determined to win you back. Knowing the man's reputa-tion for persistence, I'm surprised he hasn't found you."

Camille wondered why Justin wanted to know about her ex-husband, but she didn't ask. She turned the focus of the conversation back onto Justin. "How did *you* find me?"

"By using my magical powers, of course."

"Be serious," she said, though Justin didn't appear amused.

"All right. Through Max."

"But my own father doesn't even know where I am!"

"You sent him a postcard from Iowa. That was all I needed. I found out that a magician called Clever Cammi had played the university there." His expression was a little smug when he added, "In case you've forgotten, I gave you the nickname when you were fourteen."

She hadn't forgotten anything about that time when they'd worked together for Max. And to think she'd changed to a new stage name, assuming no one would recognize it. But of course she could not have known that Justin would come looking for her.

"You found me only by knowing I played the University of Iowa five weeks ago?"

"I'm very persistent and determined when I want something," Justin said softly, his expression filling her with a strange kind of apprehension. "And I want *you* . . . for my partner."

Whipping back to the mirror, Camille smeared makeup remover on her face and began wiping it away with tissues. She was reading mixed signals in everything he said. Well, why not? How could she view his unexpected arrival without suspicion? And yet Camille admitted that Justin might want to know about Richard merely because he was interested in *her*. Then why did she feel like running from him?

But she was so tired of running. Maybe it was time she stopped and put her life back together. For all she knew, no one had ever discovered the truth. *That* would be ironic! She might have been safe all this time if not for her paranoia and her nagging conscience, which kept reminding her of her guilt.

Still, she said, "I'll have to think about it."

Justin could feel her indecision, could almost hear her mind working. Though she might tell herself she would be wise to turn him down, he didn't think it would take much to persuade her to go to New York with him.

"We'll discuss the possibilities over a drink. At least you haven't refused. You have no idea of what your agreeing would mean to me, Cammi."

And indeed she didn't, Justin thought, for had she been aware of exactly what he meant by that last statement, she'd run like hell.

Watching her peel away the stage disguise, he realized Camille hadn't changed much. Her features were more mature, but her mouth still seemed too large for her narrow face, and her straight eyebrows still made her look too serious. And the freckles she'd been so worried about at fourteen still decorated her small, turned-up nose.

"It'll only take me a minute to change," Camille told him, disappearing behind a makeshift screen. "Velvet can stay in here while we have that drink. I'll pick her up later."

Justin watched Camille's movements reflected in the mirror. When he realized what he was doing, he looked away. Remembering his reaction to her the night before, not to mention how quickly he'd responded to the touch of her hands on stage, he cursed himself. She was no longer the young innocent he'd grown so close to and learned to love in his own way. He couldn't get personally involved with her, no matter how tempting a woman she had become.

Camille Bayard was not what she seemed to be. He knew that, and knew why she was running. What had happened to the innocent, giving creature who'd looked up to him? Justin thought with a pang of regret. She'd made him laugh when he'd been depressed; she'd been like another sister to him, as dear as his half sister, Genevieve, had been.

Justin clenched his jaw at the mere thought of Genevieve, classically beautiful like the mother they shared. Headstrong and spoiled, perhaps, but fiercely loyal to Justin even though her own father had despised him. Now it was time for him to prove he deserved Genevieve's loyalty.

If only he hadn't recommended her to Edouard Roget . . .

"I'm ready."

When Camille stepped from behind the screen, Justin could only stare at the likable face free of artifice, at the thick auburn hair pulled up in a ponytail, at the tall, willowy body draped in loose corduroy pants and an oversized shirt.

Funny, but Camille Bayard didn't look like a murderer.

Chapter Two

"I hope you like pizza," Camille said, pulling into a crowded parking lot ten minutes later. Justin had offered to drive his rented Thunderbird to the restaurant, but she'd insisted on taking her battered, rust-encrusted Toyota. Driving her own car had given her a sense of control that had been missing from her life lately. "My landlady told me that Guido's has pretentions to being an Italian restaurant but the pizza is the only safe thing to order."

"I really don't care whether I eat or not. I'm interested in talking to you."

"Hmm. That might be a challenge," she said, looking for a place to park. "The lot is pretty packed, which means the restaurant will be crowded and noisy."

"I'd settle for a drink at your place."

The thought of being alone with Justin made Camille uneasy. "Here's an empty spot," she said, whipping her car into it. "Let's take our chances. I don't have a thing to offer you at my place."

Without looking directly at Justin, she grabbed her big shoulder bag and scurried out of the car before he could object. Hugging her unlined wrap coat around her to ward off the late March chill, she led the way into Guido's.

The place was, as she had predicted, packed. Even so, Justin volunteered to find the hostess and ask how long it would take to get a table. Camille prayed the wait would be short. Since she didn't know the Champaign-Urbana area, she had no other suggestions to offer, and she certainly didn't like the one Justin had made.

She breathed a sigh of relief when he made his way back to her, a satisfied expression on his face.

"We're in luck. There's a table for two that has just been vacated, and the people already waiting are in groups of three or more. We can go right in."

This time he led the way, the crowd parting before him like magic. The clientele consisted mostly of college students dressed in baggy sweaters and jeans, sweat suits or wildly mismatched prints. In his conservative gray wool-and-silk sports jacket and open-necked blue silk shirt, Justin certainly stood out in the crowd, but in spite of his sophistication he was utterly at home in the smoky barroom atmosphere. The gum-chewing young hostess was definitely taken with him.

"Right this way, sir," she said, ignoring Camille. She tossed her long blond hair and moved toward the only empty booth in the room slowly enough for Justin to catch up with her. "I haven't seen you around. Are you new in town?"

"Actually, I came expressly to find this woman," Justin replied taking Camille's arm and pulling her forward.

"Oh." The blonde's expression relayed her disappointment. She set the menu down on the table. "Gary will be your waiter tonight. Have a good one." She left them with another toss of her hair.

"Are you sure you didn't hypnotize the young lady into getting us this table?" Camille asked, while sliding into the

booth. She slipped out of her coat but left it draped around
her shoulders for warmth.

"I never use my expertise for personal gain.'

"Ah, yes. I remember now. I used to tease you about
being Justin the Just. Moral, upright and uptight."

"And you don't believe in those values?"

Feeling herself flush, Camille fidgeted with the menu. "
never said that. It just used to amuse me when I was fourteen years old."

Justin seemed to be staring at her seriously. He couldn'
know, Camille assured herself, or he would have said
something when she told him she'd left Paris to escape
Richard. To cover her confusion, she bypassed her landlady's advice and studied the menu.

But in the end, they ordered pizza with a pitcher of beer.

"So why haven't you let Max know where you've been all
these months?" Justin asked once the waiter had left.

Camille shifted uncomfortably, wishing she didn't have
to keep lying. "He's very fond of Richard, you know. Even
if he meant to be loyal to me, Max might have let my
whereabouts slip out."

"It seems to me that there are legal ways to keep ex-
husbands from bothering divorced women, even in Europe. Did you ever contact the police?"

"No, of course not!" Camille responded much too
quickly. Rather than meet Justin's gaze directly, she stared
at the cleft in his chin and tried to minimize her reaction to
his question. "I don't dislike Richard enough to involve him
with the police. I just wanted to be free of him."

In reality she had tried to contact Richard several times to
see if the coast was clear and she could come out of hiding,
but he'd disappeared without a trace. Though she was still
disillusioned with him and furious that he had involved her
in the mess with Edouard Roget—and after she'd agreed to

vork the Frenchman's party as a favor to Max, no less!—
she was also worried that he had gotten himself in so deep
that he had to hide even from her.

She didn't want to think about the alternative—that
Richard might not be alive.

"Your pitcher of beer," their waiter announced. He set
down the frosted mugs and poured out the beer. "If there's
anything else I can get you while you're waiting for the
pizza, just yell."

When the young man had left, Justin said, "I'm sorry
thoughts of the past have the power to upset you. I have
some fond memories of the past myself."

"Like what?"

"Remember the time we played the April Fool's trick on
Max?"

"You mean when we fixed his props so they wouldn't
work properly?"

Justin nodded and grinned, his teeth flashing white below his dark mustache. "He went through three illusions
before he figured he was being had."

"He was so angry and embarrassed at first." Remembering her father's reaction, Camille had to laugh. In the end,
Max had laughed, too, until tears had streamed down his
face. "It's a good thing we booby-trapped his props before
a rehearsal rather than a performance or he would have
made both of us vanish instead of taking the whole thing as
a joke!"

Camille Bayard was beautiful and sexy when her face lit
up, Justin thought, and felt his pulse accelerate when he realized her charms were getting to him again. Once more he
reminded himself that he mustn't think about her as a desirable woman if he didn't want to be distracted from his
purpose.

So it was with deliberation that he brought his half sis-
into the conversation. "And then there was the summ
when Genevieve worked with us. I haven't forgotten th
six weeks. Have you?"

And just as deliberately, he studied her reaction. Ca
ille's expression was closed and she looked uncomfortabl
even as she shook her head.

Relentlessly Justin continued, "We were as close as
brother and sister could be until our mother died when I w
eighteen. Genevieve was eleven. Henri Gendre made my li
so miserable that I was forced to leave home. Luckily M
took me in as his apprentice," he reminded her, perfect
aware that Camille wouldn't have forgotten. "Genevie
couldn't understand how her father could dislike me s
much when he doted on her. My having to leave home hu
her deeply."

"She worshiped you," Camille said.

She took a sip of beer, then cradled the mug in her hand
so that it blocked part of her face and let her hide behind i

"I guess her looking up to me was natural since I was s
much older than she was," Justin said, studying th
expression in Camille's eyes until she lowered her lids
"Genevieve even wanted to be a magician's assistant for
while after her summer with us. She took all kinds of les
sons—acting, dancing, gymnastics. But then, in the end, he
hero worship must have faded, because she decided to be a
appraiser of valuable collectibles such as antique coins—
much more practical profession, don't you think?"

Abruptly setting down her mug, Camille murmured
"Would you excuse me?" Not bothering to wait for an an
swer, she picked up her shoulder bag and slid out of th
booth. "I've got to find the ladies' room. I'll be right back.'

Justin watched her move stiffly through the crowd. He'
gotten a reaction out of her, all right. It made him feel les

ilty about what he was doing but not any happier. He ished Camille had been able to make him believe in her nnocence. And he hoped he hadn't scared her off.

Justin nursed his beer thoughtfully.

Talking about Genevieve had made him picture his trong-willed, capricious half sister as he remembered her: eautiful and blond with large gray-blue eyes like his own; dainty doll whom he'd cherished.

It was on her fifteenth birthday, following an argument vith her father, that Genevieve had run away to join her brother at Max's. After talking over the situation with the naster magician, Justin had allowed her to stay during the summer vacation, letting her assist in the magic act along vith Camille.

At the end of the vacation Genevieve hadn't wanted to return to her father, even though he had always spoiled her—she was his only child. Justin's own father had died when he was four, and his American mother had chosen to remain in France. Shortly after coming out of mourning, Emily St. Cyr had met Henri Gendre and married him. He had never liked his stepson, and in keeping with his character, Gendre had blamed his daughter's wildness on Justin's influence.

After working with him that summer, Genevieve had wanted Justin to start his own act immediately so that she could be his assistant. Not yet ready to leave Max, he'd told her he'd consider the idea only after she'd finished her schooling. Genevieve hadn't liked it, but that was all he would promise. Once back at her expensive private school, she'd prepared herself for their eventual reunion.

But the reunion had never come about.

Feeling a need for a smoke, Justin pulled his gold cigarette case from his jacket pocket, but the action didn't stop

him from remembering. How could it, when the case ┃
been a gift from Genevieve?

That long-ago summer was the last opportunity h┃
made to spend much time with his sister. After that the
managed a few hours here and there. Then they hadn't s┃
each other for years while he traveled the world with his o┃
act. They'd corresponded faithfully, but Genevieve h┃
eventually entered adulthood pursuing her own career.

It was her career that had gotten Genevieve killed, Jus┃
thought ruefully. And he had been the catalyst by reco┃
mending his sister's services to Edouard Roget when Rog┃
had needed a discreet appraisal of his coin collection.

Realizing that he'd been tracing the monogram on t┃
cigarette case over and over with a fingertip, Justin laid ┃
hand flat on the table. He had to shove aside his feelings ┃
guilt, he thought, renewing his determination to lure C┃
mille to New York. Thinking about his plan, he pulled o┃
a Gauloises and lit it in the conventional way—with ┃
match.

CAMILLE STOOD IN FRONT of the mirror in the crowded l┃
dies' room, brushing her hair with a hand as cold as ice.

She wondered if Justin had known what he was doin┃
when he brought up the subject of his sister and her profe┃
sion. The Justin she'd known would have been more direc┃
Undoubtedly she was being paranoid again.

The thought made her angry with herself. All men we┃
not like Richard, who had concealed a motive behind ever┃
word and action when setting up a mark. She had to sto┃
being so suspicious.

Stuffing the brush into her bag, she drew herself togethe┃
with a new determination and pushed her way out of th┃
room through the group of chattering young women wai┃
ing to use the mirror. As she passed the dark, smoke-fille┃

ar area, she rubbed her cold hands together vigorously to imulate her circulation.

It was time she took positive steps to stimulate her life, amille thought. Maybe then she'd stop imagining things nd being afraid of shadows.

The first step would be to consider Justin's offer of a rofessional partnership seriously.

The waiter was just serving the pizza when she came to heir booth. "I see my timing is pretty good," she said, eating herself.

"Perfect," Justin replied with a smile that seemed trained.

Camille ignored her uneasy reaction, ordering her imagnation to behave.

Once the waiter had left, she got right down to business. "I've been thinking about your offer. It sounds promising. Tell me more about what you have in mind."

"A new challenge."

"Every magician looks for new challenges, Justin. They're what keep us fresh."

"Romance. That's what I want to give our audience at Illusions."

He raised an eyebrow, gave her what she used to call his Svengali look. But she wasn't about to be hypnotized into committing herself to do anything rash.

"Be a little more specific, please."

"I thought that sounded pretty specific. I want to create the illusion of lovers who find magic in romance."

In spite of her determination to keep cool, Camille shifted under his gaze. "But neither one of us has any experience with that kind of act. You grandstand and use high drama while I underplay and use humor."

"And I'm ready for a major change in my professional life. How about you?"

She was ready, all right, but she wasn't about to tell h
that. Not yet. Pushing her plate to the side, she leaned f
ward and fussed with the glass-encased candle at the cen
of the table. She chose her words carefully before spea
ing.

"Have you considered that this new image might n
work if the chemistry isn't correct?"

"I don't think we'll have too much trouble in that c
partment," Justin assured her, covering her hand a
moving it away from the candle. The flame flickered, sen
ing waves of faint light across his face. "You liked me w
enough once, as I remember. And I liked you, if in a diffe
ent way. But you're all grown up now, and quite nicely,
might add." His voice was rich with appreciation. "I thir
the chemistry will be there, and what's missing won't l
hard to fake."

Shying away from his reference to her schoolgirl crush
her face aflame at his compliments, Camille pulled her han
from under his. From the way her fingers tingled at h
touch, she was pretty sure she wouldn't have to fake a thin

"Let me think about it," she said a trifle more breath
lessly than she liked. He was offering her a business prop
osition, nothing more. Nor did she want more from Justi
St. Cyr, Camille told herself. She was all grown up now, ju
as he'd said. "Give me until morning."

"It's a deal."

"Since I have all this thinking to do, I'd like to leave,
you don't mind."

"As long as you don't try to vanish on me," Justin sai
with a slow, sexy grin.

Luckily their waiter was delivering a pitcher of beer to
nearby booth, so she had a reason to look away witho
feeling foolish. Camille signaled him over

"Can I get you folks something?"

"The check," Justin told him.

The young man was surprised. "Is something wrong? ou haven't touched your pizza."

Camille glanced down at the pan and their full plates. hey'd been so engrossed in their discussion that neither of 1em had eaten a thing.

"You can wrap it to go," she told the waiter with a smile. 'My cat and I love cold pizza for breakfast."

"Sure," the waiter said, giving her a quizzical look be- ore carrying the pizza back to the kitchen.

If Justin thought her request odd, he didn't comment. As matter of fact, as if realizing that for the moment he'd lone all he could to persuade her to accept his proposal, he eemed to retreat into himself, paying more attention to his :igarette case than to her. And he had little to say during the ide back to the theater.

Camille could have sworn that he was creating a distance between them purposely, yet he insisted on accompanying her to fetch Velvet from her dressing room.

She was concentrating on gathering her makeup and throwing it into a bag in spite of Velvet's determined efforts to get some attention when Justin suddenly said, "I hope you'll give a partnership serious consideration."

Glancing up at the mirror, she noted his intent expres- sion. She turned to face him directly. "Of course."

"When I set out to find you, I was positive my pursuit was worthwhile, or I wouldn't have gone to so much trou- ble. But now . . . I think I underestimated the possibilities."

Their gazes locked, and for a second she lost herself in the depths of Justin's pale, hypnotic eyes. Camille felt as though he were trying to force her to agree by the strength of his will. She could imagine a special kind of magic developing between them that neither would find elsewhere—but she wasn't sure whether it would be professional or personal.

Her heartbeat increased just a fraction, enough for her
recognize the subtle change of rhythm. She was startled
the way he could turn on his charm so easily and by
power to affect her in spite of her caution. But then Jus
St. Cyr had been seducing entire audiences for years. W
should she be an exception?

Camille broke the spell by picking up Velvet, who w
curiously poking her head into the makeup bag, and usi
the black cat as a shield against him. The last thing in t
world she needed right now was to get involved persona
with Justin the Just. If he ever found out the truth abo
why she had left Paris . .

"It must be comforting to foresee a positive outcome
all your ventures," she murmured.

He moved a little closer, his nearness affecting her inn
rhythm once more. "I know what I want, Clever Camm
and I usually get it."

"I'm sure you do." It wasn't easy to respond naturall
"But I haven't decided what *I* want—yet."

"Then I'll have to be patient."

He backed off, allowing her to check her growing aware
ness of him. Gratefully she picked up her bag and led th
way out to their cars, giving him a cursory handshake be
fore climbing into her old junk heap and driving back to th
boardinghouse.

Balancing the squirming cat, her makeup bag and th
pizza was quite a feat while climbing three flights of poorl
lit narrow steps in a rear stairwell. But Camille made the tri
up to her rented attic room safely, setting down the bag onl
to find her keys and unlock the door. Once inside, sh
turned on the light, threw the bag on her bed and let Velv
down.

"Mr-row!"

"You smell the pizza, huh? I guess you wouldn't con-
der waiting until the morning, would you?"

From the way the cat danced around her feet, looking up
 her with pleading wide eyes, Camille figured she'd best
tisfy Velvet's craving now if she wanted to get any sleep
at night. As if she could sleep at all with what she had to
ink about! Carefully opening the paper bag and alumi-
um foil, she tore off a piece of pizza with a large chunk of
ausage on it and dumped it in the cat's dish next to the
ighboy.

"That should keep you busy for a while," Camille said,
miling at Velvet's obvious enthusiasm for her treat. The cat
mmediately dug in, her sleek black tail held straight up and
witching.

Camille thought about eating a piece of pizza herself, but
he'd lost her appetite, so she put the bag on the dresser and
wandered to the window. If ever she needed some good advice, it was right now. Staring out at the night sky while
slipping out of her coat, she wished the stars could tell her
what to do.

They couldn't, but maybe Max could!

Checking her bedside clock, Camille noted it was well past
midnight. It would be early morning in Paris. Too early for
Max to be awake? Since her father had retired last year, he
wasn't likely to be indulging in many late nights. She'd take
a chance and call him. A pay phone was right outside her
door. There was one on every floor.

Once she'd set up the collect call with the operator, Camille took the receiver into her room so that she wouldn't
disturb the next-door boarder. Impatiently she listened to
the phone ring over and over again. Finally she heard an
answering click and recognized her father's voice accepting
the call. She was vaguely surprised that Madame Bouchoux, Max's housekeeper, hadn't answered.

"Yes," Max said, his tone testy.

"Max! Can't you put a little more enthusiasm into you[...] greeting for your favorite daughter?"

"My only daughter, you mean. Although I was begin[...]ning to think I was childless."

"Now, now, don't play the aggrieved parent. You kno[...] why I left Paris," Camille said, though in fact her fathe[...] didn't know her reason at all. Max believed exactly wha[...] Justin believed—that she'd been trying to avoid her ex[...] husband. "Has Richard been hanging around and bother[...]ing you again?"

"No. I haven't heard a word from him. Or of him, as [a] matter of fact."

That was both good and bad. She was worried that something dreadful had happened to Richard, but at least no police or private investigators had been around asking questions. Max would have said so if they had.

Knowing her father would expect a reaction from her, Camille said, "Maybe he's finally given up."

"I guess he took the hint when you signed the divorce papers. He's probably consoling himself with some rich widow on the Côte d'Azur."

"Richard always took advantage of what the Riviera had to offer, though I was too naive to notice until we'd been married for a year."

"Now don't go blaming yourself again. That Richard Montgomery is the smoothest con man I've ever met. And believe me, I've met quite a few."

Her ex-husband was right up there with the best, Camille silently agreed. When they'd married, he'd convinced her that he made a living from international investments. And he had in a way. While pretending a flattering interest in her career as a magician, he'd used her performances in several

uropean countries to make contacts and set up marks for
is various cons.

"Max, I don't want to waste your time and money talk-
1g about Richard."

"Good. Let's talk about your coming home to Paris."

"As you well know, the States are as much my home as
rance, but that's not what I called about."

"All right, Camille. Let's hear it. What's bothering you?"

"Justin St. Cyr wants me to work with him in a new act."

"Justin?"

"Yes. You sound surprised."

After a few seconds of silence, Max asked, "How in the
world did he find you?"

"You showed him that postcard I sent you from Iowa.
He's a determined man when he wants something."

"Obviously. But what about his grand plans for an early
retirement?"

"He's lasted longer than I thought he would," Camille
said. "He got bored with inactivity and decided to open a
new magic club in New York called Illusions. Next month.
And he wants me to be his partner, to help him put a little
magic in romance. Or is it romance in magic?"

"And how do you feel about it?"

"I'm not really sure." Camille sighed, knowing she could
tell Max only part of her doubts. "A partnership would be
fresh and challenging and exciting, and yet, since I struck
out on my own, I've never had to share the decisions with a
partner, never had to compromise."

"Well, at least if you decide to work with Justin, you'll
know his standards are the highest," Max assured her.
"And you two certainly get along well enough."

"That was fifteen years ago."

"Some outer things might have changed with time, but
not the real you and the real Justin."

Camille wanted to believe him. "Thanks, Max."

"For what?"

"For helping me make up my mind. I'm going to give [a try." *And get on with my life.* "You'll be there for th opening, won't you? I'm not sure of the exact date, but I'] let you know."

Max didn't answer immediately, nor did he sound as en thusiastic as she expected him to be. "You know I wouldn' miss it unless I had a good reason. Of course I'll be there i I can."

Camille frowned, wondering why he sounded so sub dued. But rather than question him, she tactfully decided to change the subject.

"How is Madame Bouchoux doing?" she asked, remem bering that the housekeeper hadn't answered the phone. "Any more grandchildren in the offing?" The old French woman had been grandmother of eleven when Camille had left Paris.

But obviously she hadn't picked the best of subjects.

"Actually, Madame Bouchoux hasn't worked for me for the past few months," Max said, his tone cautious. "I be lieve she's living with one of her daughters."

She could tell her father didn't want to talk about Ma dame Bouchoux. And after exchanging a few meaningless pleasantries, he said goodbye, as though he were anxious to hang up before she could think to question him further.

Camille slipped the telephone receiver back into place in the hall, then closed and locked her door.

Thoughtfully she crossed the narrow room to the win dow, picking up Velvet, who had been trying to tangle her self around Camille's feet. Perhaps her father was having money problems. She'd thought he'd retired in style. And right before she left Paris, he'd told her that he expected to make a fortune soon from some new investments. They might have gone bad instead.

Madame Bounchoux had worked for Max for nearly twenty years. She had sworn she would quit working for The Magnificent Maxwell only when she was no longer breathing. So presumably Max had been forced to let his housekeeper go because he couldn't pay her. And maybe he'd hesitated about coming to the opening of Illusions because he couldn't afford the price of the airfare.

Impossible, Camille told herself, hugging a purring Velvet to her chest. She was worrying for nothing. She and Max were so close that surely he'd tell her if he was in a bind. She had to stop imagining things.

Besides, at the moment, instead of worrying about her father, she ought to be worrying about herself—figuring out logistics, making plans, deciding whether she should get the props for her larger illusions out of storage.

Even if she played out her engagements for the following weekend, she could fly to New York a week from Monday. The thought set her pulse racing, but Camille wasn't sure if her excitement was due to the challenge of a new act or to the prospect of working with Justin St. Cyr.

JUSTIN PULLED HIS RENTED CAR up to the curb across from the boardinghouse just as the lights went on in Camille's attic room. He did not stop to analyze why he'd followed her at a safe distance so that she wouldn't see him.

He should be at his hotel, not waiting outside her building—and waiting for what?

Justin turned off his headlights and killed the engine only seconds before Camille came into sight at the window. He sank in his seat slightly, just in case she glanced down at the street and spotted the Thunderbird. He didn't want to make her suspicious.

He had suspicions enough for both of them.

He had neglected Genevieve for years before her death even though he'd loved her, and he'd involved her with his long-time acquaintance Edouard Roget, a wealthy patron of the magical arts. Justin couldn't bring Genevieve back to life and prove to her how much he loved her, but he could help bring her murderer to justice.

During the time when Genevieve was making her appraisal of Roget's collection of antique coins, one of the coins had been stolen and a fake put in its place. Genevieve had called Justin in London and told him she was on to the thief. Concerned for her safety, Justin had begged her to stop playing amateur detective, but Genevieve had merely laughed at his fears. A little danger would be exciting, she'd told him. She was going to find the thief.

By the time he'd arrived in Paris, determined to stop his headstrong sister from getting into trouble, she'd been murdered.

The police had been baffled, and so Justin had done a little detective work of his own. He'd gone to Genevieve's apartment, where he'd found a notebook in her jewelry box.

In it she'd made several entries about the missing coin and about Camille, Richard Montgomery, Max and Edouard Roget himself. Genevieve must have decided which of them was the thief, Justin figured, and the thief had become a murderer when she confronted him—or her—with the truth.

Justin had sworn to be as ruthless as necessary in order to find out which of them was guilty....

Suddenly realizing that Camille was no longer at the window, Justin got out of the car and moved into a position from which he could see her. She was on the phone, no doubt talking to Richard or Max, asking for advice about his proposition. Good. His plan was in motion.

Using Camille as the bait—having no doubts that she would perform with him—Justin planned to bring his suspects together. Max would want to see his only daughter perform. Richard, the ex-husband who hadn't learned to let go, would be drawn to Camille. And Justin knew Edouard Roget wouldn't miss the opening of a prestigious magic club.

Camille reappeared at the window, hugging her cat in her arms. She stared out, seeming to focus on nothing. What was going on in that beautiful head of hers? Realizing he was starting to think of her as an attractive woman again, Justin took himself in hand.

When all of his suspects were finally gathered together, he would learn the truth about his sister's death. Then, and only if she was absolved, he would allow himself to become involved with Camille Bayard.

Chapter Three

Nine days later Camille hopped enthusiastically out of the taxi that had brought her from the airport to Manhattan's Soho area. After paying the driver, she made her way into the black cast-iron commercial building that was soon to house Illusions, while juggling two suitcases, an overnight bag, her shoulder bag and Velvet's carrier.

A workman abandoned the sign he was installing so that he could hold open the door for her. "Need some help?" he asked. "Those bags look pretty heavy."

"The door's more than enough. Thanks."

Passing two more workers who were busy putting up silver-and-black wallpaper in the half-finished foyer, Camille hesitated only a second before turning right and heading for the lounge area. Behind the empty Art Deco bar, a man who looked to be in his mid-twenties was shuffling cards with professional expertise. His café-noir face was intent with concentration, so she hesitated to disturb him. She set down her baggage and waited for a minute, but the man didn't seem to realize she was there.

"Excuse me."

"Not today," he said before she could ask for Justin. He didn't look up but continued to manipulate the cards with long, nimble fingers. "Auditions are Wednesday."

"I'm not here for an audition. I'm here to see Justin St. yr."

"But I do the hiring."

Annoyed now, Camille said, "That's no reason to be ude."

Finally the man looked at her, his dark eyes slowly travling from her ankle boots, up her fuschia-and-green calf-ength flowered skirt and matching sweatshirt, which were evealed by her green, open wrap coat, to her wind-tossed uburn hair. Recognition registered, but his expression still vasn't exactly welcoming.

"Camille Bayard. You and Justin should make an interesting team. You're very talented. I saw you perform in France two years ago."

"Thank you. I think." Since the man didn't seem to realize anything was wrong with his behavior, Camille tried to make a friendly overture. "While you were in France, I assume you must have been performing as well."

"That's why I went, but your father wouldn't hire me to be his new assistant."

"Oh."

"Justin should be in his office." With a nod he indicated a closed door at the opposite end of the lounge, then went back to his cards. "Through the door and up the stairs."

Bending down, Camille checked on her cat, who looked distinctly bored in her small carrier. "Stay, Velvet. But if anyone threatens you, attack," she whispered softly. Then she straightened and spoke directly to the unsmiling would-be magician. "I assume you won't mind if I leave my luggage and traveling companion here."

Without waiting for an answer, Camille strode across the lounge, wondering what part this man played in the scheme of things.

Beyond the door was a flight of metal steps. When Camille reached the second floor, she found an apparently empty office with an open door. Assuming it was Justin's, she walked in.

"Justin?"

"Hello." A small, slender woman with short curly brown hair rose from behind a filing cabinet. Peering intently through her owlish glasses, she exclaimed, "You're Camille Bayard, aren't you? Of course you are. Who else would you be?" She rushed forward, holding out her hand and in a pleasant Southern accent announced, "I'm Vivian Lewis, the bookkeeper's assistant. I don't get to do any of the fun work around here, but I assure you, I am an important person on the Illusions staff, since *I* cut the pay checks."

Laughing at the rapid monologue and charmed by the bubbly personality that contrasted so strikingly with a quiet brown suit and sensible low-heeled shoes, Camille took the slight hand in her own. "I'm doubly happy to meet you then," she said. "I'm sorry if I wandered into the wrong office. I was looking for Justin, but the man downstairs wasn't very helpful with his directions."

"You must be meaning Kipp Walker." Vivian rolled her brown eyes. "Heavens, don't let him get you down. He's just as sweet-tempered to everyone else."

"He thought I'd come for an audition. For what?"

"Kipp wears many hats around here. He's one of the managers of the food-and-liquor service. Justin had a wonderful idea that all our waiters, waitresses and bartenders should know a little close-up magic so they can entertain their own customers as well as work as assistants in the shows. Kipp's in charge of auditions and training. He also acts as stage manager."

"He handles the cards well."

"Yes, but talent does not necessarily make up for lack of manners, does it?" Vivian headed toward the door, steering Camille in front of her. "I know you must be eager to find Mr. St. Cyr. His office and dressing room are right over there."

As Vivian pointed, Camille saw Justin come through a doorway a dozen yards down the hall. "There he is."

"I'd better get to work," Vivian murmured, slipping back into her own office.

Before Camille could thank her, Justin called, "I was beginning to wonder if you'd changed your mind."

"I had to switch flights because of Velvet," Camille said, walking toward him eagerly. In a mere nine days she'd almost forgotten how attractive Justin was. "Only one small animal is allowed in the cabin per flight, and wouldn't you know there were two of us who had cats. I certainly wasn't going to let my performing partner ride with the baggage, so I took a later flight."

"Well, you're here now," he murmured, his pale eyes sweeping over her appreciatively. "That's what counts. Do you feel like a grand tour of the club or would you rather get to your apartment right away?"

"Grand tour, please, then the apartment. Justin, how can I thank you for finding a place for me to live?"

"It wasn't any problem. The owner is a friend of mine who has to be out of town on business for the next couple of months. Rather than leaving the place empty, he's delighted to rent it to someone . . . trustworthy."

He emphasized the word "trustworthy," but then Justin the Just would, Camille thought. She had to stop wincing when he said things like that or he'd begin to notice. When he took her arm and led her in the direction from which he'd come, she forced herself to smile up at him. It wasn't a hard task, when her eyes were being entertained so nicely. From his cleft chin to his widow's peak, Justin was an example of masculine perfection. And the rest of him wasn't bad either.

"The offices and dressing rooms are all on this floor Yours is right across from mine." He let go of her to open the door. Then he stood back and indicated she should enter. "What do you think?"

Green eyes wide, Camille walked past him and slowly turned so that she could take in everything. The Art Deco dressing room was the largest and most luxurious she'd ever been assigned. Plush pale-gray carpet underfoot echoed the delicately patterned gray-and-mauve papered walls. In between two fan-pleated torchiere floor lamps sat a mauve couch with a shell-shaped back. Its beautiful lines were reflected in a large makeup mirror on the opposite wall. But the most impressive piece in the room was a black lacquer dressing screen with handpainted mauve and lilac waterlilies.

"I'm astounded, astonished and amazed!"

"Damn. I was hoping you'd like it."

Camille laughed as she turned to Justin, who had come up behind her and stood mere inches away. She tipped her head back to look up at his serious face, wondering for a second why he wasn't laughing too. At least he could let his mustache twitch a little.

"You knew I'd love it. But you couldn't have had this done in the nine days since I agreed to work with you. What if you hadn't found me? Or what if I'd decided I wasn't interested in your offer?"

"I'm a magician, remember. I would have used a powerful spell to find you," he teased, his low voice sending a thrill through her. "And as for your not being interested— I would have hypnotized you into agreeing."

He was hypnotizing her now, Camille thought. She wanted
to move away from him to lessen his effect on her, but her legs
wouldn't obey. "What about your ethics?" she managed to
ask.

His face—and his mouth!—inched closer, making Camille wonder if he planned to kiss her, especially when he
arched a dark brow and murmured, "Some things are worth
making compromises for."

That certainly didn't sound like the upright, uptight Justin she knew.

Still held in his gaze, Camille speculated on whether Justin had changed in the past fifteen years. Or what he wanted
might have changed, which was a different thing altogether. Perhaps he wanted her now; perhaps now he thought
of her as a desirable woman.

After all those years, maybe he'd finally realized she could
be more than an adoptive sister to him.

She parted her lips, wanting him to kiss her, just to see
what the experience would be like. Sure that her wish had
registered with him, Camille was distinctly disappointed
when he moved away, his sorcerer's eyes gleaming. She felt
an unsettling heat creep through her at her own foolishness.

"Whew, it's warm in here," she said, slipping off her
coat. "Where to now?"

She was relieved when Justin led the way out of the room
and down the corridor, saying, "I'll show you the other set
of stairs leading to the rear of the stage. They're on the other
side of the dressing rooms."

What in the world was wrong with her? Camille wondered, catching up with him. Before agreeing to the partnership she'd instructed herself to keep the relationship
strictly professional, and now she wanted Justin to kiss her.

As they descended the stairs to the crowded backstage area, she realized Justin had withdrawn, just as he had on the night he'd found her. Once more he was issuing mixed signals.

"It's a shame it took me so long to locate you," Justin was saying while he guided her through the maze of props and set pieces toward the stage. "Since we have less than three weeks before the grand opening, we'll have to combine old illusions with new."

"A practical solution," was all Camille said, her mind still busy sorting out the emotional complications.

Perhaps Justin, too, thought they should keep their relationship professional in spite of a mutual attraction. Then again, he might not be attracted to her at all. He could be trying to create that chemistry they needed for a satisfying romantic performance.

Somehow, that Justin might be creating an illusion merely for the benefit of the act didn't sit well with her.

"I already have ideas for a couple of illusions we could perform together, Cammi. We can fill in with individual pieces from our separate acts until we can develop others."

As he parted the curtains and she stepped onto the semicircular apron of the stage, Camille was distracted from her uncertainties about Justin. The club spread out before her in various shades of gray. Charcoal walls were softly lit by triangular wall-washer lamp fixtures with hand-blown glass covers. Medium gray plush booths topped by narrow strips of illuminated etched glass were arranged in ascending tiers so that every seat in the house would be a good one. The floor itself was carpeted in pale gray.

"It's gorgeous," she told him. "Who's your decorator?"

"I designed it. Farraday and Johnson carried it out." Ignoring her awed look, Justin went on, "The kitchen is to the

ght, the dance floor to the left. You can get onto the dance
oor both from here and from the lounge. And the sound
ooth for the dance music as well as for the show is right
ehind this wall."

Camille grinned at him. "How about if I forget renting
our friend's apartment and live right here?"

This time his mustache did twitch just a little. "Don't
nake any rash decisions. Wait until you see the place."

And what a place it was! Though they took a taxi to ac-
commodate Camille's luggage and Velvet, the flat was lo-
cated only a short walk from Illusions. It, too, was housed
n one of the old commercial buildings. While the green facade was quite ordinary, the apartment itself was a real
dazzler, quite as stunning as Illusions if as far removed from
Art Deco as it could be.

It was decorated in contemporary Eurostyle. Its white
walls and tile floor set off the sleek black and red furniture.
The main area was designed as a free-flowing unit taking in
living room, work space and dining nook. The full-sized
kitchen, bathroom and huge bedroom were all decorated in
the same style and color scheme.

"After the places I've been staying in, this seems like a
dream," Camille said, coming out of the bedroom, which
was double the size of anything she'd stayed in since returning to the States. "Do me a favor. Don't wake me up."

"Not until my friend comes back, anyway."

"I'll be thoroughly spoiled by the time I have to get my
own place."

"At least you'll be able to settle into the club without
worrying about finding an apartment." Justin seemed to be
enjoying her excitement with more enthusiasm than was
usual in a mere business partner, reminding Camille of those
mixed signals she'd been worried about. "Once Illusions

opens, you'll have plenty of time to find something on you own."

Then, after giving her a rundown of the stores and ser vices in the area, Justin left, asking her to be at the club b ten the next morning.

Camille let Velvet out of her cage, so that the cat coulc explore her temporary new home, and trailed after her.

Suddenly everything seemed to be going her way, start ing with the job and the work surroundings and now con tinuing with this place. If she had been a less suspicious person, she might have been able to relax and enjoy her good fortune.

But as she wandered slowly through the apartment, she felt oddly apprehensive. While the furnishings were com plete right down to the original artwork on the walls, there was something not quite right about the place. Something was missing. Absent were the little personal touches that would have told her that a real person had lived here. Everything was so new, so shiny. . . so sterile. It was almost as if the apartment were an elaborate setting for an illu sion.

Now she was being ridiculous, carrying her paranoia to new heights, Camille scolded herself. The apartment be longed to a friend of Justin's, and there was no reason in the world for him to try to fool her.

"ARE YOU SURE you don't want to have dinner and see a movie with me tonight?" Vivian asked, going up to Ca mille where she sat cross-legged on the stage, manipulating wooden matchsticks to warm up her fingers.

"I sure could use a night out, but Justin wants to re hearse a while longer."

"In my opinion, Mr. St. Cyr has been working you too hard. You're going to collapse if you don't demand some time off."

Camille smiled at Vivian reassuringly. "It hasn't even been a week since we started rehearsing. I doubt that I'll collapse so quickly. But thanks for your concern."

Watching her don her drab olive coat, Camille wished she could spend the evening with Vivian. She was drawn to her. The bond between them was forged by Vivian's wholehearted openness and Camille's pleasure in having a friend with whom she could share things, a luxury she'd had to do without for a long time.

"Well, some other evening, then."

"How about tomorrow night?" Camille suggested. "We could do something wild, go to a couple of the clubs, maybe. It's been so long since I've had a really fun night out."

"Oh, no, I just couldn't. I mean, club-hopping is really not my thing." Vivian frowned and pushed at the tortoiseshell frames of her glasses, adding softly, "I don't enjoy meeting men that way."

Camille wondered if she'd guessed the real reason Vivian wore nondescript clothes and hardly any makeup. She'd be pretty if she fixed herself up instead of playing down her looks. But then, in general Vivian seemed to be a little shy around men. She must have had some bad experiences with the opposite sex. Remembering Richard, Camille wondered whether any woman hadn't.

"How about that dinner and a movie, then?"

"All right," Vivian agreed, brightening.

Camille would have gone on to ask her which restaurants she recommended, but at that moment Justin and Kipp Walker came noisily into the club from the kitchen.

"I'm going to work late tonight, Justin," Kipp said. "I've got to finish filling out the orders for the staff's costumes and props."

"Good. I'll probably talk to you before leaving."

Justin stopped in front of Camille. "Ready?" he asked.

"Sure." Camille rose, waving goodbye to Vivian, who was already heading toward the street door. "Nice seeing you, Kipp."

On his way out, Kipp looked her way without saying a thing. At least he was consistent.

While Justin turned on the stage lights and found his portable audio cassette player and the music for their act, Camille tended to the props. After stowing some small articles in various pockets in her muted-gold calf-length skirt and baggy suit jacket, she set an artist's easel and canvas in position at the left side of the proscenium. She also set out a bird feeder.

Each of their illusions was to be a romantic story. This one, a tale of an artist painting in the park, was to be the simplest of their routines. So far, it was the only one they'd rehearsed.

"I told Sandra she could go home," Justin said, taking his place at the easel, where he donned his costume: baggy sweater, beret and a scarf around his neck.

"No sense in keeping her," Camille agreed. "We can pretend our new waitress is here." She sat down, picked up a book and slipped on a pair of lensless glasses. Looking over the glasses toward the empty bench, she said to the absent Sandra, "You look terrific tonight, Sandy, old girl." Then, to Justin, "We're ready when you are."

Determined not to let Camille get to him this time, Justin refused to smile at her whimsy. He started the cassette player.

The audio began with sounds characteristic of a park: children at play, birds singing, dogs barking occasionally. Camille pretended to be engrossed in her book while Justin painted.

On cue, he turned the easel to show the audience his completed painting of a cool-looking blonde: Sandra. With a grand flourish, he covered the canvas with a square of silk before turning the easel to face the back of the stage. Moving to the empty bench, he mimed a plea that the model for the portrait should take a look at his work. At this point, Sandra would snub him and walk off the set. Justin mimed despondency.

Violin music replaced the park sounds. Though his back was to her, Justin knew that now Camille was looking up from her book, in time to notice the artist being rejected. He steeled himself. This was where he'd been getting into trouble the past couple of days, letting her get to him in a very basic way. Though he'd found it impossible to resist Camille's charms so far, he wouldn't stop trying.

He heard her rise behind him. A moment later she tapped him on the shoulder. When he turned, Camille indicated she'd like to see his work. He feigned dejection and lack of interest. Making it clear that she wanted to cheer him up, Camille began to do close-up magic.

She retrieved coins from various places on his body, as she had the night he'd found her. This time she dropped them into the beret she took from his head. Her movements were choreographed into a romantic dance meant to put the smile back on his face. It worked all too well. The next time she touched him with her clever hands, his body flamed and he jumped back reflexively.

Her eyebrows flattened in a scowl of concentration as she tried again, and he slipped farther away. "Hold still, would you?"

"Well, watch what you're doing!"

"I'm not supposed to. I'm supposed to be staring lovingly into your eyes, remember? Now, do you want me to get into your pants or not?" Camille's green eye widened as she heard what she said, and a rosy flush spread up from her neck. "Uh, maybe we'd better start over."

Not wanting to do the last part again until he had some control over himself, Justin said, "Let's go on from where you've found all the coins."

Though she was obviously disconcerted, Camille recovered nicely, casting her spell over the coins in his beret to turn them into a bunch of fake flowers.

Justin wished Camille wouldn't look at him so sexily when she handed him the bouquet. Her gaze was that of a woman looking at her lover. He told himself to ignore his body's natural responses, but unfortunately he wasn't persuasive enough.

At least he wasn't alone in his trouble. Justin was sure Camille felt the attraction as strongly as he did. He saw it in her eyes. Now she danced behind him and twined her arms around his neck so that she could loosen the knot in his scarf. Somehow he survived the feeling of her arms around him, and her softness pressed against his back.

Twirling around to face him again, Camille covered his hands and the bouquet with the square of silk. She laid her own hands over his, shaping and pressing while the bouquet seemed to diminish in size. When she finally removed the scarf, the flowers had vanished and a live dove was found in their place. Together, Camille and Justin moved to the bird feeder, where he set the dove down.

Then they continued the dance. Now, the choreography had Justin chasing Camille until she turned and caught him. Suddenly, she broke away from him, heading for the painting. Justin cut her off, drove her away from it, touched her some more as he had to for the act until he thought he'd go crazy. Whose idea was this romance-in-magic nonsense, anyway?

When it was time to give in to Camille's stage seduction and agree to let her see his painting, he sighed with relief. The torture was almost over. He removed the silk scarf from the easel and showed the portrait first to her, then to the audience. Magically he'd replaced the blonde on the canvas with a flame-haired Camille.

Then came the final pose, for which the lights would dim: Camille's arms wrapped around Justin's neck, her face tilted up for a kiss.

Justin was sorely tempted to complete the action, but instead he pushed Camille away so vigorously that she said, "Is something wrong?"

"No, nothing." *Yes. You. You're driving me crazy.* "Actually I thought it went quite well."

Justin turned his back on her to set the easel in position once more. Could he really go through this routine again and again?

"But you had such an odd expression. I thought—"

"You were wonderful! Perfect!"

"Well, you don't have to snap at me!"

Justin turned to glare at her, but Camille's hurt expression softened him. He was having a difficult time dealing with his emotions. Opening night was two weeks away, yet he was having second thoughts—and all because he couldn't control his physical response to a woman who might be guilty of his sister's murder.

"Let's try it again," he growled.

"Yes, sir!"

What was the matter with Justin tonight? Camille wondered as she took her place on her own bench. He'd been going hot and cold on her all week, but she didn't intend to let him scald her with his stupid temper. She was sorely tempted to tell him what he could do with his new act and then walk out on him. But what would that accomplish? In spite of his fluctuating personality, she wanted to work with Justin St. Cyr.

In fact, she was beginning to think she wanted Justin himself.

Camille sighed in frustration. She might as well admit it, at least to herself. Justin St. Cyr was an extremely desirable beast, and if she weren't careful, she was going to fall in love with him all over again.

Heaven help her!

CAMILLE LEFT ILLUSIONS around midnight. Fed up with Justin, who'd gone cool on her after his short flash of temper, she didn't think anything could worsen her mood.

She was wrong.

It was miserably wet and cold outside. A freezing drizzle fell, coating the deserted sidewalks and streets with a thin but treacherous film of ice. She wished she'd listened to the weather report that morning so she would have been better prepared. She had neither hat nor gloves. Luckily she was wearing crepe-soled flat shoes.

Though she waited in the shelter of the club's canopy for several minutes, only a few cars passed by, and not a single taxi. She'd have to walk home, unless she wanted to sleep in her dressing room. The thought was tempting—it would be warm and dry—but Velvet was waiting for her evening meal, which had already been delayed for several hours.

Camille dug into her purse and found her keys so that she wouldn't have to fumble for them later while standing in the rain. She put them in her pocket, where she could get to them more easily. Then, tightening the belt of her coat and pulling the collar close around her neck for maximum protection, she bravely set off from under the canopy, her head bent against the wind-driven drizzle.

Before she had gotten half a block down the street, her hair was wet and operating like a transport mechanism to send rivulets of icy water down her back. Her ankles and feet were soaked, her shoes probably ruined. And it wouldn't be long before the wet penetrated her unlined coat.

April showers bring May flowers. At the moment, she wouldn't have cared if she never saw another flower in her life.

The drizzle turned into a steady downpour, and she could hardly see anything. Even the streetlights were almost obliterated, mere hazy haloes of faint light too far from the ground to illuminate it. Camille had to concentrate just to keep herself going, negotiate the right curbs and cross the right streets.

And so it was no wonder that it took some time for the steady beat of footsteps behind her to register.

At first she paid no attention to the sound. It was merely evidence of another unlucky soul who was having to walk somewhere in this miserable weather. But when she slipped on the icy pavement and stopped for a moment to steady herself by holding on to a garbage can that had been set out at the curb, she realized she couldn't hear the other set of footsteps. Instinct made her listen carefully as she went on.

There they were again, far behind, but keeping to the same slow pace as her own feet.

Camille turned the corner and kept going, still listening carefully. Nothing at first, then she heard the footsteps again. Her heart was thudding in strong, deep strokes. She speeded up. And so did whoever was following her.

Good Lord, someone *was* following her!

How far did she have to go? A block and a half. Wildly looking over her shoulder, she couldn't see anyone until a

passing car's beams illuminated a shrouded figure from behind, making it seem huge and ominous.

Terrified of the unknown, Camille ran for all she wa
worth, thrusting a hand into her pocket to find her keys s
that she'd be prepared with them when she got to her build
ing. It was just as she pulled them out that she tripped on a
uneven spot in the pavement and went sprawling. Auto
matically breaking her fall with her hands, Camille couldn'
stop the keys from flying out of her grasp. They jangle
across the sidewalk and shot into the street with a splash.

Panic-stricken, still down on her knees, she felt for the
keys, groping along the curb and into the icy stream of water rushing in the gutter. The search made her lose precious
seconds of her lead, but she found the keys.

Grabbing them, she took off, her mind racing as fast as
her legs. She had to find a place to hide.

The steps!

She thought of them as she reached the next corner. In
stead of crossing the street as she normally did to reach her
building, she turned the corner and ran a few yards to a set
of steps leading to a basement entrance. As she descended
she hugged the wall, then forced her breathing under control.

She could hear him coming.

Her back flattened against the streetside wall, Camille
listened intently. She didn't have long to wait for the muted
sound of leather soles slipping and sliding on the slick
pavement to draw closer. Her pursuer stopped, cursing
softly—a frustrated male growl.

Splashes alerted her he was coming toward her. She froze
and held her breath when he stopped and stood still inches
from her hiding place. He was almost directly above her.
She sensed that he was trying to decide which direction to
take, and until he did, she didn't dare move or breathe.

Don't let him turn around and look down. Don't let him find me, she prayed, breaking out into a cold sweat.

A minute or two later, he was off again. Panting for air, Camille forced herself to wait twice as long as she thought was necessary, even though every nerve in her body urged her to run. But what if he turned back and saw her as she left her shelter? Finally she decided that she'd given the man more than enough time to return if he was going to do so, and crept up the steps, cautiously peering around her as she rose to street level.

All clear.

Camille scrambled up the last few steps and headed for her building at a breakneck pace. Intent on getting herself to safety, she crossed the street blindly and didn't stop running until she got to her door. By then her chest was heaving painfully and her lungs felt as if they were ready to burst.

Fingers numb with cold, she fumbled with her keys, but she finally got the door open. She ran all the way up to the second floor and got into her apartment in less than a minute. Throwing the metal bar of the police lock into place, she sank to the floor with her back against the door, icy water puddling around her.

It was only then, when she began shaking with the wet and cold and fear, that she considered the identity of the man who had followed her.

Who the hell was he? He might have been a stranger, but he might also be someone she knew. He might even have come from Paris. Heaven help her, she was all alone in this.

The irony of the situation got to her. Camille began to laugh, and once started, she couldn't stop. It was hilarious. Someone was stalking her, and she couldn't even go to the police for protection!

What was she going to do?

Chapter Four

Her first instinct was to run. She could pack her things an[d] steal into the night like a thief before she was caught. Th[e] analogy amused her with its irony. And yet it was no laugh[-]ing matter. Camille was like a claustrophobic; she had a[n] abnormal fear of walls closing in on her.

Prison walls.

Escape-proof, even to a magician.

Angry that her frightened mind was creating such dar[k] fantasies, Camille challenged herself.

She couldn't be sure her pursuer was connected with wha[t] had happened in Paris. Only the day before, the *New York* *Times* had carried an announcement that the newly forme[d] team of St. Cyr and Camille would be the headlining act fo[r] Illusions. There had hardly been enough time for the infor[-]mation to get back to Europe and a pursuer to cross the At[-]lantic and pick up her trail.

Maybe someone from the club had followed her. But tha[t] didn't make sense, either. Only Justin had lingered s[o] late...and Kipp, she added thoughtfully, even while won[-]dering what motive he could possibly have to follow her[.] Merely to frighten her? Ridiculous. The man might be un[-]friendly but he treated everyone at the club with equal dis[-]regard.

Obviously some street criminal had been planning to rob er. If she hadn't had a secret to guard, she would have ome to that conclusion immediately.

Still, Camille couldn't help but look over her shoulder all he next day, even in the Chelsea restaurant where she and Vivian had met for dinner. While they were waiting for a able, her green eyes constantly roamed the lounge area— along the mahogany bar, past the blazing fireplace, toward small tables lit by Tiffany lamps—though she saw nothing suspicious.

"Are you all right, Camille?"

"What?" Realizing she'd been caught closely inspecting the bar's clientele, Camille said, "Yes, of course."

Vivian frowned and pushed her glasses back to the bridge of her short nose. "You seem distracted, as though you'd rather be somewhere else." As if she were trying not to sound too hurt, she added, "You could have canceled dinner if you had something else you wanted to do. I'm a very understanding person."

"I wanted to have dinner with you." Camille hesitated even as she felt the need to talk to someone about what had happened the night before. Vivian was the most likely person in whom she could confide. "I'm just a little nervous tonight."

"About what?"

"Someone followed me home from the club last night."

Vivian gasped, and her eyes widened. "Who? Why?"

"I wish I knew. I got away from him before he got to me. Both Justin and Kipp were still at the club. You've known Kipp longer than I have," she said. "Do you think he'd do something like that to scare me?"

"Surely not. Heavens, Kipp Walker might not be a sociable man, but I don't think he'd do something so malicious." Vivian looked down at her drink. Her Southern

accent was stronger when she added, "It was probably so
inner city pervert, Camille. I had a similar experience wh
I first moved to New York."

"What happened? Did some man steal your purse?"

Vivian looked up at her, and Camille thought her brov
eyes seemed haunted. "I only wish that's what the man h
been after. He tried to—" Vivian pulled up her sleev
Camille swallowed when she saw the ugly scar a few inch
above her wrist. "He had a weapon, but I stopped hir
Then a couple of kids came along and I screamed." Vi
an's lips turned up into a tight smile. "Luckily the wom
in my family are all good screamers."

Able to empathize with her, Camille said, "Luckily t
women in my family are all good runners. I didn't let t
creep get close enough for me to find out what he wanted
Remembering how her pursuer had been mere inches awa
from her hiding place on the steps, she shuddered. "Than
goodness."

Camille took a swig of her predinner brandy withou
really tasting it. It warmed her all the way down to her toe
When she set the glass down on the table, Vivian patted he
hand comfortingly.

"Try not to think about it, Camille, honey. Why, ever
time I see a man with dark hair and a mustache . . . Believ
me, it won't do you any good."

"You're right. I won't dwell on it," Camille agreed. Bu
she was no fool; she would keep an eye open. "Thanks fo
making me feel better."

"Friends are supposed to make each other feel better
Unfortunately I didn't know anyone here in the city whe
that man attacked me. I wish I'd had someone to talk to."
Vivian's lips quirked. "But now I have you, haven't I?"

"We have each other."

The quirk turned into a satisfied smile.

Having someone to talk to was a great feeling, Camille decided, and Vivian seemed equally relieved to be accepted as her friend. Too bad that Vivian hadn't had a friend to confide in when it would have counted. If someone had helped her through her horrible experience then, she might be more comfortable around men now.

But speculating on might-have-beens was useless, as Camille well knew from personal experience. Neither of them could go back and change the past. And so no matter how much she comforted herself with the idea that she was just another of Richard's victims, no matter how hard she tried to convince herself that she'd come out of this thing unscathed, Camille suspected she'd better get used to the idea of looking over her shoulder for the rest of her life.

"WHAT A WAY TO START the week," Justin muttered to himself. He had been setting up props for publicity stills when Camille strode onto the stage, and this was one of the times that he found it impossible to think of her objectively. His temper was sorely tested.

He was mesmerized by the skin of sparkling turquoise sequins molding her body and arms from her bared shoulders to her snug waist and the swag of silk encircling well-curved hips. Low-slung purple skirts spun out in a full froth that swished around her long legs as Camille glided toward him on high-heeled sandals. Her projected image of elegant sexuality was marred only by the expression below the mass of wild auburn curls streaked with bright purple and turquoise glitter.

Camille Bayard was distinctly unhappy and was unwilling to disguise the fact.

"I'm ready." She stopped a full yard away from Justin, her arms crossed under the tempting breasts that threatened to spill from the low-cut costume. Brows flattened, she

eyed the array of equipment at the edge of the stage. "
where's the photographer? Did you make him vanish
amuse yourself while waiting for me?"

Justin silently cursed his traitorous mustache, which h
twitched in amusement. "He's talking to Kipp. He'll
getting pictures of the staff in costume later. I didn't real
you were so anxious to be photographed."

"I'm anxious to get the ordeal over with. I never did li
sitting still for so long."

"Funny, but I don't remember that about you."

"Perhaps your memory is rusty with age."

"Cruel cut," Justin said, "especially since you said thirt
eight wasn't so old." He knew that Camille would like
avoid being photographed—photographs increased h
chance of being found by the wrong people. She didn
know that she'd been found already. So, unable to sto
himself from torturing her a little, he went on before sh
could respond. "Amazing that you can't bear to sit still fo
a photography session, yet you have to sit still even long
for some of your illusions."

"That's different."

"How did I know you were going to say that, Cleve
Cammi?"

"Because you can read my mind?"

He realized that she was smiling in spite of herself, an
Justin felt the blood swell rich and full through his veins i
response. This woman had the ability to set him on edg
while she turned him on, then to challenge him while mal
ing him like it. It was going to be a long haul till openin
night, when his plan would be fully implemented.

"I know I approved the sketch, but do I really have t
wear this costume in our act?" Camille asked suddenly, ir
specting the front of her gown.

"What's wrong with it?"

"Nothing, I guess. It's gorgeous, but it's not something I would normally wear to perform in."

She met his eyes, and he was no more able to stop himself from being snared by the emerald depths of hers than he was able to stop his pulse from racing. What would happen when he had to touch her, for God's sake?

"I'm kind of uncomfortable working in anything that's not loose on me." Camille broke the spell by looking down once more to inspect the gown's snug lines.

"Would you really want to wear one of your usual costumes with me in these tails?"

"Actually, you look as uncomfortable as I feel," she informed him—unnecessarily, although she couldn't possibly know that something other than his formal clothes was bothering him. "We could both change into something more casual."

"Image, Cammi, image. Remember that we're creating new stage personas together."

"You're right, of course."

She fluffed out her skirts, fidgeted with her tight sleeves and fussed with her hair, all the while pacing the length of the stage. Justin was beginning to suspect she'd be a basket case by the time the photographer returned and set up. He pitied the poor man, who would have to use magic to get a smile out of his lovely subject.

To his amazement, however, Camille seemed to calm down at first sight of the photographer, almost as if she figured she might as well give in to the inevitable. And when Trevor began to explain the various poses he wanted them to try, she turned on the charm Justin remembered so well.

"Now don't be nervous, Trevor." Camille aimed a mischievous, teasing smile at him. "If we don't like the pictures you take, we can always change them with some hocus-pocus. We're magicians, you know."

Trevor winked at her in what Justin thought of as a ph[c] naughty little boy manner, and his voice was smooth as [c] of Justin's prop silks when he said, "Let me be a tad s[e] ish, Camille. I'd like to think all the magic today will be my hands." Trevor flourished his camera, then attache[c] to its tripod.

"Why, I'm sure it will be," Camille agreed, her full l[i] softening into a very different kind of smile.

Starting to get irritated by what seemed like his partne[r] deliberate flirtation with the photographer, Justin scowl and was about to offer a tart suggestion that she should [ ] Trevor get the show on the road. But then he noted a fle[e] ing vulnerable expression on Camille's face while Trev[or] adjusted his tripod. She was merely covering her nervou[s] ness. She was a good actress; he'd always known that.

He almost felt sorry for her.

That didn't lessen the tension that tightened him up th[e] moment Trevor said, "All right, let's start with some po[r] trait shots. I want you both to face the camera, Camille back to your front, Justin." Gingerly Justin and Camille g[o] into position. Trevor looked into his viewfinder and sai[d] "Yeah, that's good, but get a little closer. Wrap your arm around this lovely woman's waist, would you?"

Justin complied, and Camille seemed to melt into h[is] chest, making it difficult for him to remember that for a[ll] practical purposes, she was the enemy. The thought suff[o] cated him: he was supposed to pretend interest, not ac tually feel it.

At least that had been the plan.

"Hey, can you two manage to look like you're enjoyin[g] each other?" Trevor asked from behind his camera. "Yo[u] both look as if I'm torturing you."

"It's a little difficult to relax when your oxygen supply [is] being cut off," Camille murmured.

Justin immediately loosened his grip. "Sorry."

"That's all right." This time her mischievous smile was aimed at him. "If you ever get tired of magic, you could always go into wrestling with a hold like that."

He couldn't resist smiling at the enemy.

It was difficult to stay relaxed with Camille in his arms; her softness stirred up all kinds of sensual illusions for him. But once they got going, Justin had to congratulate himself on a job well done. Obviously he must be as good an actor as Camille was an actress, because Trevor seemed satisfied with their improved expressions. He shot the first roll of film quickly, contenting himself with placing their bodies in glamorous poses and adjusting the angle and the tilt of their heads.

"Lift your chin a little more, Camille. Hold it! Good. You're going to love this one," Trevor informed them. "Now relax while I change the film. I'd like to get some movement next." He reverted to the naughty little boy to add, "Justin can twirl you about so that those skirts flare up and reveal a lot more of those long, luscious legs for me."

"Or I could be the twirler rather than the twirlee." Camille turned an innocent expression on Justin. "Do you think your trousers would flare properly?"

Goaded by her teasing on top of the effects of their recent close proximity, Justin growled, "I don't think I'm Trevor's type."

The photographer merely snorted. Camille's lips twitched, but she bit back a further reply.

At that moment Justin noticed that some of the waiters who would be doubling as magicians' assistants were already in costume and sitting at tables here and there. And Kipp was watching the photography session from the floor, obviously waiting for a chance to speak to him. He stood with his arms crossed, his face set in a dissatisfied frown.

"Kipp, something the matter?" Justin asked, walkin downstage toward him.

"You could say that. Leotie, one of the new waitresses developed a sudden case of nerves when she realized she wa going to be photographed. Sandra told me Leotie didn' want to come out here, so I figured I'd better talk to her.' Kipp shook his head disgustedly. "I found her in the dress ing room, huddled in a chair like a little kid."

"What's wrong? Is she sick?"

"Yeah. Stage fright. Leotie's strictly amateur. She ad mitted lying about her stage experience on her application She'll have to go. I just thought you'd want to know."

"Wait a minute." Camille came down to the front of the stage, stopped next to Justin and looked down at Kipp, her expression appalled. "You're going to fire this woman just because she doesn't have any experience? She must have talent or you wouldn't have hired her in the first place, right? Everyone's got to start somewhere."

"Not here, not now," Kipp insisted. "She shouldn't have lied."

"Look," Camille said reasonably, "she probably figured she didn't stand a chance of working here if she told the truth."

"You're right."

"Well, since you did hire her, why not give her a chance?" Justin thought the suggestion made sense and admired Camille for making it, but Kipp seemed more determined than ever to have the last word.

"For one, because her knees gave out and she won't be able to make it onto this stage."

"Maybe all she needs is someone to build up her confidence rather than take it away!" Camille snapped. She turned to Justin, touching his arm with a pleading hand. "I'd like to talk to her, if you don't mind."

How could he say no when she was appealing to him so fervently? "All right," Justin said, nodding his agreement, though he knew that Kipp would stew about the decision. But then Kipp stewed about everything. The guy probably had been born unhappy. "Give it a shot. But I'm warning you, if she can't make the grade right away, she'll have to go."

"But at least she'll get her chance to try something that's obviously important to her. That's what counts." Camille stood on tiptoe and kissed his cheek, whispering, "You're okay, partner," before heading for the dressing rooms.

Shocked by the way his heart thumped after her, Justin stood staring at the wings long after she'd disappeared, not caring that Kipp was silently fuming a few feet away.

Justin was disturbingly light-headed, but not because he could still feel the imprint of soft lips against his cheek, soft breasts against his arm. Camille's physical attraction had become meaningless for the moment, transposed into something far more precious.

Her letting down her guard had forced him to face her real worth.

He'd recognized the old Cammi he'd known fifteen years before: charming and loving, concerned about others, champion of the underdog. She'd always been ready to listen to someone else's troubles, make that someone—*him*—feel wanted and worthwhile. She'd helped him get through the rough spots when he'd needed help most.

Of all the people who'd touched his adult life, she'd been his truest friend.

Justin told himself to be wary of that Cammi, the one who couldn't possibly hurt someone else—the one who made him uneasy about the way he was using her.

It was too late for doubts.

"Hey, there are a few things I've got to take care of,"
Kipp said, interrupting Justin's thoughts.

"Go ahead. Thanks for keeping me informed."

The manager backed away from him, radiating still
lingering displeasure. "I'll let you deal with the situation.
don't think we should condone someone trying to fool u
like that, but you're the boss. I just hope you know wha
you're doing."

"So do I," Justin said fervently, thinking of the way he'c
been fooling Camille.

Pushing back the insidious guilt that crept along his gut
Justin knew he couldn't let his growing feelings for Camille
throw a wrench into his plans. Even if she was innocent of
murder, he had to use her as bait to get the others to come
to New York or all the energy and money he'd invested into
the previous six months would be wasted.

And more important, Genevieve's murderer would still be
walking the streets.

Trying to salve his conscience, Justin told himself that
Camille might be playing a part, molding herself into what
she figured he expected of her. He was sure she had something to hide. His instincts were finely honed. He could
sense the wariness in her and had brief glimpses of it when
he looked deep into her eyes, the pathways to her soul. She'd
always been a fighter. She wouldn't have left Paris merely to
get a persistent ex-husband off her back.

And yet, no matter how much he tried to be tough and
realistic, Justin had a hard time believing that the part of her
that was still the Cammi he used to love was an illusion.

Camille came back into the club just then, urging on an
obviously frightened but determined-looking young Native
American woman. Justin swallowed hard. Against his will,
his mind flashed back to a fourteen-year-old girl who had
bullied him, a grown man, when he'd doubted himself.

Justin lit the last Gauloises in his pack, hoping the cigarette's harsh smoke would help clear away those memories,
help him steel himself against her—but he suddenly found
it impossible to think of Camille Bayard as the enemy.

DURING THE NEXT HALF HOUR, Camille's awareness of
Justin as a man and of herself as a woman heightened with
each posed embrace until she grew uncomfortable. Suppos-
edly this was a professional photography session, but she
was being seduced onstage in view of all the gathering waiters and assistants, who could tell, she was sure.

Her brain waves must be out of kilter today, she thought
as she got down off the floating-woman apparatus, where
she'd posed for the last few shots. That would explain why
her reactions to Justin seemed more intense and less con-
trollable than usual. Not that she wasn't always attracted to
the man . . .

Then again, maybe it wasn't her brain that was acting
peculiarly, but her heart. Justin's kindness in letting her talk
to Leotie and his fairness in giving the inexperienced woman
a chance over Kipp's objections had touched her.

"Break time," Trevor called. "Why don't you change
into another dazzling costume, Camille."

"Do I have enough time?"

"Take all the time you need. I can start posing your assistants for individual head shots. They all seem to be here."

"Terrific. Coming?" she asked Justin.

"Not yet. Go on up without me. How about wearing the
beaded red number?"

"Terrific," she grumbled to herself. "I can't breathe in
that one, either."

Even so, she was glad to escape to the serenity of her
dressing room, if only to change into another uncomfortable costume—until she found the door slightly ajar.

Having something of a photographic memory, an advantage in her profession, Camille distinctly remembered closing the door securely. It couldn't have opened again by accident. Perhaps someone had been looking for her.

Trying to suppress a slight rush of adrenaline, Camille pushed the door hard; it thumped back against the wall. At first glance, everything seemed to be all right—a little messy just as she had left it. But then Camille noticed the waste basket leaning crookedly against the wall as though someone had bumped into it.

She scanned the room quickly. Her breath caught in her throat when she noticed other small irregularities: her lacquered screen pulled slightly forward at the right; a drawer in her dressing table that she hadn't used that day not quite closed; a makeup bag lying on the wrong side of her cosmetics; a prop turned upside down.

Someone had been in here searching through her things, not openly, but clandestinely. Whoever it was hadn't wanted her to know that a search had been made.

As she tried to guess what the searcher had been after, a feeling shuddered through her that was neither anger nor fear.

She felt violated.

"I've been looking for you."

Camille jumped slightly at Vivian's unexpected arrival. "I came up here to change my costume."

"That's what Mr. St. Cyr told me—" Vivian stopped and gaped at her. "Heavens, is something wrong? You're as white as bleached cotton."

Camille hesitated only for a heartbeat before making up her mind to share her discovery with her friend. "My dressing room's been searched."

Vivian stared at Camille in shock for a moment, then walked by her into the room. She looked around, obviously inspecting it for damage, but when she turned back to her friend, she seemed perplexed.

"Everything looks pretty normal to me." Vivian smiled and drawled, "I have noticed that you are not the neatest person in the world, Camille, honey. Did you forget where you put one of your props or something?"

"I wasn't looking for a prop." Camille entered the room herself, closing the door behind her. "Believe me, I know what I'm talking about. Someone was very careful about putting things back where they belonged, but I can tell certain things have been moved slightly."

Pushing up the bridge of her glasses, Vivian peered around more intently, a frown puckering her forehead under her froth of brown curls. "Are you sure you aren't imagining things? I mean, you have a right to be nervous after what happened to you on Friday night. You know, after that man tried to assault me, I'd go home and turn on the lights, check my closets and look under the bed so I could relax and get a good night's sleep."

"I'm not being paranoid," Camille insisted. She wasn't. Not this time. She could feel the invader's presence almost as though he were still in the room. "And I'm not imagining this. Someone was in here, looking through my things. But who?" she whispered, more to herself than to Vivian. "And why?"

"Hmm, I wonder..."

"What? Did you see anything—anyone—who looked suspicious out in the corridor?"

"No, not exactly." Vivian walked over to the assortment of magician's props strewn across one end of the dressing table. Looking down at them thoughtfully, she picked up a pack of oversized cards, turned them over and set them down again. She leaned against the table, facing Camille. "I was just thinking that there are a lot of aspiring magicians around here, what with the policy about the waiters and bartenders, and all. Maybe one of them was trying to discover some of your secrets or something.''

Camille could see no reason to disagree. ''You're probably right.'' The whole thing just gave her a spooky feeling. ''I would have sworn Justin would be a better judge of character when it came to hiring his help—''

''Justin hires only the managers. They hire their own staff. You know, the bookkeeper hired me, the chef hired the cooks and kitchen help, Kipp hired the waiters and waitresses.''

Kipp. The name set up an instant alarm—well, not an alarm, maybe, but a little warning buzz.

Camille remembered the way the man had glared at her when she'd challenged him. He had not been pleased. And yet she didn't think his searching her dressing room would put a smile on his face. Besides, he was open about his dislikes. If he'd had something to say, he would have said it, right then. She was sure of it.

''Listen, Vivian, I'd better get changed before someone comes looking for me,'' Camille said, not wanting to discuss the situation with her friend after all. She had some serious thinking to do that was best done alone. And so she asked, ''Was there something important you wanted to discuss?'' as she pulled pins out of her hair.

''I just thought you might want company for dinner tonight.''

''Not tonight.'' Camille leaned forward to the mirror to disentangle an earring that had got caught in her hair, and from the corner of her eye she saw an unhappy expression pass swiftly over Vivian's face. ''We're going to be working late again,'' she added quickly, trying to assuage her friend's hurt feelings. ''I'll probably get something to eat with Justin. Maybe some other night this week.''

"Sure." Vivian headed for the door, muttering, "Well, 'd better get back to work myself."

"See you later."

Camille unzipped her gown and slipped out of it huriedly, the search of her dressing room whirling through her houghts. She'd promised herself that she would not be paranoid, so there was no reason to suppose that the search had anything to do with the coin.

Or was there?

No, she was not going to start that again!

Camille removed the hanger from the red-beaded gown, rading one exotic costume for another. A simple invasion of privacy was no reason to start worrying. One of the aspiring magicians must have been peering into her secrets, just as Vivian suggested. She'd better check her close-up props to make sure nothing was missing.

Red beads splashed against the mauve couch as Camille threw down the dress and crossed to the table where her props lay. Everything seemed intact. Cards, ball and cups, coins, book, fake glasses. Sorting through everything, she noticed a folded piece of paper in the midst of her silks.

What in the world had she stuck in there? Probably a receipt or a list of groceries. But she hadn't left any lists or receipts on the table among her props. Or maybe she had and her photographic memory was beginning to break down. She unfolded the note quickly, her lips quirked into a smile at the thought of Velvet who would be quite miffed if her mistress had forgotten to buy cat food.

But the handwriting on the paper wasn't hers. And it wasn't a receipt. It was a note, addressed to her, written in French. She scanned the unfamiliar handwriting. The message stole the smile from her lips, and a renewed feeling of violation almost suffocated her. The invader had searched the room while looking for the perfect place to leave this

ugly missive for her. Swallowing hard, she reread it, auto
matically translating into English as though the words would
make more sense in another language.

"If you're very clever, Cammi, you will make yourself
vanish before it's too late...."

Her heart beating with increasing rapidity, Camille care
fully folded the note, as if hiding the writing would make it
message vanish, just as it told her to do. It was a macabr
joke, nothing more. It couldn't be a serious threat agains
her. She didn't have any enemies.

A picture flashed through her mind, of a threatening
stranger illuminated from behind by a set of car lights. He
pursuer. Were the pursuer and the invader the same man
A man who meant her harm?

Realizing she'd folded the note over and over until she
couldn't fold it any more, she searched for a place to hide it.
Her makeup box, that was it. Finding a cylinder of stage
makeup that was nearly empty, she inserted the paper and
replaced the top of the tube securely, then stuck it under her
eye shadows and lipsticks.

Carefully putting the disturbing words from her mind,
Camille started calmly to prepare herself for Trevor's camera.

But a few minutes later, staring at herself in the mirror—
decked out in a brilliant red-beaded costume, her face arti-
ficially beautified with layers of paint and powder, her hair
tortured into an exaggerated theatrical style—Camille
couldn't help but wonder if someone was choreographing
her entire life into one horrific illusion from which there was
no escape.

Chapter Five

Later Camille convinced herself that she'd merely had a moment of quiet hysteria caused by her overactive imagination acting on her guilty conscience. Any lone woman leaving the club late at night might be followed. And the note must have been a macabre joke, as she'd first assumed. She felt a little foolish about blowing it out of proportion, even to herself.

That's why she hadn't told anyone about the threat.

She grew adept at looking over her shoulder, however. Always vigilant, Camille awaited the occurrence of another unusual incident, all the while telling herself she was not being paranoid, merely cautious. Several days passed and nothing untoward happened. Only once during that week did she pull the tightly folded paper from its hiding place to study it and speculate about its author. Anyone at the club might know French, but duplicating the distinctive handwriting wouldn't have been quite so simple.

She'd been tempted to throw the thing away, better yet, to burn it. Instead, not knowing why, she had refolded the paper as tightly as before and returned the note to its hiding place.

Now, a week after she'd received it, Camille wondered if she'd made a mistake in keeping it. The secret missive had

become her albatross, its mere existence preventing her from
taking much satisfaction in the way her life was going. Ma.
had called to say he'd be there to give her all the support sh
could want on opening night. The act was becoming mor
polished and more pleasurable with each rehearsal. She wa:
already filled with delicious butterflies at the thought o
opening night. And Justin . . .

Justin seemed to be treating her with a new deference. She
was beginning to think the man was more than physically
attracted to her. Still, there was some reserve in his attitude, as though he might be fighting his feelings. Perhaps he
didn't believe in mixing his personal life with his business.
Or maybe he too had been disappointed by someone he
loved. But there was always a time for new beginnings.

The thought—while not one she wanted to inspect too
closely just yet—put an extra spring in Camille's step as she
hurried to join Justin on stage, exchanging quick greetings
with assistants and crew members as she passed. When she
saw her partner decked out in a black pirate shirt, tight pants
and high boots, Camille didn't conceal her appreciation.

She whistled.

Justin faced her, an eyebrow raised as though he disap-
proved of whistling. His twitching mustache gave him away,
and Camille grinned happily. "Did I ever tell you I've had
this pirate fantasy for years?"

"Saucy wench," he muttered. Then, registering the fact
that she was dressed in a green jump suit and a three-
cornered hat instead of a complete eighteenth-century
highwayman's outfit, he demanded, "Why aren't you
ready?"

"My costume's being altered. The breeches didn't fit
right—too tight in the hips," she told him, grinning wider
when his gaze dropped to that portion of her anatomy. "The
seamstress said they'll be ready for tomorrow."

"They'd better be."

"You always did hate leaving things until the last minute, always had to have absolute control."

"I admit it. I'm a person who prefers to be in control."

"Of everything?"

Before he could answer her teasing question, Leotie, their new assistant, interrupted. "The guys and I are ready to start if you are." She eyed Camille's green suit. "I guess not, huh?"

"No costume tonight," Camille told her, admiring the other woman's period dress and hairdo, which went well with her dark, exotic looks. "So I guess we're ready to rehearse our big epic."

They'd gone through the scenario several times during the past few days, using minimum props, but now the set was in place. With a painted backdrop of a sailing ship in harbor, and crates and barrels and coils of ropes scattered around, the stage had been turned into a dock.

"Places!" Justin yelled. "Let's do it as if we have an audience to play to," he told the performers as they took their places. "No matter what happens, keep going. Cover mistakes just as you would during a performance."

"Does that mean we really kiss tonight?" Camille asked with interest, her pulse picking up at the thought.

"I said we're doing the whole performance." Justin quirked an eyebrow at her.

The delicious thought distracted her slightly as she took her position and tucked up her hair under her highwayman's hat. What would it be like to be thoroughly kissed by Justin St. Cyr? He'd barely brushed her lips in previous rehearsals. She could hardly wait.

The music started, and the pantomime began. On cue a group of aristocrats swept onto the stage. Camille went on after them and used close-up magic to distract them—unsuccessfully. She mimed a bungled attempt to rob them, and they chased her offstage. From the wings she watched a spotlit Justin descend the gangplank from his pirate ship and then she ran on again, fleeing from her pursuers, straight into him. She dislodged her hat neatly. Camille could feel a tingling in her veins as Justin ran his fingers through her tumbling hair and expressed his wonder that she was a woman. Then he helped her into a crate. Camille crouched gingerly in a corner of the crate, keeping her feet away from a hole cut in the floor and covered with black elastic webbing. Justin lowered the lid. She knew that he would then drop a big pirate flag over it.

Now came the hard part.

The crate was constructed of a hinged top and four wooden sides hinged to a wheeled floor that had been placed exactly over an open stage trap. Underneath her was an elevator platform that was fitted with a control panel positioned at the top of a long shaft lined with wooden slats.

Listening intently, Camille heard the sound of running feet signaling the return of the pursuing aristocrats and the music that accompanied their demand to know what was underneath the pirate flag.

Quickly she pulled the pins out of the hinges and slid through the webbing onto the elevator as the top and sides of the crate collapsed inward above her head. She knew that Justin was keeping the pirate flag in position and then whipping it away to reveal an innocent flat wooden platform.

As soon as her feet touched the elevator, she hit a button on the control panel to start its slow descent. She swung the trapdoor into position. The first bolt on the underside of the trapdoor slid easily into place, but she had to force the second bolt home. She made a mental note to check on that bolt after the rehearsal was over.

Since she had time to breathe for a few minutes now, Camille told herself to relax if she could. This was the least enjoyable part of performing illusions—being stuffed into a dark hole of a place with only a couple of dimly lit switches for comfort. At fourteen, she'd had to spend several hours stuck in one of Max's cabinets until Justin had come along to rescue her. She'd never forgotten the awful experience. Camille had never gotten over her abhorrence of being shut up in the dark, but the task came with the territory, so she'd learned to deal with her fear in her own fashion.

To that end, Camille tried to distract herself with thoughts of Justin and the upcoming kiss, but soon realized she wasn't making any headway.

She was warm, perspiring, short of breath. She wanted out.

She heard Justin moving aside the wooden platform to show a bare stage. Feet again, moving away—the aristocrats trooping into the wings.

Not much longer. Good. She couldn't wait to get back up on stage, to breathe fresh air, to feel Justin's arms around her, to taste his kiss.

A clunk overhead—a second crate, which had been dangling above the stage in full view of the audience, landing on the trapdoor—and a tiny light glowing green on her control panel: those were Camille's signals.

She punched a button, which made the elevator move upward with a soft hum. She would unbolt the trapdoor and climb up into the second crate. Justin would whip away the pirate flag and hand her out of the crate, and she would reward the pirate with a kiss.

Split-second timing was important in this illusion. Bending her knees to avoid hitting her head on the trapdoor, she slipped open the first bolt, then tried the second. It moved slightly, then stuck.

She had to get down on her knees to be able to give the bolt a good yank. The knob came off in her hand.

"Damn!"

Suddenly sounds were amplified in her head: the jagged beat of her pulse; the whimper escaping her lips; the inner rush of her own fear.

Camille hit the emergency switch to stop the elevator from continuing its journey upward. The hum didn't stop. The switch didn't work! Camille could sense the bolted trap slowly drawing closer, knew it was too late to use the escape route at the bottom of the shaft.

"Justin!" she screamed, even as she sank to the floor, frantically clawing at the knobless bolt overhead. "The trap won't open! Help!"

A muffled curse and a confusion of quick footsteps assured Camille that those above knew of her plight, but what could anyone do in time to save her? Her fingers felt raw. She tried to get a grip on the bolt, all the while sinking lower until she was flat on her back on the elevator floor, her knees pulled against her chest. Her heart thundered against her ribs and exploded through her head. She'd never known such dizzying fear.

She was about to be crushed to death.

"God, no!" she cried, furiously kicking out at the slats of her prison, knowing that she wouldn't be able to budge the two-by-fours. Futilely she pounded at the trapdoor above her face. "No, not like this! Why?"

The note.

... make yourself vanish before it's too late ...

If only she could. If only she'd believed. Now it *was* too late. Flattening her body, she turned her bent legs sideways until she thought her knees were being pulled out of their

sockets and tried to protect her head with one arm. There
was no room to maneuver, no way to help herself. The
trapdoor was pressing against her hip, the jammed bolt
against her arm. The pressure increased fractionally...

And then suddenly the movement stopped and the soft
hum of the elevator died.

Camille cried out, one long, low wail of released fear.

"Cammi, are you all right?"

"Justin! Yes. Get me out of here."

Her plea was answered without words, though she was
aware of raised voices all jumbled together. Wood chips and
dust sprinkled her face as the trap was pried up. Camille
closed her eyes against the grit, but her choked coughs
mingled with the sound of ripping wood. Then she was freed
of her prison, pulled up into strong, warm human arms. For
the moment she was oblivious to the others crowding them,
whispering in low, shocked tones.

She was wrapped tightly against Justin's chest, and his
arms around her felt as good as she'd always known they
would. He'd saved her, just as he had that summer long ago!
Grateful tears stung her eyelids, and her fingers clutched at
his pirate shirt.

"You saved my life."

"Thank God," he murmured into her hair. "I didn't
think Kipp was going to get to that master power switch in
time. I'm not hurting you, am I?" He loosened his grip
enough for her to see the worry lining his face.

"What happened?" someone asked.

"Honey, you aren't hurt, are you?" a Southern voice demanded, its owner parting the small crowd with determination. Camille reluctantly pulled away from Justin, and his
expression closed as Vivian arrived beside them, her be-
spectacled gaze shifting back and forth from one to the
other. "Shall I call a doctor, Mr. St. Cyr?"

"That's a very good idea."

"No!" Camille protested. "I'm fine physically, just a little shaky inside."

"Then perhaps you should lie down for a few minutes in your dressing room," Vivian suggested.

"Would you go with her, Vivian, and make sure she *is* okay?" Justin asked.

"Of course." Vivian took Camille's arm. "Come on. I can even make you a nice cup of mint tea. My mama always said there was nothing like mint tea to soothe the nerves."

Still in shock at her close call, Camille let her friend lead her away from the knot of people who stared after them. She tried to focus her thoughts, concentrating only with difficulty.

"I don't understand how you got stuck like that. Sandra said the trap wouldn't open, but one would think there'd be some kind of emergency system."

"There is one. It didn't work."

"Oh, honey, how awful it must have been for you."

"Awful" was an understatement. The experience had been the stuff of which nightmares were made. Camille shivered and rubbed her clammy palms against the jump suit. Thank God she hadn't been wearing her costume with all its extra material to take up more room and get caught on moving parts. Clearly whoever had tried to kill her had known what he was doing and so must have firsthand knowledge of illusion construction. And if he'd rigged one accident without anyone catching him, what was to stop him from rigging another?

Next time she might not be so lucky. Justin might not be around to save her.

Vivian had been silent as they climbed the stairs, but now, halfway down the upper corridor, she whispered, "You don't think there's a connection, do you?"

Since Camille hadn't told Vivian about the note and the threat, this question startled her. How had her friend found out about the note? "Connection?" Camille said cautiously.

"Well, yes. First there was the man who followed you, then your dressing room was searched." Vivian was ticking off the incidents on her fingers. 'And now you've had to suffer this ghastly near-disaster.'

Of course Vivian didn't know about the note, which was proof positive of a connection. And Camille wasn't about to tell her, either. Her friend already knew too much, and more information could only endanger her.

"I'm sure there'll be some kind of logical explanation for this accident," Camille finally said, trying to make light of the whole thing. "Do me a favor. Don't tell anyone about the other incidents."

"But, Camille, honey, someone might be playing with your life. Surely Mr. St. Cyr—"

"No one. Promise."

"Oh, all right. I promise. But I can't help worrying about you." Vivian seemed almost embarrassed when she added, "I can't afford to lose a friend, you know."

Camille stopped in front of her dressing room door and gave Vivian a quick hug. "Thanks for your concern, friend. Listen, I can take it from here."

"I really shouldn't leave you alone."

"I'm fine. I insist."

"What about the tea?"

"Maybe later. I'd just like to lie down so that I can close my eyes." *And think,* Camille silently added. "That'll be better medicine even than mint tea."

"Well, then . . ." Vivian backed away toward her office. "You give a holler if you need company."

"I'll do that."

But Camille had no intention of involving Vivian further. She had to figure this thing out for herself.

Her mind already churning with thoughts of the attempt on her life and trying to discern the possible reasons and suspects, Camille opened the door and stepped into her dressing room. She stood stock-still on seeing the golden-haired man stretched out on her couch as though he had every right in the world to be there.

After what she'd gone through, this was one shock too many. "What the hell are you doing here?" she demanded tersely.

The slow, sexy smile turning up the corners of Richard Montgomery's perfectly sculpted lips irritated the hell out of her, but not as badly as the words that came from them. "Is that any way for a loving wife to greet her husband?"

Fighting the rising adrenaline that bade her throw something at the man, Camille balled her hands into fists and glared. "If you hadn't disappeared, Richard, you would have been informed that we were legally divorced six months ago."

Rising, he moved slowly toward her. "My, you do sound miffed," he murmured, turning on the charm. Too bad it didn't work on her anymore. It made her stomach knot rather than flutter. "I think I like it. Were you very devastated when you couldn't find me?"

"Don't flatter yourself." Camille slapped at the hand that tried to tuck a stray strand of her hair behind her ear, a familiar gesture of endearment. "And don't touch me!"

"Afraid?"

"Don't be ridiculous."

"If lines worked on you, I'd tell you you're beautiful when you're angry," Richard said, his brown eyes appreciative.

"You're right." The knot in her stomach tightened. "Your lines don't work on me anymore."

But they had in the past, and she'd always remember the last time she'd allowed him to con her.

"You look even better than you did in yesterday's *Times*."

"So that's how you found me."

"You don't seem pleased. *I'm* pleased." He paused, as though waiting for her to agree. "Well, if you won't observe the amenities, then I will. I'm fine, thank you. How's Max? Does he still have that bad-tempered Madame Bouchoux working for him?"

Barely holding on to her temper, Camille stewed at her ex-husband's colossal gall. Only Richard Montgomery would have the nerve to show up in her life as if nothing were wrong, and after everything she'd suffered because of him, right up to an attempt on her life.

"As far as today's rehearsal is concerned, let's call it a night," Justin told the others as he watched Vivian lead Camille away. He ignored their questions about the incident and refused to entertain any of their speculations. "Performers can go home. Crew members take a break and come back for repairs in ten minutes."

He turned to the stage trap. He wanted to inspect all the equipment immediately, while there might be some evidence to be found. His instincts told him that disaster had been too close to have been an accident, too perfectly executed to have been planned haphazardly. Justin wasn't about to give the saboteur a chance to make it look like anything other than what he felt it was in his gut—some kind of gruesome warning.

At least, he hoped it was a warning. Better a warning than an aborted murder attempt.

Picking up what was left of the wooden trapdoor, he examined it carefully.

"Find anything interesting?" Kipp asked.

"Not yet."

"I'll check the emergency switch."

Keeping an eye on Kipp, who was stepping down onto the elevator platform, Justin twisted the trapdoor in his hands and slipped the bolt free. Its metal housing had been slightly misaligned. That would account for the bolt's sticking, he supposed, and Camille was probably strong enough to rip off the knob if she was in a panic. She must have been terribly frightened. Though she hadn't said a negative word about this illusion when he'd suggested it to her, Camille might not have outgrown her fear of tight places.

"I found it," Kipp muttered.

"What?" Immediately Justin stooped and looked over Kipp's shoulder. Kipp had removed the cover from the switch box and was inspecting the contents. "Did someone cut the line?"

"No. Someone could have tampered with it, I guess, but I don't think so. Look here. See that tiny gap between the wire and the contact point? It looks like a case of sloppy workmanship. The metal housing probably wasn't bolted down securely, and the elevator's motion eventually vibrated it free." Kipp turned to stare at Justin, his dark eyes unfathomable. "Or were you thinking someone arranged this accident?"

Not about to admit any such thing, Justin replied evasively, "I merely wanted to make sure I considered all the possibilities. Someone might have a reason for not wanting this club to open. A serious accident would do the trick, wouldn't it?''

"Or someone might not like your partner?" Kipp said, his tone challenging. It seemed as if he expected Justin to point an accusing finger at him.

"That, too, is possible," Justin admitted, rising from his crouch. "I think I'll go see if the lady's all right. Would you make sure the crew gets started on the cleanup?"

He felt Kipp staring after him as he headed for Camille's dressing room.

Suddenly plagued with doubts, Justin wondered if he could continue with his plan which would put Camille in more danger. For he was sure that's exactly what he'd done. Perhaps he'd set her up as his bait all too well. She might indeed be innocent, as all his instincts kept insisting, but might know something she shouldn't. That might be why she'd been hiding and why someone would want her to have an "accident": so that she wouldn't—or couldn't—talk.

Justin would never forget the panic that had flooded over him when he'd heard Camille's terrified screams from the trap and the sense of relief he'd felt when he held her in his arms. She'd been so vulnerable. He'd wanted to press her to him forever. Damn! He couldn't continue blindly with his plan after all, after what had almost happened. Not feeling as he did

Unbidden thoughts of Genevieve made Justin try to harden himself so that he wouldn't define exactly what he felt for Camille.

But if he were to choose a word to describe what he felt, would it be love?

Not wanting to explore that train of thought, Justin took the stairs two at a time. He was anxious to talk to Camille, to find out exactly what she might know. She'd have to be honest with him if he was to protect her.

But from the certainty in her raised voice, which he heard clearly as he headed down the hall, he could tell that Camille didn't need protecting.

"Richard, cut the small talk," she was saying, her tone unnaturally hard and impatient. "You didn't come here to chat with me about my father or his housekeeper."

"You're right. I guess I should be direct after all these months I've spent looking for you, my elusive love."

"Get to the point, Richard."

Justin quietly approached the dressing room, stopping at the half-open door. He could see the two of them reflected in the makeup mirror, Richard cool and sure of himself, Camille stiff and obviously angry.

"The point is I came to chat about us," Richard continued. "About our future. And about the fact that Edouard Roget never reported the missing coin?"

"So?" she demanded, while Justin tensed at the mention of the coin and its owner.

"Don't you think it strange?"

"I don't want to think about it at all anymore."

"Why would he give up the insurance money?"

"Maybe he never figured out the coins were switched."

"He's not stupid."

"What's stupid, Richard, is your thinking I'd want to see you after all this time."

Justin recognized from her tone that Camille was hurt. A woman thwarted by love? He couldn't help himself. He watched the mirror-image man gather Camille into his arms and kiss her passionately. She neither protested nor struggled to free herself.

What a fool he was! Justin thought, backing away from the dressing room door. He'd been feeling guilty about using Camille; he'd wanted to protect her. Thank God he hadn't confessed all his feelings to her before finding out she was a criminal after all. Furious with himself, he whipped

around and headed for his office, where he could think
straight.

So Richard and Camille had been in on the theft of the
coin together. The question was: had they murdered Genevieve together as well?

REALIZING HER LACK of participation wasn't getting
through to her ex-husband, Camille turned from his kiss
angrily. "Don't."

Richard dropped his hands to his sides, but he didn't
move away. "Whatever you say."

"You never cared for what I had to say."

"That's a lie. I've always cared. I still care, Camille."

"As much as you did when you made me your accomplice in crime?"

"More."

"Really? Was that a turn-on for you?" she asked, suddenly as furious with him as when he'd pulled the coin
switch and expected her to go along with it. "I foolishly ruined my life to protect yours. Did that make you realize I
was the only woman in the world for you?"

"I've always known that," he said quite seriously. "And
if our situations were ever reversed, I'd give my life to protect you."

"How comforting." She didn't even attempt to keep the
bitterness from her voice. "Except we both know I'll never
be in that sort of situation."

"I hope not, Camille. You have no idea of how much I
love you."

"Then why the hell couldn't you have gone straight, like
you swore you would if I gave up the idea of a divorce? Why
did you lie to me and involve me in one of your cons? I was
giving you a second chance, for God's sake!" she cried, reliving the pain of Richard's betrayal. It was a hurt that
seared deep, all the way to her soul. She wanted to strike out

at him and wished she had a hefty object at hand. "You sa
you loved me then."

"Everything I said was the truth, you know. I real
meant every word.'

"You had a fine way of proving it!"

"I tried to go straight for your sake." Richard move
away from her, sat on the couch, ran a frustrated han
through the fine golden-blond hair falling over his for
head. "But I guess I was born bent out of shape if no
downright crooked. It took more incentive than I had at th
time to straighten me out." His eyes were pleading for u
derstanding when they met hers. "I thought you loved m
enough to forgive me anything."

So had she. Camille turned away from him, memories o
his betrayal haunting her.

Even though she'd left Richard and filed for divorce af
ter finally catching him in one of his scams, Camille ha
listened to his lies. A short while before the separation be
came final, he begged her to come back to him. He swor
he'd changed his life-style because of his undying love fo
her. Like a fool, she'd wanted to believe him. In spite of he
devastating disillusionment with her playboy husband, sh
hadn't been able to stop caring.

But caring and romantic love were not necessarily tn
same thing. She'd known that even then. That's why, when
she'd agreed to a trial reunion, the cautious part of her ha
kept Richard at a platonic distance, telling him directly tha
he would have to put up with it until she was satisfied he'd
really gone straight.

When Richard had presented her with replicas of val
able coins for her act, she'd thought nothing of it. He'd a
ways been so generous. She'd accepted them as a peace
offering.

Not until she was working a private party given by
Edouard Roget had she realized that Richard had set her up.

While everyone had been busy with cocktails and hors d'ouevres, Richard had disappeared for a while. She'd wondered why she hadn't been able to find him.

He was making the switch—one of her props for an antique coin worth one hundred thousand dollars.

Then, acting as her assistant during her magic act, he'd boldly passed the real antique on to her in front of a roomful of witnesses. Her sensitive fingertips had known the difference immediately.

Camille had realized then that the only feelings she could trust were those she experienced through her fingers. Her heart had allowed her to be betrayed.

She had gotten Richard away from the guests and faced him with his trickery. He'd refused her demands that he should return the coin to Roget's collection, in spite of her threat to turn him over to the police. Better to be jailed than dead, he'd insisted. He needed the money to pay off gambling debts, to stay alive.

She'd been guilt-ridden and fearful, yet unable to turn him in. Not reporting the crime made her an accomplice.

That was when Camille had divorced herself both from her husband and from the glamorous European life-style to which she'd become accustomed, and had started looking over her shoulder. And now, six months later, she was still paying for that mistake.

Camille frowned as she remembered her close call in the elevator shaft, and a bizarre thought occurred to her: she hoped she wouldn't ultimately pay with her life.

Suddenly, realizing Richard was speaking to her, she turned to him, frowning. "What?"

"I asked if you hated me for involving you in the theft."

"No, Richard, I don't hate you," Camille responded tiredly. She leaned against her makeup table and ran the sensitive, still-raw pads of her fingers along its crisp edge.

"I might always care what happens to you, but don't m
take that for love. You ruined that for me."

"You're still angry."

She didn't bother to respond to the obvious. Sighing. s
asked, "Why are you here, really?"

"Because I want you back."

"I'll never give you another chance to hurt me, Richar
I don't trust you." Camille was actually talking to hers
when she added, "I prefer a man who's moral, upright a
uptight." She preferred Justin, maybe even loved him. S
remembered how safe she'd felt with his arms around he
"I would never trust a man who's used me, no matter ho
he tried to justify it. You must believe that."

Richard stood and crossed the room to her. He tucked h
hair behind her ear. She didn't bother to pull away. I
couldn't affect her now. The kiss had proved that.

"I hope you'll change your mind, Camille, for my sak
If you do, I promise I'll really try to be what you want n
to be this time."

"I don't believe you."

"At least think about it. I'll give you time . . . until ope
ng night, anyway"

"It's too late for us. You must believe that." Camille w
almost sad when she murmured, "Go away, Richard. Don
come back."

"I'll go for now, but nothing will keep me away," h
promised, cupping her shoulders in his hands. "I want t
hold you in my arms again, Camille. I want you so that I ca
make love to you, cherish you, protect you. I'm willing t
do whatever I must to get you back where you belong."

He kissed her cheeks and went away.

Camille forced back her anger and sadness so that sh
could think about the aborted rehearsal.

Who had tampered with the stage trap?

It had to be someone who spoke French, who could have written that note and who was familiar with the staging of illusions.

Those qualifications fitted Richard perfectly. Though he was British, he spoke and wrote French like a native. Forgery was one of his nefarious talents, so he could easily have created a handwriting she wouldn't recognize. He also knew quite a bit about magic, because she'd taught him herself. And he'd been here in her dressing room, conveniently waiting for her to show up after the accident. Perhaps he had rigged the elevator and trap, hoping she'd be frightened enough to run into his arms—and back into his life—for protection.

Camille couldn't quite believe this theory.

But neither could she believe that anyone else at the club would want to do her harm.

She thought of Justin, a magician who also spoke French and could get into her dressing room at any time. But he'd certainly have no reason to try to frighten her after bringing her to New York to form a new act. Of course, she had reason to want to believe in his innocence, Camille thought, as old feelings for him stirred within her.

Something told her there had to be a connection between the trap incident and the coin theft. Edouard Roget? Had he figured out how the robbery was done and, rather than go to the police, decided to handle the situation himself? That, too, seemed unlikely. Surely someone would have spotted the stranger in the club. Except, of course, that Richard had apparently got in unnoticed.

Whoever it was, the guilty one was clever and devious. Wondering if the person merely meant to frighten her into vanishing or really meant her harm, Camille felt a chill crawl up her spine.

How would she ever identify her invisible enemy?

Chapter Six

"The elevator incident yesterday may or may not have be[en] an accident."

Sitting at the edge of the stage, Justin made his a[n]nouncement loudly and clearly. He'd called a general mee[t]ing of the entire staff to take place prior to rehearsal, and [h]employees were before him now, spread out over the club['s] various levels. Perhaps he couldn't spot the guilty party, b[ut] he could put everyone on the lookout so that nothing of t[he] kind could happen again.

"We were lucky," he went on. "Camille was only bruise[d] but she might have been killed."

A murmur filled with speculation rose in every directio[n.] All eyes turned to the woman seated next to him. Cami[lle] hunched her shoulders uncomfortably, and Justin guesse[d] she hadn't forgotten those frightening minutes. It had be[en] the memory of her trembling in his arms that had made hi[m] soften toward her, made him reevaluate what he'd seen a[nd] heard in her dressing room. She couldn't have faked h[er] terror when he'd helped her out of the stage trap. He wante[d] to believe there was some explanation for Camille's know[l]ing about the coin that would absolve her of all guilt. Per[]haps she was a pawn in some deadly game, just as Genevie[ve] had been.

Camille's voice sounded strange to him when she said, "Why don't we just forget about yesterday and get on with the rehearsal."

"I think it's a good idea. No one would want to hurt Camille," Vivian insisted from her seat in the front row. "She's a wonderful person." The bookkeeper's assistant surprised Justin, since she usually didn't venture an opinion. "Everyone around here likes her."

And some people more than liked her. Justin thought of the way he himself felt in spite of everything he had against Camille. "But each of us has a potential for making enemies, and for any number of reasons that may have nothing to do with our personal worth."

"But you couldn't prove the control box had been tampered with," Kipp reminded him. "You saw it with your own eyes."

"True. The bolt's sticking at the same time as the elevator's emergency switch gave out might have been an unfortunate coincidence." Justin thought Kipp seemed awfully anxious for him to accept the incident as an accident, a fact he'd keep in mind. "As a matter of fact, even if someone did deliberately sabotage the illusion, Camille might not have been the intended victim."

"Then who else might have been the target?" Kipp asked, his face set into a disbelieving expression. "You?"

"Or the club. I don't know." Justin had to raise his voice to be heard over the increasing din. "The point is, I want you all to keep your eyes open. Report anything suspicious to me. Don't make any assumptions about our props and staging. Check and double-check everything." He paused, letting his words sink in, waiting for any objections. When there were none, he added, "Rehearsal in twenty minutes."

Justin rose. Before he could go backstage to inspect the arrangements for their first illusion, Camille stopped him

Gently she placed a hand on his arm. Steeling himself, [
tried to remain unaffected, but willpower wasn't any u:
Her touch was warming, her smiling green eyes bewitchin

"I haven't really had a chance to thank you proper]
Justin."

"For what?"

"For coming to my rescue. For the second time. R
nember Max's cabinet?"

"You'd better thank Kipp as well," Justin said, trying
forget everything about their former relationship in Pari
He had to be objective where she was concerned. "He's tl
one who pulled the power on the elevator."

Her smile faltered. "Yes, well..." After hesitating a se
ond, she asked, "After rehearsal, can we get together
talk?"

"About what?"

Shrugging, Camille seemed a little embarrassed. She a
lowed her gaze to slip away from his, down to the middle c
his chest. "Old times. New times." Her eyes met his di
rectly and he could swear they glowed with challenge. "Us.'

Justin realized his mouth had gone dry. And he couldn'
help glowing from the inside out when her full lips curve
into a seductive smile. How he wanted to cover them wit]
his own!

Then he remembered the way Richard had kissed he
Having had time to think things over, Justin wasn't sure i
he'd been witness to her ex-husband's attempt at outrigh
seduction or if the scenario had been part of a well-though
out plan. What if Richard had rigged the illusion to elimi
nate Camille so that she couldn't tell anyone about the coi
theft and thus link him to Genevieve's murder?

Maybe if he had some time alone with her, he could de
cide how deeply Camille was involved.

"I haven't made any other plans for tonight," Justin finally said. "Why not get together? I've got a well-stocked bar in my dressing room. We can have a preopening toast celebrating the future success of St. Cyr and Camille."

She seemed relieved. "Good. It'll be fun. It'll give us an opportunity to do some catching up."

Justin didn't think that catching up was on Camille's mind at all. She had some other motive for wanting to spend time with him. An irrational part of him wanted to believe that motive was pure.

But the rational part wondered exactly how wary of her he should be.

A FEW HOURS LATER, Camille stood in front of Justin's dressing room door, wondering what in the world had possessed her to suggest this little get-together. If she'd wanted someone to talk to, Vivian probably would have been glad of the company. Besides which, Camille knew she didn't need to complicate her life any more than it was already. And getting involved with a man, especially one as aboveboard and honest as Justin, would only load it with further complications.

Then Camille remembered how safe she'd felt in Justin's arms. For a few moments he'd been her oasis in a rising sea of fear. Aching to feel his warmth surrounding her once more, she knocked three times.

Justin called to her from a distance. "Come on in and make yourself comfortable. I've just got out of the shower. I'll be out in a minute."

Opening the door, she called into the dressing room, "I could come back in a few minutes."

"No! Don't go anywhere. I'll be right out. Fix yourself a drink."

"I'd rather wait for you."

"Anything you want."

That was a tempting offer, Camille thought, grinning as she closed the door behind her. Justin might be shocked to know she'd rather have him than a drink.

She strolled the length of his dressing room, so very different from her own. Though it had been decorated at the same time as hers and by the same firm, it had an entirely different atmosphere. The pale gray sectional sofa and footrests had simple, modern lines, as did the halogen floor lamp. What made the room arresting for her was the history lining its main wall. Posters and pictures detailed the career of the great St. Cyr. There was even one of Justin, Max and herself...

"Find my souveniers interesting?"

"Very."

Justin was interesting, too, wrapped in a long black terry robe, his dark hair still wet from the shower, a black towel hung around his neck. Noting the enticing sprinkling of hair curling from his chest around the edges of the robe, Camille was hit by a sudden attack of nerves that made her knees weak.

"Mind if I sit down?"

"That's what the furniture's for."

She tried to make herself comfortable. Justin sat next to her. Too close. Not close enough.

"I remember when that was taken." Trying to distract herself, Camille pointed to a familiar picture. "It was Max's birthday. You and I bought him the escape cabinet that was supposed to have belonged to Houdini."

"Max didn't have the heart to tell us we'd been ripped off. Do you remember when The Amazing Ambruster told us we'd bought an expensive fake with mechanisms too new to have been used by Houdini?"

"Max couldn't bear to hurt our feelings."

"Your father was some kind of man," Justin said quietly, then confirmed something Camille had only guessed. 'I can't tell you how many thousands of times I wished he was *my* real father. I even used to pretend that he was."

They had their love for Max in common—among other things. Camille squirmed uncomfortably when she tried to enumerate those things, however. She had to leave out certain positive characteristics, such as rigid moral values, since she'd allowed Richard to disappear with a coin that didn't belong to him, even if she'd done so reluctantly. But at least she and Justin had their work in common.

"So you would have liked Max for a father," she said, suppressing the nagging guilt that she couldn't make vanish like one of her props. "Is that why you thought of me as your little sister?"

Justin shook his head. "You were fourteen. I was almost twenty-three. How else did you expect me to think of you?"

"And now?"

"You're not a child anymore."

Camille experienced a tingling expectancy that she tried to counter with a humorous, "I should say not. I'm a woman of the world. Married. Divorced."

Available, she wanted to add, but she couldn't force the issue. Justin was either attracted to her or he wasn't. Somehow she thought he was, even though he hadn't stopped sending her those confusing mixed signals since the day he'd tracked her down.

"What about Richard?" The question was personal, but Camille could have sworn he was trying to keep her at an emotional distance. "Is he out of your life for good?"

"Yes."

Justin frowned as though he didn't believe her. "You're sure?"

"I'm sure." Camille hesitated only a moment befo
adding, "Richard's here, you know, in New York City. H
came to see me yesterday." Justin seemed to relax. He'
known! She realized he'd been waiting for her to tell hin
about Richard's reappearance. "I told him to go away, bu
I don't think he believed me."

"Why did you divorce him?"

"Irreconcilable differences." Justin certainly was curious about Richard, almost as though he were sizing up his
competition. That thought cheered her and allowed her to
keep her tone more flippant than she actually felt when she
added, "Just like our illusions, Richard was not everything
he seemed to be."

"So he disappointed you badly?"

"That's an understatement," she murmured more to
herself than to him.

"Care to explain?"

Camille didn't see how she could tell moral, upright Justin that she'd been married to a con man and thief and
expect him to have any regard for her afterward. She was
afraid he hadn't changed, that he still saw the world in black
and white, without any shades of gray in between. Besides,
it wasn't her place to discuss Richard's illegal profession
with Justin.

"Let's just say my ex-husband's business practices were
not what I would have liked them to be," she said as truth-
fully as she felt she could. "Richard didn't see the harm in
what he was doing, so he wasn't willing to change. I, on the
other hand, was, so I left him."

"And how would the authorities feel about these du-
bious practices?"

"I have no idea." Camille lied with a bold face, yet the
doubtful way Justin stared at her compelled her to add, "I
was a wife, not an informant."

And that was the heart of her problem, the reason she had best not encourage a more personal relationship with a man who'd probably condemn her if faced with her secret. If Justin despised her for being morally weak, however, he didn't show it. As a matter of fact, she thought his expression had lightened.

"Justin, if you don't mind, I'd rather not talk about Richard."

"That's right. You wanted to talk about us."

Eyes widening at the change of inflection in his voice, Camille wondered if she was being influenced by wishful thinking or if Justin really had softened toward her. He seemed to have moved closer to her, not only physically, but also emotionally. She was receiving those mixed signals again, and they made her doubly cautious as she tried to interpret his interest in her correctly.

Aware of the male hand that had slid its way along the back of the sofa until it was almost touching her, Camille shivered and tried to tell herself not to let Justin's nearness affect her. Then, looking into his pale, hypnotic eyes, she thought better of her resolution. She wasn't about to make herself any promises where Justin was concerned. It would be impossible to remember good intentions around this man.

"You offered me a drink," she reminded him, unsure if she was trying to distract him or herself.

"So I did." She was relieved when he stood and went to a liquor cabinet, part of a narrow wall unit on which were displayed more magic memorabilia. Revealing his well-stocked bar, he asked, "How about a Kir?"

"Fine."

Preparing the white wine and cassis, shrouded in black as he was, Justin would have seemed as mysterious and magi-

cal as his stage image if it hadn't been for the very human
bare feet peeking from below his robe.

And it was his human side that appealed to Camille.

A dark lock of damp hair had fallen onto his high forehead, hiding the widow's peak that was usually so prominent. It gave him a boyish look, which made poignant
memories rise within her. Camille did her best to stifle them,
but her heart beat faster when, drinks in hand, Justin turned
to her. She slid her eyes down, past his, focusing on the cleft
in his chin.

Wordlessly he handed her a glass. Wordlessly she accepted it.

And as he sat down—closer to her this time—she kept her
gaze focused on his chin, hoping he wouldn't be aware of the
sudden inner tension that made her want to toss down her
drink and run away from him as fast as she could. Her instincts were working overtime, she told herself. They were
being too protective for once.

Purposely forcing her eyes back to his, Camille felt herself falling into a timeless void where there was no black or
white, only blessed shades of welcoming, hypnotic gray-
blues. Those eyes held her spellbound, seemed to probe
through her, searching for her soul. She held her breath,
wondering what they would find there.

"To opening night," Justin finally said, the softly spoken words echoing hollowly through her head as though
from a distance. He lifted his drink in a toast.

Still snared, unable to disconnect the current that held her
gaze fast, she lifted her own glass. "To St. Cyr and Camille." *To Justin and Cammi.* Then her free hand did
something impossibly bold completely of its own accord: it
reached out to touch his face. A fingertip grazed his mustache.

At contact, his eyes heated like molten steel. "Cammi!" The whisper was as urgent as the iron grip suddenly encasing her wrist. Justin's lips and tongue worked an earthy magic on her palm, sending her body rhythms wild. Her heart beat jaggedly, her inner temperature skyrocketed, her breathing became shallow. And she thought something had gone awry with her hearing when, still holding onto her wrist, he said, "Perhaps you'd better leave while you can."

Taking a shaky breath, Camille boldly returned, "And what if I don't?"

"Then be prepared."

"A good magician is always prepared. No, wait a minute, that's a Girl Scout motto," Camille murmured, attempting to counter their escalating physical awareness of each other with a little humor.

But Justin didn't smile. Eyes narrowing into unreadable slits, he released her wrist only to wrap his hand around the back of her neck. The flesh there tightened, the exciting sensation spreading downward to tease her breasts. Camille caught her breath, anticipating his next move.

With firm but gentle pressure, Justin inched her toward him until the tips of her breasts brushed his chest. Now their lips were but inches apart. She could feel his ragged breath on her face, could count his irregular heartbeats in her tightening nipples, yet he didn't force her closer. Suddenly her overactive instincts warned her to stop him now, before it was too late.

But too late for what?

She was more than ready for this to happen. It seemed they'd been tempting and teasing each other with searing looks and touches during each and every day of their rehearsals. Camille had wanted to taste Justin's unrehearsed, passion-filled kiss so many times.

And then she had her wish. His mouth was on hers, urging hers open, his invading tongue exploring, conquering, seducing. She lost herself in the kiss, pressed against him, wrapped her arms around his back without considering the drink in her hand. The Kir trickled from her tilted glass, wetting her free hand as well as his robe. Immediately flustered, she pulled out of the embrace.

"Sorry."

He didn't respond to the choked word except to take her half-empty glass. He set both their drinks on the floor next to the plush couch. Then he pulled the towel from his neck to dry her wet hand, somehow making the gesture more sensual then practical. He tossed the towel away. All the time he hadn't taken his eyes from her face.

His movements were slow but deliberate as he reached for her again, this time tangling his fingers in the wild auburn curls that had scattered across her cheek. Swallowing hard at his touch, Camille admitted that she wanted more than a kiss from Justin, and from his intense expression, she realized that he was more than willing to take everything she'd offer.

Now that she was faced with the very thing she'd fantasized about, she had a moment's reservation about making love with a man she really didn't know.

But she did know Justin St. Cyr, an inner voice argued. She'd known him forever, since she was little more than a child. He was an honorable man. He'd never use her as Richard had. She was sure of that, just as she sensed Justin must still care about her as she did him.

Old feelings were hard to destroy.

And so it was with a sense of déjà vu that Camille willingly slipped back into Justin's embrace. She felt as if she'd been there before and knew she wanted to remain there forever.

She wanted so much more from him than physical intimacy, and this surprised her. She'd thought her trust in men had been stolen from her for good by her thieving ex-husband. But Justin could restore it to her.

Justin took her mouth again, the kiss hard and hungry as he pressed her back against the couch, making her forget about everything but him—his scent, his taste, his touch.

Then he stripped her, quickly vanishing articles of clothing like magic. *He* was magic, Camille decided, untying his robe as he settled himself over her so that the black terry tented them both. Whimsical imagery sparked her imagination: Justin as a conjurer using his wizardry to transpose sensual heat from himself to her until she was aflame, ready to surround him with her own searing magical fires.

He slid into her, his cry of pleasure mingling with hers. Camille arched into him, wrapped her legs around his thighs. He stiffened, his head bent, his ragged breath feathering the hair around her ear. He was striving for control, and the realization gave her a sense of power she couldn't resist.

She urged him into movement with exploring hands, increased his excitement by nipping the soft flesh of his shoulder. He seemed frenzied, as spellbound as she, as they climbed together toward that elusive rapture experienced only by lovers. They peaked together quickly, and with such intense sensation that Camille could hardly believe she was experiencing reality rather than the culmination of some exquisite illusion.

But their joining had been real. Justin was real. Her emotions were real. This was an experience she didn't need to question.

She felt so safe with him wrapped around her.

JUSTIN LOOKED DOWN into Camille's relaxed, sleeping fac
and wondered how he'd let things get so out of hand. He'
invited Camille into his dressing room to elicit informatio
from her. He'd begun by doing just as he'd planned. Bu
she'd turned the tables on him by telling him partial truths
By showing her vulnerable side.

Her eyes flicked open. She squinted, as though trying t
focus on him. "Justin? You're dressed."

"It's late."

"Then you shouldn't have let me fall asleep." Camille'
attempt to rise was almost comical because she wasn't quit
awake. Unsuccessfully she tried to keep herself covered with
the robe he'd spread over her, shielding one part of her body
after another with the black terry cloth as she moved
around. "I'm keeping you from your own bed and a good
night's sleep. I'll get dressed immediately, unless you made
some of my clothes vanish for good, that is."

"They're all there," he said, ignoring her attempt at humor.

Justin turned his back as though he were allowing her
privacy. In reality, he could see her every movement in his
dressing room mirror.

Dropping the robe, Camille bent over to climb into a pair
of flesh-colored bikinis, then into peach-colored trousers.
God, she had a tempting body, long and elegant, yet well
rounded in all the places that counted. As she raised her
arms to pull on her matching sweater, he was reminded of
how exquisite those full breasts had felt in his hands. Renewed desire coursed through him, forcing Justin to divert
his attention to lighting a cigarette.

Even so, he couldn't stop himself from saying, "I'll walk
you home."

Her "Fine" didn't sound as though she meant it. He
sensed Camille was feeling awkward with him.

And why not? He was feeling awkward with himself.

He'd made love to a woman who might have been involved in his half sister's murder, for God's sake.

Could Camille have responded to him so passionately if she was guilty?

He couldn't—didn't want to—believe it.

Yet he couldn't bridge the awkward gap that he'd made between them while they covered the few blocks to Camille's apartment. He concentrated on the Gauloises rather than on her. They walked silently side by side, a foot apart, as if they hardly knew each other.

And indeed, Justin felt he'd barely scratched the surface of his partner's sensual self. What they'd shared had been nothing more than a quick release of the tension that had been building between them since he'd found her. He grew embarrassingly hard just by thinking of how good it could be if they had enough time to really explore each other.

But that would never happen. He wouldn't lose control so easily again, he promised himself, flipping his cigarette butt into the street.

When they entered Camille's apartment, her green eyes were filled with uncertainty and hurt. "I guess I'll see you tomorrow, then. And, uh, maybe it would be best if we forgot about what happened earlier."

Thick auburn lashes were lowered, hiding her inner self, and Camille backed away awkwardly. She seemed so vulnerable that Justin couldn't help himself. Before he could think about what he was doing, he reached out and caught her arm, then pulled her to his chest and hugged her in what he realized was an honest embrace.

"I don't want to forget about it," he said.

And there was more to that truth than the sexual satisfaction he'd experienced. He hadn't wanted to admit it, but Justin knew he cared for Camille. He cared whether or not she was innocent of Genevieve's murder, cared that he'd been using her and that he would go on using her in spite of the guilt that nagged at him even now.

"I don't want to forget either," Camille said, looking up into his face. "And I don't want you to leave."

Her words made him flush with desire. He shut and locked the door, then pulled his lovely partner back into his arms and covered her eager mouth with his own, wanting nothing more than to explore fully her special magic.

Yet, their surroundings reminding him of the illusions he'd woven through her new life, Justin wondered how Camille would feel when she discovered how badly he'd used her.

Chapter Seven

Camille turned away from the purring noise that invaded her sleep-fuzzed brain, but the furry body that was pressed against her neck followed her movement. Whisker tips tickled her face, making her pull a protective pillow over her head.

"Knock it off, Velvet, it's not time to get up yet. It's still dark."

Gradually the realization that it was evening rather than morning sank in.

Camille remembered other things: that she and Justin had arrived at a satisfying new relationship the night before; that he'd stayed with her till morning; that they'd come to her place "for dinner" after rehearsing all day; that her stomach was empty because they'd never gotten around to eating; and that he'd gone to run an errand before tonight's full technical rehearsal while she'd allowed herself to fall asleep on the couch where they'd made love.

Justin had worn her out. She could probably sleep till morning. As if to chastise her for being such a lazybones, the doorbell rang.

Groaning, she pushed herself up from the couch and quickly pulled on the pants and shirt that lay crumpled on the floor. This was beginning to be a familiar routine, she thought, though not without satisfaction. Padding across the cool tile, she tried to stifle a large yawn.

The buzzer sounded again.

"All right, all right," she muttered irritably. "I'm coming." Velvet sprang from the couch to dance around her feet. "Since you're so excited about having company, why don't you answer the door?" Camille asked the cat. "Or is it kitty chow you're after?"

"Meow!" came Velvet's agreeable reply.

"Well, you'll just have to be patient." Camille demanded of the intercom, "Who's there?"

"Your favorite father."

"Max!"

Sleepiness vanquished, she pressed the buzzer to let her father into the building. Camille had known Max was scheduled to arrive that evening, but she'd figured he'd call from his hotel, then maybe meet her at the club.

It was a good thing that Justin hadn't stayed longer. Wouldn't they have had some quick explaining to do if they'd been found together, tousled-looking and sleepy! Not that her father would disapprove of her new relationship. Max loved Justin almost as much as she did.

Love? Justin? Did she?

Before she had time to think about this idea, Max was at the door. Opening it, she took a long, hungry look at her distinguished parent, whose tall wiry form was topped by hair that seemed to show more salt than pepper these days. Then she flew into his arms and was crushed by his enthusiastic hug.

"I'm so glad to see you, Max."

"You could have been seeing me every day for the past seven months if you hadn't vanished into thin air."

"Max, don't start. At least not until after you've come in." It was then that Camille noticed the luggage that lay at

er father's feet. "Didn't you even stop to check in at your
otel?"

"I decided to skip the Algonquin this time. Too pedes-
rian," Max said with a wave of a hand. "If it's all right with
you, I thought I'd stay here. That way we can spend more
ime together."

Hesitating only because she was taken by surprise, Camille came to her senses and picked up Max's bags. She
headed for the bedroom, Velvet following curiously.

"Of course you can stay with me. You can have my room.
I'll sleep on the couch."

"No. Now, I don't want to put you out of your bed. I'll
take the couch."

"It's all right," she assured him, setting the bags inside
the bedroom door. After scooping up the pesky black cat,
she rejoined her father in the living area. "I really don't
mind giving up my bed. As a matter of fact, I'm getting used
to sleeping on couches. I was just napping on this one when
the doorbell rang."

Max eyed her suspiciously, but all he said was, "If you
insist, the couch is all yours, dear daughter."

"Well, I do insist. Come on into the kitchen. Velvet won't
let me alone until I feed her. And I need a cup of caffeine to
pop these eyes open fully."

Max followed her lead and sat himself on a stool while
Camille poured crunchies into the cat's bowl and found the
coffee can and filters.

"This is a stupendous place you have here, Camille."

"It is nice, isn't it? I sublet it, furnishings and all, from a
friend of Justin's who has out-of-town business. I'm not
sure when he'll be back. I really should start looking for a
new flat soon."

"Moving is such a bore. I don't look forward to it myself," Max told her as she turned on the electric coffee

maker. "I've been thinking of selling the Paris town house It's a trifle large for one person to rattle around in all by himself."

Almost knocking over the open can, Camille was startled into thoughtful silence. Max was planning on selling his town house! He'd owned the place for more than twenty years, ever since her mother had divorced him and he'd gone off to Europe. What was going on?

"You could close off the upper floors," Camille suggested carefully.

"I did think of that. I even considered renting them. But I'm not making definite plans just yet. Who knows what city I'll be working next month," her father said with a flourish of his hand. "Everything hinges on my bookings."

"Bookings? Max, what are you talking about?"

"I'm going back to work."

"Why?"

Max frowned at her, his salt-and-pepper brows flattening over green eyes so like her own. "Now, Camille, I hope you're not intimating I'm too old."

"No, of course not. But I thought you were enjoying your retirement."

"Justin got bored in a couple of months. It took me a couple of years, but there you have it. I can't stand not having anything to do. If I don't go back to work, I *will* be old before my time," he insisted, but he didn't seem to be able to meet her eyes directly. "I've made an appointment with my old agent Freddie Patterson tomorrow."

"I'm sure you won't have any problem in getting bookings," Camille said faintly, though she wasn't sure of any such thing, knowing fame could be fickle. "Your reputation as a master magician won't have been forgotten by anyone."

"I should say not. I was—I *am* the best in the world at what I do."

Camille wasn't about to argue with that. She didn't want to argue with her father at all. She wanted to ask questions, serious ones. But Max had his pride, and she couldn't question him about money. For surely lack of money must be the problem that was forcing him out of retirement.

She was thoughtful as she poured two cups of coffee.

Things began to make sense: why he'd hesitated about coming to the opening of Illusions; why Madame Bouchoux no longer worked for him; why he wanted to stay with her rather than at his usual Manhattan hotel; why he'd even consider selling the Paris town house. That investment return he'd been expecting to come in must have bombed royally.

Camille quickly came up with what she hoped was a solution. Max could work at Illusions to help him get back on his feet. Justin had plans to book other acts to supplement their own in the future, and she was sure he'd be eager to help the man he'd thought of as a father. She'd talk to him about it as soon as she returned to the club.

But for the few minutes she could afford to spend with Max before heading back for a technical run-through, Camille would try to take his mind off money.

Handing him one of the coffee cups, she said, "You're really going to enjoy Justin's and my act."

"I'm sure I will. I've always been proud of my daughter's skills. I taught her everything she knows."

"Well, she might just surprise you. Maybe she's learned a few new tricks," Camille said with a grin. "Or a new presentation."

"There was nothing wrong with your old style, but it was quite different from Justin's. It will be amusing to watch the two of you rehearse."

"Listen, I'm going to have to get over to the club as soon as I finish drinking my coffee. I'd invite you, but I know how horrible jet lag can be. Why don't you stay here and sleep it off, then come to dress rehearsal tomorrow night."

"Don't you start treating me like an old man, Camille Bayard."

"I promise." Camille kissed his cheek. "To me, you'll always be The Magnificent Maxwell."

But she couldn't help worrying about him, which was exactly what she did all the way to the club. Less than four years before, he'd retired nicely with a portfolio of stocks and bonds and a healthy bank account. How could he have run through so much capital in such a short time? He must have gambled it all on one bad investment.

Upon entering Illusions, Camille checked the lounge first, then headed for the club itself, but Justin was nowhere to be found. Leotie was the only person near the stage, practicing one of the card tricks she'd use to entertain her customers.

"Have you seen Justin?" Camille asked her anxiously.

Leotie's exotic face lit and her lips tilted into a friendly smile as she looked up from her spread deck. "I heard him say he was heading for his dressing room to clean up and change. That was about ten minutes ago."

"Thanks." Camille climbed up onto the stage and headed for the rear stairs. "I'll look for him there."

"Before you go, I want to thank you for giving me the courage I needed the other day," Leotie said, making Camille pause in the wing of the stage. "I wouldn't still have this job if it weren't for you."

"I didn't do anything but give you a push."

"You did much more than that. I heard how you persuaded Mr. St. Cyr to give me a chance over Kipp Walker's objections."

Not wanting to discuss that unpleasant man, Camille said, "I was glad to do it. But now the rest is up to you. If it helps, you have my vote." She backed away, adding, "Listen, I've got to find Justin. I'll see you later."

A thrill ran through Camille as she rushed up the stairs, as eager to be alone with her lover as she was to discuss solutions to Max's financial plight with him. She had no doubt that Justin would be pleased to have his mentor appear at Illusions.

But when she knocked at his dressing room door, there was no answer. Thinking Justin was probably in the shower, Camille entered uninvited, with an anticipatory grin at the thought of surprising him. She wouldn't mind a shower herself.

Opening the bathroom door, she peeked in. "Justin?" He wasn't there.

Well, he had to be somewhere. He hadn't been in the lounge or in the club. Perhaps one of the assistants or a member of the crew had stopped him for last-minute instructions. No doubt he'd be heading this way at any moment.

She'd wait.

To amuse herself, Camille decided to inspect the wall unit of shelves loaded with old props. Assuming they'd all been used by Justin at one time or another, she poked through the magic memorabilia with increasing interest. She wanted to know everything she could about the man. It wasn't until she'd worked her way down to the bottom shelf that she spotted an object that brought a smile to her lips.

"He's kept it through all these years," Camille murmured to herself happily as she reached into a back corner and pulled out a tray holding a fake goldfish bowl.

Camille was touched. She'd given this magic prop to Justin as a going away gift fifteen years before, when he'd finally decided to leave Max's employ to set out on his own.

The prop in fact was a half bowl, behind which was secreted a load chamber faced with a portion of a buttoned white shirtfront. It had been designed to make the observer think he was seeing through the bowl to Justin's shirt-covered stomach. Turning the prop in her hands, she heard something solid slide within the load chamber. That was odd. Usually the chamber would contain nothing heavier than silks.

Curiously, she tilted the prop. A flash of red flew out of it and fell on the floor, revealing itself to be a red leather-bound notebook. Setting the tray back on its shelf, Camille picked up the notebook, which had fallen on its spine, its pages opened to the well-worn middle. She would have returned the book to its hiding place had she not noticed the handwriting. It wasn't Justin's, yet it was familiar. And the language was French. Taking a closer look, she realized the entry could have been written by the same person who'd sent the threat to her. She scanned the page.

Camille froze when she read her own name in the middle of the text. Then Richard's. And Max's. Her heart thundered in her breast when she found a reference to Edouard Roget and the missing coin. Paging through the small book, she quickly read various entries about the author's search for the thief.

But who was the author and what was the notebook doing in Justin's dressing room?

One indecipherable page contained only abbreviations of words combined with letters and numbers; it looked as though it had been written in a code. Then Camille found several pages of notes on Justin's search for her, written in his own hand.

"God, no! Justin!" she cried, the sharp sound seeming to mock her as it echoed through her head.

Feeling as though the red leather cover was burning her fingers, Camille threw the notebook at the wall, where it landed on a middle shelf.

Justin had been using her!

A chill ran through her flesh, settling into her very bones. She sank down onto the couch on which she'd made love with Justin St. Cyr only the night before. The memory made her want to deny the evidence of his betrayal. She stared at the red notebook, which was barely visible from where she sat, as though it could tell her a truth she would be able to accept.

Camille squeezed her eyes shut against the anguish that made her want to cry.

Edouard Roget must have hired Justin to find her and the coin.

But that didn't make sense. Roget could have set the police on her instead of seeking her privately. And Justin could have demanded she turn over the coin outright if he'd believed she had it.

What kind of a weird and dangerous game was he playing with her?

Then she had an even more awful thought: perhaps Justin wasn't working for Roget.

Perhaps he was planning to use her in some illegal gambit for his own profit, just as Richard had done. Justin had certainly put on a good enough act to fool her.

More than once lately Camille had had the feeling that her life was being cleverly manipulated. Now she knew why. Justin St. Cyr was a master of misdirection, the central principle in the art of magic, the thing that made deception work and illusion seem real.

The things that had happened to her suddenly made sense. The man following her, the threat, the rigged elevator: probably all Justin's doing. He'd terrified her so that he could set himself up as her protector. He'd saved her from harm, hypnotized her into believing he cared.

Was Justin's making love to her nothing more than a superb example of misdirection, another of his dangerous illusions?

He must have planned everything right from the beginning, Camille thought bitterly. Opening her eyes, she stared at herself in the mirror opposite, searching for some sign of her own gullibility. It must be in her face somewhere. Justin had recognized it and used it against her.

Suddenly the thought of running into him here in his private dressing room with no one else around made her sick to her stomach, so she hurried out, heading for her own dressing room.

Calm down. Get hold of yourself. Think, for God's sake!

"There you are!" Vivian called, catching up with Camille. "I just came from—"

"I don't have time to talk to you now, Vivian."

They stopped in front of Camille's quarters. Vivian's brow furrowed, and her brown eyes grew serious behind her owlish glasses. "Honey, is something wrong? Has something else happened to upset you?"

"No, nothing." Realizing her tone was clipped, Camille smiled and excused herself as best she could while opening the door. "It's just that I'm going to be late for rehearsal if I don't get changed in a hurry."

Though Vivian seemed uncertain, she didn't object. "You go ahead, then. I'll talk to you later."

"Later," Camille echoed.

Rushing into her dressing room, she slammed the door behind her. Her heart pounded like crazy, urged her to run, to get as far away from Illusions and Justin St. Cyr as she could. But he'd found her once, and he could do so again. And she was through with running!

Camille stripped off her clothes and grabbed her costume from the rack. No, she wasn't about to run away. Once again she'd been disillusioned by a man and was fearful for her own safety, but this time she would stay and play out whatever game Justin had created.

"But the rules are about to change," she muttered while jerking on the glittery costume. "You didn't nickname me Clever Cammi for nothing."

Camille didn't know exactly what she was going to do, because she hadn't figured out what the man was after. But she would. The one thing she did know for sure was that if she was successful, Justin St. Cyr would be trapped in his own illusion.

THROUGHOUT THE TECHNICAL REHEARSAL, Justin had taken care to double-check every piece of equipment they used and to keep his eyes open for anything unusual. So far, nothing out of the ordinary had occurred.

Now, in the midst of the finale—the illusion using the elevator that had almost crushed Camille—he was tense and wary. She was hidden below the stage trap, and they were at the point where things had gone wrong last time. Justin eased the rope that made the second crate slide down its cable. Settling the crate in position over the trap, he listened intently for Camille's voice.

But all he heard was the music changing, preparing the audience for the production of the missing woman.

Justin went through all the correct dramatic motions, yet he hardly breathed while opening the crate. When Camille popped out of it and into his arms immediately, relief flooded him, softening his rigid stance, and he felt like crushing her himself.

They kissed briefly, Camille as stiff and unnatural in his arms as she'd been throughout the entire rehearsal. He could hardly blame her, considering the circumstances. Probably she, too, had been waiting for another "accident" to occur. Still, now she should be as relieved as he that their performance had gone without a hitch.

Justin led her upstage to the pirate ship. Then, with them clasped in each other's arms at the rail, the stage went as black as the club. Camille pulled free of him immediately.

When the house lights were turned on, Kipp Walker approached them, clipboard in his hand, his face void of expression. "Do you want any technical changes in this illusion?"

"Just one small lighting addition at the end," Justin told him.

He snaked an arm around Camille's waist, but rather than moving into his body as he expected her to, she seemed to hold herself apart from him, making him wonder if Kipp's presence made her nervous. He'd had his own suspicions of Kipp, yet he now admitted they didn't make sense. Kipp was not the friendly sort, but Justin couldn't believe he would try to hurt someone merely because he didn't like her.

"Keep a spot on us and dim the other lights gradually as we walk toward the ship," Justin told Kipp, who penciled the request into his notes. "When we board and stop at the railing, I'll take Camille into my arms and kiss her. That'll be the signal to bring out the spotlight."

"I'll tell the lighting man before we leave. Are we done for tonight?"

"Done with rehearsal." Then, when Kipp moved away, telling the technical crew to call it a night, Justin lowered his head to Camille's and whispered, "But you and I aren't done for the night, are we?"

"Actually, we are."

"What's the matter? Afraid I won't let you get your beauty rest?"

Turning her into him more squarely, he inhaled her fragrance, her special Cammi-scent that was as tantalizing and unforgettable as the woman herself. The stagehands and assistants had all wandered away, and sure no one could see what he was doing, Justin slipped a hand under her highwayman's coat and purposely brushed her breast. Her slight shudder delighted him.

"I don't think you need sleep anyway, Cammi. You're beautiful now."

Taking a deep breath, Camille wedged a hand between them and flattened her palm against his chest. Her lips turned up at the corners, but there was no invitation in the smile. "Don't get any ideas. You can't come with me tonight."

But Justin needed her tonight, and he had to protect her. Only two days to go until the opening, until he could face his suspects and reveal Genevieve's murderer. He was sure Richard Montgomery was the guilty one. He didn't want to think about the fact that he might never be with Camille again once she discovered the truth about the way he'd used her to bring her ex-husband to justice.

He was tempted to tell her himself. Now.

Maybe he would explain everything tonight, when she was in his arms, softened, emotionally open from their lovemaking. He would never have a better opportunity. Surely she'd understand his reasons and forgive him.

She had to forgive him.

He loved her.

Coaxingly he murmured, "Give me one good reason wh
I can't come to your place."

"Max."

Immediately releasing her, Justin looked out into the au
dience, searching it for his mentor. Everyone had cleare
out. They were alone. "He's here somewhere and you didn
tell me?"

"Not at the club, at my apartment. He's sleeping off hi
jet lag."

Relieved that she wouldn't be alone tonight, disap
pointed that he wouldn't be the one to keep her company
Justin asked, "When will I see him? What about lunch to
morrow?"

"Max is planning to be here for dress rehearsal." Ca
mille seemed to be studying him closely when she added
"But I don't know what his plans are for the day. He saic
something about having a meeting with his old agent, Fred
die Patterson. Max is talking about coming out of retire
ment."

"He is? Well, why don't you tell him to see me? If he
wants to perform, why not here? I told you I was planning
to book other acts for the future."

"Maybe you should suggest it," she said faintly. "Lis
ten, I've got to go. I really do need some sleep."

"Don't I get a kiss good-night?"

He could have sworn he noted a fleeting expression that
was not one of pleasure before she agreed, "One kiss."

Justin pulled Camille into his arms, his body responding
to hers instantly. "Lady, if that's all you'll allow, let's make
it one to last us."

He cupped her chin and tilted it, raising her face to his.
Brushing his mustache across her lips to open them, he made
his move slowly, savoring every second of contact. Her
breath was shallow, attuned to the irregular beat of her heart

against his chest. Her mouth was so tempting. When he captured it and explored its intoxicating moistness, he never wanted to let it—or her—go. He kissed her deeply, telling her of his love with action rather than words.

Camille seemed just as captivated. She wound her arms tightly around his neck, and she kissed him with a fervor he hadn't before tasted. She made his body flame with remembered magic.

But the kiss was over before he had enough of her. Camille pushed him away suddenly, then stood before him for a few seconds, trembling, her hand to her mouth, her emerald eyes wide and filled with uncertainty. Backing away, she turned and ran toward the stairs.

"Camille, wait a minute!" Justin called, starting after her. "Let me walk you home."

"No! I'll see you tomorrow," she yelled in return, not bothering to slow down.

Justin followed her up the stairs to the dressing rooms at a relaxed pace, wondering why Camille was acting so oddly, as though surprised by her own feelings. Maybe that was it. Could she have finally realized that she loved him? Undoubtedly the realization would be as great a shock to her as his own revelation of love had been to him.

Once in his own dressing room, Justin stretched out on the couch and worried about how he was going to find a way to be alone with Camille so that he could tell her the truth before the opening of the club. He couldn't risk losing her. He knew that now. He'd never loved another woman as he loved Camille. Justin wanted that love to last forever.

If only Max had stayed at a hotel.

The problem reminded him of the notebook. It was usually kept in a wall safe hidden behind one of his performance posters. He'd been reading it again tonight, as though it could tell him new truths, when he'd been sum-

moned to resolve a minor emergency. He hadn't had time
reopen the safe, so he'd hidden the notebook temporarily
the goldfish bowl prop. Now he thought he'd better put it
the safe at once.

Justin drew the bowl from its corner.

The load chamber was empty!

Hastily he checked all the shelves in case he'd been mi
taken about the hiding place, but the red leather noteboc
was gone, and with it his only clue to his half sister's mu
derer.

Someone had stolen it.

The guilty party must have known it existed and woul
have realized the significance of the entries. His min
worked feverishly. At least three of the suspects were i
town. Richard, Max and Camille. .

"Camille. God, no!"

Justin didn't want to believe she was guilty, but he coul
no longer eliminate Camille from the list. Though Richar
or Max could have sneaked in undetected and found th
notebook while everyone else was rehearsing, she was th
most obvious choice since she had free access to his dress
ing room.

Grimly he dropped back onto the couch, feeling as i
someone had punched him in the gut. Whether for hersel
or to protect Richard Montgomery, Camille must have sto
len the evidence. Sick at heart, Justin knew the theft mus
have been the real reason she'd been acting so strangely al
night.

Now that she had what she wanted, would she run?

Chapter Eight

Camille spent a restless night full of disturbing dreams. Justin refused to leave her alone, even in sleep. He was always there, waiting for her, trying to hypnotize her with his depthless pale eyes. Trying to trick her, to use her.

Though she tried to run, she could escape neither him nor the dangerous illusions he created to seduce her. They awaited her at every turn. A dark sorcerer, he cast an evil spell that drew an invisible net around her tighter and tighter until ultimately Justin had her in his power in some dark, underworld place that smelled of death and decay.

She awoke in a cold sweat, her heart pounding with her fear. Clutching the blanket to her chest as she sat straight up, Camille felt the depressing gray morning close in on her through the windows. She wondered why she'd been sleeping on the living room couch again. As confusion cleared from her mind, she remembered offering her bedroom to her father.

"Max?" she called out anxiously, barely able to take a steady breath. "Max, are you there?"

No answer came from the bedroom. He was still asleep. Realizing that she'd just sought her father's protection like a scared child, Camille was embarrassed. She'd merely had a bad dream, after all.

Still, she couldn't help being frightened.

A thump on her feet startled her, but it was only Velvet. Camille scooped the cat to her, taking comfort in the furry warmth. Obviously hungry, Velvet alternately purred and protested.

"You'll just have to wait a minute, you purr monster. I don't think my knees would hold me at the moment."

Camille took a deep breath, willing the shakiness away, wishing she could as easily will Justin to be the moral, upright man she had once known and loved. It was only natural that having been taken in by Richard, she had been drawn to the honesty she had believed to be the foundation of Justin's character as much as she had been to his charisma.

Her naïveté had remained intact in spite of her experience with Richard. She'd been so easily fooled, so easily betrayed. Her disappointment with Justin as a person was exceeded only by her disillusionment with him as a friend and lover.

"You really know how to pick them, don't you, Clever Cammi?"

Thinking about her own gullibility depressed her.

Glancing at the wall clock, Camille was surprised to see it was almost noon. This was no time to be maudlin. She had to form a plan of attack right away before leaving for the club. She had to figure out what Justin was up to, so that she could foil his plans and ensnare him in his own illusions. But how? Where should she begin?

Max. Her father probably knew Justin better than anyone. He could help her. Camille scrambled off the couch, ignoring Velvet's protest that she was heading for the bedroom instead of the kitchen.

But peering through the open door, she was faced with an empty bed. She went in to find open suitcases, male toile ries spread on her dresser, and a robe tossed over a chair. He had already left.

"Damn!"

Not knowing Max's plans for the day, Camille figured she wouldn't be able to talk to her father until he arrived at the club to watch the dress rehearsal.

But waiting wasn't as easy as she would have liked.

Camille spent the afternoon worrying and ignoring the telephone, which rang insistently at regular intervals. Sure it was Justin calling, she didn't want to answer in case she should inadvertently give him a hint of her suspicions. Eventually she unplugged the phone, thinking she would try to get some rest. She couldn't sleep, because she couldn't stop worrying about hurting Max with the truth.

Though she was anxious to have her father's help, in order to get it she would have to tell him everything, starting with the stolen coin and the real reason she had had to leave Paris. Max would stand by her, she was sure of it, but his loyalty didn't make the prospect of telling him the story any less difficult. He'd want to know why she hadn't been honest with him in the first place.

By the time she entered Illusions early that evening, she was in a fine state of nerves, which were calmed only a little by the fact that her father had arrived before her.

"Camille, there you are!" Max was standing with Justin in the club's entryway. Taking her in his arms, he crushed her in a fatherly hug and kissed both her cheeks. "Justin has been showing me around the place."

She avoided looking directly at the man who'd betrayed her. As determined as she was to foil Justin's plans, she felt weak in his presence, just as she had the night before, when she'd let him kiss her. She'd betrayed herself for a moment then, responding with all the love he didn't deserve

She wouldn't be so foolish again.

"So what do you think of your protégé's club?" Cami
asked Max.

"This is what I'd call a class act."

"You're the classiest act I've ever watched, Max," Ju
tin assured the old man, while Camille focused on her f
ther so that she wouldn't have to look into Justin's dange
ous eyes. "If you ever think of going back to work, let m
know. I could use you here."

Since she distinctly remembered telling him her fath
wanted to come out of retirement, Camille was startled in
meeting Justin's gaze anyway. He was staring at her, h
expression unfathomable. She refused to let him know h
bothered her. Glad that she had taken acting lessons, sh
smiled at him as though nothing were wrong, whereas i
reality her heart was racing and her mouth had gone dry
Wondering what game Justin was playing now, she was eve
more surprised when Max seemed willing to join in.

"I'm honored, Justin, but I don't know. I've gotten use
to taking it easy. Performing would mean another majo
change in my life-style." Max paused artfully before add
ing, "I have to admit I do miss the old profession. Tell yo
what, my boy. I'll sleep on the idea."

"You do that."

Desperate to get Max alone, Camille interrupted. "If yo
can spare your daughter a few minutes, she'd be delighte
to show you around her dressing room."

"Lead the way." Before following, Max took a long look
at Justin. "I'll be keeping a professional eye on you to
night, my boy. Do an old man proud, will you?"

There was pride in her father's voice already, Camille re
alized uneasily. Enlisting Max's aid was going to be a mor
difficult experience than she'd imagined.

Once they were in her dressing room, she retired behind
the Art Deco screen to change into her first costume, the

muted gold suit for the artist-and-model scenario. She tried
to figure out how to begin while Max settled himself com-
fortably on the mauve couch.

"Camille, I don't think I've ever told you how truly proud
of you I am."

"You don't have to."

"But I want to. I've always been equally proud of both
you and Justin. There have been times when I've felt as
though that boy were my own, you know."

Max said this so wistfully that Camille's heart fell along
with the green knit dress, which puddled around her ankles. She shivered, the reaction coming from deep inside,
then pulled on her blouse, wishing its persimmon color
could warm her.

Max's tone was cautious when he added, "I love Justin
almost as much as I love you."

"That's understandable." Camille drew on her acting
skills again. She took a deep breath and pulled on the calf-
length skirt, mentally forcing her fumbling fingers to coop-
erate. "The two of you were very close for several years
while I lived with Mother in California."

"That's why I sort of adopted him, made him my protégé. I was missing you, I guess. I'm glad my fondness for
him never bothered you. I expect it was because you loved
Justin yourself." Camille froze behind the screen, the skirt's
zipper halfway up. As if her father could sense her reaction, he added, "You didn't have any idea I knew how you
felt, did you?"

"No."

"I was a lot more perceptive than you gave me credit for,
my dear daughter!"

He gave a delighted chuckle that upset Camille's equilib-
rium. She put a hand against the wall to steady herself as she

realized that her girlish love for Justin didn't displease him
She was sure she knew what was coming.

"I can't tell you how much it pleases me that the two of
you are working together now. I never thought it would
happen." Max cleared his throat noisily, the sound seeming
to convey something he was embarrassed to say directly.
"And I'd be just as pleased if your relationship developed
into something more than business."

Camille closed her eyes and whispered, "Oh, Max..."

"Don't say anything, Camille. It may be nothing more
than the heartfelt illusion of a sentimental magician, but let
me create it, at least in my mind, would you? I guess I must
be getting old," he said with a sigh. "And who knows?
Maybe some day those magical feelings you once had for
Justin will be rekindled and returned. As a matter of fact, I
distinctly felt something going on between the two of you
before we came up here."

If only Max knew the truth! His heart would be broken
when he learned how Justin had used her.

Though she felt a little like crying, Camille got control of
herself for her father's sake. She couldn't tell Max about the
things that were troubling her, because she no longer had the
heart to involve him in a scheme to trap Justin. She'd go it
alone. She couldn't bear to see Max as disillusioned as she,
not yet, at least.

She'd let him dream a little longer.

After zipping up her skirt, she stepped out from behind
the screen as though nothing were wrong.

"Ah, Camille, you're more beautiful than your mother
ever was."

"You old flatterer." She leaned over and kissed him on
the cheek. "You know I look like you, not Mother. You just
wanted me to assure you you're still as handsome as ever."

"Well?"

She tugged at his tie. "Don't you know men get better ooking as they mature?"

"Now who's the flatterer?" Max chuckled as he rose and headed for the door. "But then who am I to argue with my beautiful, intelligent daughter? I'll leave so that you can finish getting ready. Besides, I want to make sure I get the best seat in the house," he added, as though he'd have to fight hundreds for the privilege when in reality the rest of the audience that night would consist only of members of the cast and crew. "Break a leg."

Opening the door after this parting shot, he almost ran into Vivian. As Max passed by, she turned to Camille, looking quite alarmed. "I didn't mean to interrupt anything."

"You didn't." Feeling guilty at having brushed off her friend the day before, Camille said, "Come in," then headed for her makeup table, wondering how she was going to deal with Vivian when she had so much on her mind. Realizing that Vivian was hovering in the doorway, Camille asked, "What's wrong?"

Vivian slammed the door shut. "Nothing's wrong. Not with me. But that man looks very familiar. As a matter of fact, I'm sure I saw him around the club the other day. Why did he tell you to break a leg?"

"Saying break a leg means wishing good luck in show business," Camille said, wondering if her friend had been eavesdropping. "He looks familiar because he's my father, and you couldn't have seen him around the club before because he came into town only last night."

"Oh. I thought maybe he was the one who . . . you know, followed you and then tried to—"

"Hardly," Camille said with a laugh tinged with bitterness.

"Well, I just wanted to let you know I was staying to watch the dress rehearsal." Vivian paced the room as though she were still uneasy. "Anything I can help you with?"

"You could get my jacket. It's on the clothes rack."

When Vivian slipped behind the screen, Camille checked her makeup. It needed very little attention, since she'd applied it just before leaving her apartment. Vivian really must be suspicious of men if she thought Max could frighten anyone. Wouldn't she be surprised if Camille told her Justin was the culprit.

"Found it." Vivian reappeared and set the jacket on the couch, then disappeared once more while Camille chose a blusher. "Honestly, honey, you have to learn to be a little neater. I'll hang up this dress you left on the floor."

"Thanks," Camille said, tinting her cheeks and hairline with copper powder.

A swish of fabric and scrape of hangers along the clothes rack was followed by Vivian's wistful, "These costumes are so beautifully designed, especially the red-beaded gown."

"You know, that color would look good on you." Camille was a little surprised by her friend's unusual interest in clothes. She knew she'd love to help Vivian replace her dowdy wardrobe, especially the unflattering olive suit on view today—if she was around long enough to do so. "Try it on sometime. If you like it, we could shop for something similar for you."

"Maybe I'll do that," Vivian said, reappearing from behind the screen. "I'm getting sick and tired of looking like the ugly duckling."

"So we'll turn you into a swan at the first opportunity." Camille gave her full mouth a fresh coat of burnt orange lipstick, then threw the tube onto the growing pile of makeup on the table. She grabbed her jacket and pulled it on with suddenly shaky hands. "I'd better get downstairs. Justin is probably waiting for me."

"Yes, you mustn't keep Justin waiting."

Camille knew that Justin was indeed waiting... but she didn't know why or for what. She would ferret out the truth, she promised herself, even if she did have to do so alone. Absently she picked up her prop book, stuffed her silks and coins into her pockets and left the dressing room, her stomach churning at the thought of having to work so closely with a man who might mean her harm.

If only she could figure out where to start her investigation or what incriminating evidence to look for. Camille realized that even if she found a clue to the truth, she wasn't sure she'd recognize it.

The one thing she *was* sure of was that she'd be damned before she let a man use her again!

As though her thoughts could summon his presence, Justin was waiting for her at the foot of the backstage steps, his face schooled into a casual expression. She slowed her gait, not anxious to be alone with him.

"Too bad you got down here so quickly," he said as she stopped on the stair above him so that they were eye to eye. "Max came down to the club a few minutes ago, so I was hoping I'd catch you alone in your dressing room."

Camille was sure he forced the note of personal interest into his voice. Her pulse raced annoyingly. "Why?" she asked, trying to disguise her suspicions by making the question a sultry challenge.

A dark eyebrow winged upward, but there was no smile in the gray-blue eyes boring into hers. "So I could do this."

His hands burned into her upper arms as he drew her to him and forced her to suffer his kiss, his lips mechanically crushing her own. Mercifully the embrace was brief, void of any true emotion. Realizing that all their kisses had been just as false without her knowing it left a bitter taste in her mouth.

When Justin released her, Camille decided that if he was determined to play a part, she would go one better. Sliding her fingers along his cheekbone, she was gratified to feel his slight shudder. So he wasn't totally immune to her touch after all. Good.

"Maybe you could come to my dressing room when rehearsal's over."

And by that time, she'd have figured out some excuse not to be there herself.

Eyes hooded against her, he asked, "What about Max? He suggested we split a bottle of champagne and talk about old times afterward."

She pouted, pretending disappointment, then trailed one nail down his neck to his sweater. Perhaps she imagined it, but she thought something at the back of his eyes flared at her touch.

"Things are getting complicated, aren't they?" she asked, purposely brushing up against him. Justin jerked as if hit by an electric shock. "It's a shame, but I guess we'll have to wait a while longer to be alone."

"Pity," Kipp said from where he stood a few yards away, staring at them with his arms crossed over his chest. "But can you wait to make personal plans until later? I'd like to start this dress rehearsal on time."

"You're right, of course," Justin said as he stepped away from the near-embrace, "even if you can't find a more civil way to let us know."

Irritated by Kipp's familiar rudeness, Camille stared at him, crossing her own arms. "I'm ready, but I didn't hear any calls for places."

"Places!" Kipp repeated. "But if you're ready, where are your glasses?"

Camille's hand flew to her face and she felt herself flush. She'd forgotten her glasses. They were still in her dressing room. "I'll get them and be right back."

"Make my day."

While Camille ran up the stairs two at a time, she was sure Justin was chastising Kipp further about his attitude Though she would have liked to have told Kipp a thing or two herself, Camille thought Justin had a lot of nerve chas tising anyone about anything.

He'd turned out to be no better than Richard, who be longed in jail for his nefarious deeds. Justin St. Cyr had stolen her hopes, her trust and her love, so that all she had left was suspicion and bitterness.

Furious with him, herself and the whole situation, Camille threw open her dressing room door with a vengeance, so that it bounced noisily off the wall. She heard a woman shriek.

"Camille!" Vivian exclaimed, a hand over her breast. "You startled me. You aren't angry with me, are you? You said I could try this dress on."

Vivian was standing at the mirror, glamorous in Camille's red-beaded gown, which accentuated a well-proportioned figure. She'd sleeked her hair back and added bright slashes of makeup to what was a really beautiful face and had been admiring herself in the mirror when Camille had flung open the door.

Camille shook her head. "No, of course not. I'm just surprised."

"I-I'll take the dress right off. I never should have tried it on in the first place."

"Vivian, don't be silly," Camille insisted as she reached for her prop glasses, but the other woman had already slid behind the screen. "It was my suggestion. I promise I'm not angry with you. It was Kipp,'' she half lied. "The man is impossible. He made me lose my temper.''

As soon as she put on the glasses, she realized they weren't hers because they weren't lensless. They had to be Vivian's. Yet Camille could see through them perfectly. The lenses were plain clear glass. How odd. Was Vivian so determined to hide from men that she'd even wear glasses she didn't need?

Before she could question her friend about it, Camille realized Sandra was standing in the doorway.

"I was just on my way down,'' Sandra said. "Are you ready?''

Nodding, Camille returned Vivian's glasses to her dressing table, then found her own pair. At the moment she needed to keep her mind on the upcoming rehearsal in case there were any nasty new surprises with which she'd have to deal.

She'd worry about Vivian's problems later, after she'd solved her own.

THE DRESS REHEARSAL went smoothly. No hitches and no accidents, minor or otherwise. As he changed back into his street clothes, Justin figured he should be grateful for the respite and hoped his own plans for the next evening would go as well. He didn't know how they could, though, now that the notebook was missing.

He could imagine the disaster. He'd have his suspects gathered together in his dressing room, just as they are in a mystery story when the detective is about to rehash the clues and reveal the criminal. The only problem was that his one piece of tangible evidence was gone. His suspects would laugh at his suppositions, and the guilty person would walk away, a free man.

Justin would have to rely on being able to probe Camille's conscience until she broke and incriminated Richard as the thief and murderer.

Or was he?

Through his own investigations Justin had learned Richard Montgomery was not what he seemed to be, exactly as Camille had admitted.

But she could have stolen the notebook to protect herself or her father, who was having financial difficulties. Maxwell Bayard was an old acquaintance of Roget's and had been at the party at which Camille had performed. Perhaps the old magician had pulled the coin switch so that he could pay off some debts. Though Justin had heard Richard and Camille discussing the fact that the missing coin hadn't been reported, neither had indicated who had stolen it.

And then again, it wasn't beyond possibility that since he hadn't called in the police, Edouard Roget himself might have had some reason to kill Genevieve. There was a chance that she had stumbled onto some dangerous information while playing amateur sleuth.

Maybe a good night's sleep would make the puzzle pieces fall into place, only Justin wasn't so sure he was going to get any sleep at all this night.

With that thought, he left the dressing room to join the preopening-night-celebratory party Max had instigated. Walking along the corridor, he could feel the floor under him pulse with the beat of sultry music that came from the dance area. Happy voices carried to the stairs, but as he descended, Justin was aware of nothing but Camille, who was looking on while Max performed a close-up trick for one of the crew members.

Her auburn hair and green dress were bright spots against the grays of the club. He was drawn to her in spite of himself, a moth drawn to the flame.

"Dance?" he asked, standing above her.

Camille's green eyes flicked upward, and he saw the same self-protective shadows that he'd noted earlier, when she'd teased and tortured him on the back stairs. "I'm already being entertained nicely, thank you."

"But by your father." Max interrupted his trick to nudge his daughter out of the booth. "You'll have a better time in this young man's arms."

Camille had the air of a woman bravely facing a firing squad. Her posture was too erect, her smile too forced, her eyes too haunted.

Not waiting for any objections, Justin swept her toward the half-filled dance floor and into his arms. The music was heavy with sensuality, seducing him into holding her closer. He had to be crazy to torture himself like this.

Neither was Camille unaffected. He was aware of a genuine physical response from her before she stiffened slightly. She seemed to be trying to put a mental distance between them.

"We're in public," she murmured. "Not in your dressing room."

Unable to resist torturing her as she had tortured him, he stroked her spine, leaving his hand pressed to the small of her back. Her immediate reaction was undisguisable through the thin cotton knit. "Are you ashamed to let the others know we're lovers?" he whispered, his breath feathering her hair.

She didn't answer immediately, but he could feel the quickening of her heart, since she was pressed against his chest. "It's none of their business."

He swung her around in tight circles, his thigh wedged firmly between hers, his body a traitor to his mind, his heart a traitor to his soul. He wanted her. He loved her. Even if she was capable of murder. Even if he had to see that she was locked behind bars.

Since this was probably the last time he'd ever hold her in his arms, Justin decided to make the most of the opportunity. He crushed Camille to him, for the moment losing himself in her softness and scent. He wished things could be different. He wished he could love her without guilt.

And as if she recognized his momentary sincerity, she clung to him as if she never wanted to let him go. They moved together intimately, true lovers for a brief time. Then her hands stroked his body discreetly, one trailing up to his neck, the other down to his waist and around to the inside of his jacket.

His wits were so befuddled with love and desire and despair at knowing he could never have her that Justin almost missed the clever movement of the hand on his hip.

Almost.

Though he forced himself not to stiffen, not to betray the knowledge, Justin was thoroughly aware of exactly when his pocket lightened.

Camille had lifted his keys.

What the hell was she up to now?

He wanted to curse her, to shake her, to force her to tell him the truth. He did nothing but hold her in his arms as naturally as possible until the music ended and she escaped from the dance floor and him.

Only as practiced an eye as his could have picked up her covert movement when Camille slipped his keys under the left shoulder pad of her dress while pretending to smooth her long hair away from her neck.

By that time Justin had already figured that she wanted access to his apartment to find and remove any clues that would link her to the crimes. Following her back to Max's table, he sadly decided to give her enough rope to hang herself.

Camille put his plan for her self-execution into motion immediately upon arriving at the table. She gathered up her purse and coat and remained standing, obviously anxious to leave. Justin couldn't help himself. He stopped next to her, casually draping his arm around her back, making sure his hand covered her left shoulder pad. He would have been surprised if she hadn't immediately tensed.

"Aren't you going to thank me?" Max asked her. "Wasn't that a lot more fun than watching a trick you've seen a thousand times?"

"It would have been great if the music hadn't been so loud," Camille answered in a shaky voice. "I'm afraid it gave me a splitting headache."

After patting her shoulder and hearing a slight metallic noise, which made Camille jump, Justin slid into the booth to watch the rest of her performance. "Sit down and have another glass of champagne. That'll cure what ails you."

"No! Champagne would only make my head feel worse," she insisted, fidgeting with the strap of her purse before settling it over her shoulder.

The strap would hold the keys firmly in place until she was able to retrieve them, Justin thought. How clever of her. But then he'd been the one to nickname her Clever Cammi.

"You're probably right about the champagne," he said. "But I'm sure we have aspirin at the bar."

Camille shook her head. "I'd better go home. I haven't slept well the past few nights—you know, the excitement of the opening and everything."

"And everything," Justin echoed.

"But I thought we were going to celebrate and talk about old times," Max complained. "It's been fifteen years since the three of us were together."

"But we'll be together tomorrow too."

"All right," Max grumbled, returning a few props to his pockets. "I guess I can wait."

"I don't expect you to come with me. You and Justin can entertain each other with your stories tonight." Camille put out a staying hand, since her father seemed determined to rise anyway. "Please. You'll make me feel guilty if I drag you away when you're having fun. I promise you I'll be fine."

"You're sure?"

"Positive," she said, already backing away. "Stay as long as you like."

Heading for the door, Camille seemed oblivious to the cast and crew members who wished her a good-night. Justin watched her go, knowing that the longer he and Max talked, the better for her.

But he would only allow her enough time to set the noose firmly in place.

CAMILLE FORCED HERSELF to calm down once she stepped into the cool April air. Taking a deep breath, she removed the keys from her dress surreptitiously, just in case there was anyone around to see her. Then she put on her coat, belting it tightly around her waist. Relieved to be out of the club and away from Justin, she hurried down the street toward his apartment building, wondering how much time she had for her search.

Though she tried not to think of the way she'd almost panicked when Justin had put his hand on her shoulder and then again when he'd made the keys jingle, Camille was nervous. She hated this intrigue, yet she was determined to learn the truth at any cost. Maybe she'd find it in Justin's personal belongings, a logical assumption, since he'd never invited her to come to his place. Luckily she'd had the foresight to check his address while waiting for Max that afternoon.

Within minutes she stood in the slightly dilapidated entryway, trying the various keys on the ring. She found the correct one just as another tenant came down the hall. Had she still been fumbling around, he would have been suspicious and undoubtedly would have challenged her right to be there. Her mouth went dry at the thought.

Taking the elevator to the fourth floor would have been practical and faster than using the stairs, but Camille preferred to climb to Justin's apartment under her own power. She hadn't forgotten the incident at the club, and she doubted that she'd feel really safe in any elevator for a long, long time.

Thinking about the way her life was going, she doubted she'd feel safe ever again.

Focusing on the task at hand, she found the correct apartment. To her relief, she had no trouble with the keys. Once inside, she closed the door before feeling for a light switch. The room revealed to her came as a shock. After seeing the club he'd designed and the apartment he'd found for her, she had assumed Justin would live equally well. But it was obvious that no thought had gone into decorating this place.

The few pieces of furniture filled only a portion of the space in the living room. A couch and chair. A coffee table. A desk. It was a functional room at best.

When she'd searched it without finding anything she could consider a clue, Camille entered the bedroom, guided by the spill of light from the living room. There'd be more to look through here, judging by the personal effects strewn around. But even in the semidarkness she could tell the room was far from being luxurious or even particularly attractive.

Snapping on a dresser lamp, which gave light that spread softly into the dim corners of the room, she opened a drawer and rummaged through it. Nothing interesting. The next two were equally unrevealing, but when she got to the bottom drawer, Camille found something other than clothing.

Pulse fluttering, she picked up a faded photograph. Holding it in both hands, she slowly sank onto the bed behind her. She was staring at a much younger Justin. He looked cocky, poised, ready to take on the world, and he had his arm wrapped around a blond teenager whom she recognized instantly.

An uneasy feeling snaked through her as she suddenly realized that Justin had never once talked about Genevieve since their conversation at Guido's on the night he'd found her. He hadn't even mentioned his half sister in the three weeks Camille had been in New York City—not that she wanted to be reminded of a young woman whose looks belied the reality beneath the glossy exterior.

Camille would never forget the summer the spoiled, pretty blonde had run away from her father because Monsieur Gendre wouldn't buy her an extravagant piece of jewelry she wanted. Because Justin had felt guilty for leaving her, albeit with her own father, he'd recognized his half sister's bid for attention by talking Max and Monsieur Gendre into letting Genevieve stay with them until school was back in session.

At first Camille had been delighted. She'd been in Paris for no more than a few months then, since Max had only recently talked her mother into sharing custody, and her only real friend had been Justin, who was much older than she.

That friendship had been the problem, the sole reason Genevieve had disliked Camille so immediately and so intensely. She'd been jealous of Justin's brotherly affection for the magician's daughter, which she'd considered grossly misplaced. Instead of a friend, Camille had made an enemy, but one who lurked behind sunny smiles and innocent gray-blue eyes.

Genevieve had played plenty of nasty tricks on Camille, but Max and Justin had never caught on because Genevieve was such a good actress. Only once did Camille try to talk to her father about the uncomfortable situation, but he'd gently chided her for trying to get the other girl into trouble. Max had been sure that a gawky-looking, socially awkward Camille had been jealous of the beautiful, poised blonde.

And so it was no wonder that she had never told anyone that Genevieve had locked her into one of Max's magic cabinets early one evening. No one missed Camille until late the next morning. Hour after hour she'd been trapped in that little space, terrified, the walls seeming to be shrinking around her, sure that her next breath would be her last.

Camille could taste the fear now, as if she were reliving the incident, as if the walls of the dimly lit bedroom were closing in around her. She could see Justin framed by the doors of the cabinet, the dashing hero who'd come to her rescue. She could feel his strong arms around her, his gentle fingers wiping away her frightened tears....

She'd never even thought of accusing Genevieve when Justin had muttered something about a faulty lock.

Who would have believed her?

As memories rushed through her, Camille closed her heart against them. For God's sake, this wasn't the time to remember how she'd first fallen in love with Justin St. Cyr. Nor was it the time to remember he'd once been her friend and protector. That belonged to the past.

He was the predator now.

He was her enemy.

Setting aside the photograph, she continued her search through the drawer. At first she ignored a folded piece of newspaper. But when she couldn't find anything else of value in the drawer, she picked up the clipping and unfolded it.

"Seine hides murdered woman."

Camille read the headline out loud, automatically translating from French into English. Then she studied the accompanying photograph: a Fiat perched at the edge of a river, its driver's door wide open, its windshield a spiderweb of cracks.

Her gaze dropped to the article itself, dated approximately six months before.

At half-past midnight, police found an abandoned car thought to be the scene of a gruesome murder. It lay at the edge of the Seine in the heart of Paris near the Pont Neuf. In addition to evidence of a struggle and a bullet hole in the windshield, there were traces of blood leading from the front seat of the car to the river. Police also found a handgun that had been wiped free of prints caught on the embankment several yards away.

A leather handbag lay at the water's edge. According to the identification found inside, the car is registered in the name of Genevieve Gendre, who works as an appraiser of valuable collectibles here in Paris.

Tearing her eyes from the clipping, Camille picked up the photograph again. "Genevieve! Dead?" Genuinely shocked, she couldn't figure out why Justin hadn't told her that his sister was dead. Frowning at the sympathy she felt for him in spite of his recent betrayal, she went back to the article.

Miss Gendre has not been seen by friends or family for several days.

After preliminary laboratory tests were completed, police spokesman Antoine Fouchet told the press that the blood samples taken from the front seat of the car and the ground near the river had been matched with the medical records of the missing woman.

"Though a fisherman found a single shoe floating in the river early this morning," Fouchet said, "the body has not as yet been recovered. She is presumed dead, and her body is presumed to be floating somewhere along the Seine "

Staring at the clipping and the picture in her hands, Camille frowned. Nothing made sense. If Justin had this clipping, why had he talked about his sister at Guido's as though she were alive? Straining to recall the conversation, Camille vaguely remembered him bringing up the fact that Genevieve had decided to pursue a profession more practical than magic.

She'd become an appraiser of valuable collectibles—including antique coins!

At the time, this information hadn't really sunk in because Camille had been upset by the mere mention of Genevieve's name. She'd gotten up to go to the ladies' room before Justin could expect her to indulge in warm remembrances of the summer they'd all spent together. Now she realized he hadn't been fishing for memories.

He'd had another, less innocent purpose in mind altogether.

Heart thumping, she whispered, "For God's sake, what in the world is going on?" as though the photograph or the newspaper clipping could tell her.

"That's a good question," a male voice answered from behind her.

Terrified, Camille whipped around to see a man silhouetted in the doorway. He added, "Why don't you tell me?"

"Justin!" she gasped, the fact that he blocked her only escape route registering immediately. "What are you doing here?"

"This is my apartment, remember? If you'd wanted a tour, you had only to ask."

He moved toward her slowly, menacingly, making Camille quake from the inside out. She could feel her pulse in her throat, the only sign that her bodily functions were still working, since she couldn't stand, couldn't even breath.

"You're the one who has explaining to do," Justin said softly, stopping only when his leg touched hers. "Max always bragged you were good enough to be a pickpocket if you wanted to be." He paused barely a second before demanding, "Does he know you are, in fact, a thief and murderer?"

Chapter Nine

Was Camille a superb actress or was she genuinely shocked by his accusation? Justin wondered. Her face was stunned, her eyes unnaturally wide. She stared up at him, seemingly frozen to the bed. He could even see an erratic pulse beating in her throat.

Gasping for air, she finally croaked, "What are you talking about?"

"Are you trying to tell me you don't know about the coin stolen from Edouard Roget?" Camille's gaze shifted away from his, stopping in the vicinity of his chin. He tried to bluff her into a confession. "I thought not. You're guilty, all right, or you wouldn't be here."

Her eyes whipped back to his, seeming to blaze green fire as she defended herself. "I'm here because I figured it was the only way I was going to find out the truth about why you tricked me into coming to New York."

Wanting to know for sure how she'd figured out his scheme, he softly asked, "What are *you* talking about?"

"Don't pretend innocence, Justin. I read the entries in the notebook."

He felt himself pale beneath her steady gaze. So he had been correct in assuming that Camille had stolen his only piece of evidence. He moved away from her and leaned against the dresser for support. Why did confirmation seem like an unwelcome surprise? Because he'd hoped she was innocent, Justin silently admitted, in spite of the damning circumstances. But now that he'd caught her rifling through his things, he had to find out the whole truth if he could.

"Genevieve's notebook is very revealing, isn't it, Cammi? Luckily she thought to keep notes on her investigation of the missing coin, or I never would have been able to figure out why she was murdered."

Camille sounded convincingly appalled when she said, "You can't really believe someone would commit murder just to keep a stolen coin."

Though she hadn't exactly admitted she'd stolen the coin, she hadn't denied it either.

As if she realized she should have made a flat denial, Camille blinked nervously. Her face blanched, and her generous mouth was pressed into a tight line. There was a haunted look in her eyes that begged him to believe in her innocence, but Justin steeled himself against softening and pressed on.

"That notebook implicates you, your ex-husband and your father, as well as Roget himself. I had to find out which of you was guilty."

"Of murder?" He thought she spoke more to herself than to him. "That's why you went looking for me. Not because you wanted to form a new act, but because you wanted to pin Genevieve's murder on me."

"Because I wanted to ferret out my sister's murderer, Clever Cammi, no matter who he or she might be." He made the admission coldly, not unaware of the hurt and fury reflected on her beautiful face. "I was sure your appearance at the opening would draw out the guilty party. Not a bad plan. Richard and Max have both arrived already. I figured Roget wouldn't miss the opening either, since he's such a devoted patron of the magical arts. I sent an invitation. He cabled that he'll be here.''

"You used me.''

Not bothering to confirm the obvious, Justin relentlessly pursued the truth, even as he hoped it would somehow clear her. "I wanted to confront all my suspects together, but the whole setup is pretty clear now, isn't it? You and Richard stole the coin, then you murdered my sister because she discovered the truth and planned to turn the information over to the authorities.''

"I haven't murdered anyone!''

"Then why did you steal the notebook if not to protect yourself?'' he demanded. "Or did you do it to protect Richard?''

Jumping to her feet, Camille yelled, "I don't have the damn notebook!''

In her agitation she let go of the two items she'd been studying when he'd surprised her. Her hand shook as she retrieved the clipping, which lay on the floor directly in front of her, then reached for the photo, which had landed facedown. Brow wrinkled, she stared at the loving message Genevieve had written to him on the back. Justin figured she was stalling, trying to avoid resuming the incriminating conversation.

When she looked back at him, she seemed a little puzzled and there were tears in her eyes. "I thought you knew me as well as I knew you, but I guess we were both wrong. Justin the Just, moral, upright and uptight—that's what I used to call you. But that Justin doesn't exist anymore, does he? That Justin was also honest. He wouldn't use people to salve his own guilty conscience.''

"What the hell is that supposed to mean?'' he asked, uneasy with himself.

"You always had some stupid notion that you'd failed your sister because you left home—left her with her father. I don't think you were as blind to her faults as you pretended to be. You saw what she was becoming, didn't you? And you blamed yourself, because you didn't stop her and you weren't there for her when she needed you. So you'll do anything to make it up to her now that she's dead, even if it means accusing innocent people of murder."

Ignoring her accusations, which were uncomfortably close to the truth, Justin turned his uneasiness back on her. "You haven't proved you're innocent."

"What happened to innocent until proved guilty, Justin? Do you think we're all guilty? Whether or not you want to believe it, I didn't murder your sister," Camille rasped, and against his better judgment and in spite of the fact that she knew more than she was admitting, Justin did believe her. "And Richard has never been a violent man. He may not be the most honest person I know, but he couldn't kill anyone. So who's left? Max? Or Edouard Roget, a wealthy businessman who could afford to lose ten of those coins and never feel their loss?"

"You, Max and I are all masters of illusion, Camille. How can you be so sure Richard and Roget aren't equally skillful, if less flashy?"

Remembering the way Richard had fooled her for more than a year after they'd married, Camille couldn't deny it. How could she be certain of anything anymore?

"I think it's time for me to leave," she said, setting the article and photo on the dresser.

"No."

Not liking the final sound of that, she eyed Justin uncertainly. The grim smile playing around his mouth made her stomach knot.

"Are you going to explain, or am I to assume you're in the mood for another amorous tryst? If so, forget it. That's over. I won't be used."

"Yes, you will, for a little while longer."

Justin moved toward her, and suddenly Camille was more afraid than nervous, but the hand that pushed the hair away from her face and settled on her neck was surprisingly gentle. She hated the way her flesh there responded to his touch, sending messages to other, more sensitive parts of her body. She didn't understand how she could be so weak, knowing what she did.

"No, Justin," she whispered, trying to harden her emotions as well as her heart.

"I'll continue with my original plan to confront the suspects, and I won't have you warning them. You'll stay here with me tonight."

Camille ducked her head away from the hand that taunted her, surreptitiously gauging the distance to the door. Not far, but Justin was blocking her way, so she'd have to climb over the bed to get out of the room. She could feel the adrenaline rushing through her as she readied herself.

"And what if Max alerts the police when he realizes I haven't been home?"

"I've prepared him for that. I gave him the idea you might be with me tonight." He had the nerve to smile when he added, "In case you're wondering how he took it, the old man was delighted."

"How dare you!" she cried, purposely throwing him off balance with a good shove.

Instantly Camille scrambled onto the bed in an attempt to get to the doorway. Recovering immediately, Justin wrapped a hand around her ankle before she could reach the floor He gave it a sharp tug.

She went flying, landing half on and half off the bed. Her shoulder hitting the floor jarred her teeth, but before she even had time to curse him, he had flipped her up and turned her around so that she was lying on the bed as if she'd meant to sleep there all along. Panting with the effort, she tried to fight him, but her blows were ineffectual against his determination and superior strength. He easily pinned her flailing arms to the mattress, using his own legs to stop hers from kicking.

Frustrated tears gathered in her eyes as he lay over her, demanding, "Either you agree to stay there all night or I'll tie you to the bed."

"I hate you!" she whispered through clenched teeth, knowing she uttered a lie.

Justin ignored her vitriolic words and the look of contempt she turned on him. "I'm not playing games with you. I intend to finish what I've started. Now, do you agree or not?" His voice softened. "Make it easy on yourself, Cammi. Don't make me hurt you."

Thinking that she might be able to escape him more easily if she wasn't tied up, Camille drew on her talent for acting and pretended resignation.

"All right. I agree."

Studying her expression suspiciously, Justin let her loose and rolled over to lie next to her. He stared at the ceiling for a while before getting up to turn off the light. When he undressed, she refused to protest, but she closed her eyes against the male silhouette outlined by the light glowing through the open doorway.

As soon as he settled next to her, she turned away from him onto her side so that she wouldn't have to touch him. How long would it take him to fall asleep?

How long before she could escape his presence if not her own heartbreak?

"Camille." The word came in barely a whisper, and if she hadn't been hardened to the man, she might have admitted that she heard longing in the sound of her name. "I'm sorry. Not because I did what I had to do, but because I had to do it in the first place."

"That's a real relief," Camille said caustically, thankful that her voice didn't break on the words.

His statement did make sense, though. Of course Justin was sorry his sister was dead and felt vindicated in doing whatever was necessary to catch the murderer. What she couldn't understand was how he could have misjudged her and used her so badly. She'd never forgive him. Never.

Not even if she couldn't stop loving him.

Going over the events of the past few weeks, she couldn't stop questions from roiling in her mind. She might have demanded answers, except that she sensed Justin had fallen asleep. Now was her chance to sneak away. But she couldn't move. She didn't want to, maybe because this was the last time she'd ever allow Justin St. Cyr to be this close to her off the stage.

Camille wondered what had happened to her marvelous instincts. When she'd really needed them, they'd failed her and had even led her to draw false conclusions. She'd suspected that Justin had been trying to involve her in something illegal, but she'd been wrong. She was relieved even as she was devastated that he could have thought her capable of killing his sister.

She thought about Genevieve of the sunny smiles and lying gray-blue eyes.

Careful not to touch the warm body next to hers, Camille shifted her position uneasily, knowing her instincts were trying to warn her again. Something felt wrong. Things were not as they seemed.

She was sure of it.

THEY AWOKE LATE the next morning. Justin wasn't any more willing to let her out of his sight than he had been the night before, in spite of the heated argument Camille instigated about letting the police handle the investigation. He'd gone too far to give up now, he insisted.

It was early afternoon before they shared an uncomfortably quiet breakfast.

As she tried to eat, a sense of foreboding gripped her. Camille didn't know if Justin's plans for that evening were filling her with such unease or if the sense of looming danger was due to her own imaginings. She'd fallen asleep thinking she was caught in the middle of an illusion. By the time she'd awakened, the feeling had intensified.

Instinct told her Justin wasn't directly involved in her fears this time, but she didn't trust her instinct anymore. Therefore, she didn't ask him the questions she might have—about being followed in the rain, then threatened and finally trapped in the elevator.

He said he had simply wanted to get her to New York City to carry out his plan. If he'd been guilty of those other things, his motivations weren't as pure as he'd claimed. Part of her refused to believe he was guilty—the same part that had kept her by his side all night and would keep her there through the opening night. She'd see this thing through to the end. After that, Camille didn't know what she'd do.

She kept their conversation cursory: "Pass the salt." "No more coffee." "Can I use the bathroom by myself, please?"

And all the while she avoided confronting Justin, a viable reality teased and taunted her just out of conscious reach. If only she could think clearly, Camille knew she'd recognize the clues she was certain her memory had stored. Then she would come face-to-face with the truth.

If only she could concentrate, she would be able to see t
dangerous illusion for what it was and then expose it, re
dering it harmless.

If only Justin didn't distract her so...

It wasn't until hours later that Justin gave up his sile
custody. Barely fifteen minutes before their first show, l
left Camille in her dressing room to get ready, satisfied th.
she wouldn't have time to warn the suspects, each of who
would receive a written invitation to come to his dressin
room after the performance.

Camille hardly had time to glance at the bouquet c
flowers she'd received from well-wishers. While applying he
makeup, she resigned herself to letting Justin play out h
game, sure in her own mind that his suspects were all inn
cent of murder. She only wished she didn't feel so alone.

A moment after she stepped behind the screen to chang
into her costume, there was a rap at her door.

"It's Vivian."

"Come in," Camille called, stripping herself of her gree
dress. "How are things going out there?"

"We almost had a full house when I came up. I declare
every critic and professional magician alive must be in th
audience. Kipp Walker said we are going to be in trouble i
everyone who has received an invitation tries to use it,"
Vivian told her.

"That's the chance you take with an invitation-onl
show."

"I guess. You know, we all were so worried that you an
Justin wouldn't be here on time. What kept you?"

Coming from behind the screen fully dressed, Camille sa
down at the mirror, wondering if she should involve Vivia
in her fears. She hated feeling so alone. And perhaps he
friend would be able to see things from a fresh perspective

"Vivian, you may have a difficult time believing this, but Justin kept me because he didn't want me to have time to talk to my father or my ex-husband or one particular patron who'll be here tonight," Camille began as she quickly pulled a brush through her hair.

"Why wouldn't Mr. St. Cyr want you to see them?"

"Justin was afraid I'd warn them that he suspects one of us of having murdered his sister."

"Th-that's preposturous," Vivian stated uncertainly, her voice unnaturally soft. "Isn't it?"

"Yes, of course," Camille assured her friend. She spotted a lone camellia overshadowed by the big bouquets. She picked it up. No card. "I told him that. It's a complicated story, one I don't have time to get into fully right now, but it revolves around a coin stolen from a man named Edouard Roget, the patron I mentioned. It seems that Genevieve was investigating the loss, and so when she was killed, Justin assumed the murderer was someone involved in the theft of the coin."

After pinning the flower to her jacket lapel, Camille glanced at the other woman's reflection. Vivian's face was intent, and she was absently rubbing her arm. Camille figured her friend was wondering what she'd had to do with the theft. It would take too much time to explain, so she went on with the most important part of the story.

"The thing is, my intuition keeps telling me something's not right with the picture I have of the situation. I feel as though I'm looking straight at another magician's illusion but can't quite get a handle on the clue to what's making it work because the misdirection is being so skillfully done. Does that make sense?" Still watching Vivian's mirror image, Camille thought there was something disturbing about the other woman's unhappy expression. She whispered, "Vivian?"

Abruptly Vivian was all smiles. "None of this makes sen
to me at the moment, but I shall try to understand it lat
when you can repeat everything again. I don't have tir
right now because I have to find a prop for Justin." Vivi;
backed away toward the door. "I just dropped by to wi
you a broken leg, honey. Not literally, of course," she add
quickly.

"I get the idea."

"See you after the show."

Camille continued to think about the situation while sl
sorted her props. This time her photographic memory ga
her all the help she needed. Various incidents replaye
themselves in her mind and began to fit together like th
pieces of a puzzle. She didn't have time to pursue its solu
tion, however, for Justin's reflection suddenly appeared
the mirror with hers.

"Are you ready? We should be downstairs now."

Picking up her glasses and book, Camille rose and led th
way out of the room. "Did you get that prop from Vi
ian?" she asked distractedly.

"What prop are you talking about?"

"The one she said— Forget it. My mind was on othe
things."

And those things were starting to make sense. Camill
suspected she was about to penetrate the illusion that ha
taken over her life.

Though aware of her imminent breakthrough during th
entire program, she kept it at the very edge of her con
sciousness. Camille knew she needed absolute concentra
tion to make this her best performance ever.

She and Justin had put together a mixture of three kind:
of magic: illusion, stand-up and close-up. Luckily they'(
also added a few solo performances to those they did to

ether They'd arranged the program so that both of them
would have breaks as well as time for costume changes.

Everything went smoothly, exactly as planned. The applause became increasingly enthusiastic. Then Justin left to
don his final costume, and Camille stepped down from the
stage to work the audience with close-up magic.

Though she didn't draw them into her act, Camille easily
spotted Max and Richard sitting together. A little later she
found Edouard Roget at a table on the other side of the
room. And toward the back she saw the group of nonper-
forming employees who'd been given one of the larger tables.

Vivian was not among them.

So when the stage lights dimmed, signaling Justin's major solo illusion—her cue to leave—Camille ran up the
stairs, then stripped off her red-beaded gown as she raced
down the hall. Once in her dressing room, she removed a
makeup tube from her case, grabbed the highwayman's
outfit from its hanger, and headed back into the hall,
struggling into the breeches, shirt and jacket. She couldn't
have cared less if anyone saw her.

She needed all the time she could get.

Determined to confirm her growing suspicion, Camille
entered the bookkeeper's office, which stood lit and wide
open. Pausing only a second to catch her breath and let her
pounding heart stabilize, she approached Vivian's desk.
After several minutes of searching without finding what she
wanted, she was about ready to give up in disappointment
when she spotted the desk calendar.

Everyone wrote themselves reminders on those, didn't
they?

She had to turn only two pages to find that they did!

Excited now, Camille opened the makeup tube, pulled out
the threatening message and unfolded it with shaky fin-

gers. Then she compared the message with the scribbl
fragments of words on the calendar.

Whether writing threatening notes or jotting reminders o
her calendar, Vivian had barely bothered to disguise h
handwriting.

Not Vivian, Camille told herself. Genevieve.

Unless she was crazy, Justin's half sister was alive and we
and working at Illusions. Or had been, until she had rea
ized that Camille was on the verge of discovering the trutl
That's why she'd acted so oddly when Camille told he
about Justin's plan to find the murderer. She'd immedi
ately found an excuse to leave when Camille talked abou
looking at an illusion but not quite figuring it out.

Vivian had been the illusion!

Sinking onto a chair, Camille cried, "My God, how coul
I have been so blind?"

"Blind about what? Me, I hope. Have you finally de
cided to come away with me?"

Whipping around, Camille faced Richard. He was lean
ing against the doorjamb, purposely posed that way, n
doubt, to make the most of his lean good looks. The pos
annoyed her as much as his presence. "What are you doin
here?"

"Following you. I left the club when I realized Justin wa
going to do his thing all by himself. I told you you hadn'
seen the last of me."

Pushing back her irritation, Camille decided that eve
Richard didn't deserve what Justin had in store for him
Besides, he might foul up her own plans. "Richard, get ou
of here! I have to get back to the stage!" Snatching up th
page of the calendar and the threatening note, she stuffe
the evidence into a concealed pocket in her jacket. "Don'
go back into the club. Justin knows about the coin an
thinks you killed his sister over it."

"What the . . . ?"

"Don't worry, she's not dead." Camille was already shoving him out the door, so he had no time to protest. "I can't explain now, but I think you'll be saving yourself some grief if you disappear for a while. Meet me later at my place."

"Anything your heart desires, love," Richard said as she started down the hall. "Say, doesn't that outfit include a pair of shoes?"

Camille looked down at her stockinged feet. "Good Lord!" she cried. She ducked into her dressing room to slip into the proper shoes and grab her hat. Then she was off again, her feet moving as fast as her mind.

Genevieve had been so clever about it all that no wonder Justin had never suspected Vivian was his own flesh and blood.

Hairstyle and color would have been easy to change, and she must have had herself fitted with brown contact lenses. She probably hadn't needed those any more than the fake glasses she'd worn. Plastic surgery would account for the smaller nose and for minor differences in her features as well.

But what had fooled her most had been the Vivian personality, totally opposite to that of the glamorous, poised and haughty Genevieve. Vivian's dowdy dress, physical mannerisms, insecurity and Southern accent had all added to the illusion.

Illusion! The finale was about to begin!

"Where the hell have you been?" Justin was demanding, looking as fierce as the pirate he was supposed to be.

"Meet me in my dressing room after the show and I'll tell you all about it," Camille said, stuffing her hair into her hat. "I guarantee you'll be amazed, though definitely not amused."

"You know perfectly well we're all meeting in my dressing room—"

"Not likely!" Camille replied in a heated whisper as she joined their assistants in the wing from which they were all to enter. "If you want to know the truth about your sister, you'll do as I say."

She heard Justin curse as she got into position on the darkened stage. Kipp had already provided the necessary props.

Then the lights came up on the hold-up, and she had to concentrate on being a highwayman. Nevertheless, that didn't prevent her from surveying the first few rows of tables. Max was sitting alone. Richard must have heeded her warning, she noted thankfully. Then she was chased offstage into the opposite wing, and she glanced at Roget's table. Empty. Curious but not alarming, she told herself.

When she ran headlong into Justin a minute later, she half expected him to shake her rather than steady her as he was supposed to do. But he was as professional as she onstage, never revealing his true feelings, never faltering from his appointed role. He even touched her uncovered tousled hair with a gentle hand—almost lovingly, she thought sadly—before leading her to the wooden crate.

The rest of the performance went off smoothly, from the vanish to the production—from the moment he made her disappear to the moment he made her reappear. Camille popped out of the second crate and into Justin's arms on cue. She told herself that his touch wouldn't affect her if she didn't allow it to, but when they reached the deck and he kissed her, she was anxious to be free of him in spite of her logic.

She had to endure the proximity to him for a few more minutes while they took their bows. It was only when the

urtains closed for the last time that she pulled away from
im and took off for the stairs before he could stop her.

"Are you coming, Justin?"

"Camille, wait a minute!"

She wasn't about to wait for anything. She had the lead
and meant to keep it. He narrowed the distance in the hall-
way, but didn't catch her until they were directly in front of
her dressing room door. Grabbing her arm roughly, he spun
her around to face him.

"What the hell do you think you're up to?"

"Come in if you want to find out."

"This had better be good."

"Don't worry, it will be."

She should throw the truth in his face happily, but she
couldn't. Though he'd used her badly, Camille would get no
pleasure from Justin's pain. Genevieve's being alive might
bring him joy, but only momentarily. There'd been a reason for his half sister wanting everyone to think she was
dead. He'd figure that out, just as she had.

He stopped just inside the door. "Let's have it."

She decided not to pull any punches. "Genevieve is
alive."

"Damn it, Camille, that isn't funny."

"I'm not trying to be funny. I'm trying to tell you the
truth." Camille pulled the note and the page from the calendar from her coat pocket. "Read it for yourself."

Justin grabbed the papers from Camille, expecting that
he'd be able to laugh at her ridiculous story. Then he'd drag
her to his dressing room if necessary so that he could proceed with his plan. He scanned the note first. A threat
against Camille! Then he compared it with the scribbled
abbreviations on the other scrap of paper.

They were familiar. They were like the gibberish in Genevieve's notebook.

Because he was an intelligent man, Justin considered the real possibility of his sister's being alive with mixed feelings. Hating himself for the disloyal thought, he assured himself that nothing else would matter if Genevieve was alive—but if she was, why had she pretended otherwise? What in the world was she up to? And how did he know this wasn't Camille's way of getting even with him?

Waving the papers in her face, he played dumb. "What are these supposed to prove?"

"That she's alive. You recognize the handwriting, don't you? It's not disguised very well. If you had her notebook for comparison, you couldn't deny it."

Justin forced himself to relax his clenched jaw. "I don't need the notebook. I studied it hour after hour, day after day. Those pages are burned into my memory."

"Then you believe me?"

"I believe someone is trying to play a macabre joke on me." He stared at her intently. "Forged any checks lately, Camille?"

"That was a low shot, Justin, and unworthy of you." He hated her pitying expression. "In your heart you know I've discovered the truth."

"I don't know any such thing! If this isn't some kind of hoax you're trying to perpetrate on me, then why didn't you show me this threat sooner?"

"Because," she whispered, shifting her gaze to his chin, as she always did when she was uncomfortable, "I suspected you might have sent it."

How the hell could she believe that? He loved her, for God's sake! The thought that Camille had been in danger and hadn't trusted him made him furious. But then, she'd had reason to hold him suspect.

Justin clenched and unclenched his jaw. "Maybe I deserved that." He reread the missive, concentrating on the chilling part. *If you're clever, Cammi, you'll make yourself vanish before it's too late...* "When did you get this?"

"I received it the day before the illusion was rigged so that I couldn't get out of the elevator. I didn't make the connection then, but... Genevieve knew how terrified I was of enclosed places, because she was the one who locked me into Max's cabinet."

And he had saved her, had held the sobbing girl he'd loved as a second sister in his arms, had tried to pretend she had had an accident. Justin had suspected there'd been more than a lock at fault, but he'd been as afraid to face the truth then as he was now.

Camille went on, "That clipping you kept said Genevieve was presumed dead, her body thought to be floating somewhere along the Seine. Was it ever found?"

"No, but her blood was everywhere. In the car. On the ground. Experts matched it to her records. How do you account for that?"

"She must have cut herself..." Voice trailing off, Camille frowned, her gaze turning inward as though she were remembering something. "The scar on her arm a few inches above her wrist—that would have bled enough to leave a trail, and she could easily have controlled the bleeding from there. She even had the nerve to show me the scar."

"What are you talking about? Who showed you a scar?" Glancing down at the indecipherable scribblings on the calendar, Justin suddenly felt adrenaline rush through him. "And where did this come from?"

"From Vivian's desk." Camille took a deep breath. "Vivian Lewis is Genevieve Gendre."

Whatever he'd been expecting, it wasn't this. "Now I know you're lying or crazy! Even if we haven't been close for years, do you think I wouldn't know my own sister if I saw her face-to-face? I've spoken to Vivian several times. I spoke to her after the illusion went wrong.''

"You haven't had any reason to suspect she was still alive, have you?'' Camille asked.

"No, but if she was my sister . . .''

Justin allowed himself to be silenced when Camille put a finger to his lips.

"She's so very clever. She hasn't merely changed the color of her hair and eyes. Genevieve disguised herself from the inside out. She was a marvelous actress even at fifteen, Justin, but you were always too guilty to see through her. I have to admit she's even better now than she was then. She had *me* fooled this time.'' Camille looked hurt when she added, "I really believed Vivian was my friend.''

"But what would be the point of her going around in disguise?'' Even as he continued the argument, Justin sensed his sister might indeed be alive. "Why would she want everyone to think she's dead?''

"That's the thing that's bothering me. I honestly don't know.''

"Perhaps I can answer that.'' Edouard Roget stepped from behind Camille's dressing screen, his narrow olive face pinched, his expression furious. "It was the best way to ensure no one would look for her after she stole more than two million dollars' worth of coins from me.''

As much as he wanted to deny that his sister would have done such a thing, for once Justin couldn't say a word in Genevieve's defense.

Chapter Ten

It was impossible to come face-to-face with Richard's victim and not sweat, Camille thought, feeling her palms grow damp. But why was she worried? Roget wasn't hurling accusations at her. Perhaps he didn't know he'd been robbed in two separate incidents by two different people. Or had he been? Could Richard have been bold enough to return to Roget's home to rob him a second time?

"You'd better explain yourself, Edouard," Justin finally demanded of the Frenchman, his voice more calm than Camille would have expected.

"What is there to explain? You yourself know I hired her to make a discreet appraisal of my coin collection. You recommended her."

"Genevieve's professional reputation was beyond reproach."

"Perhaps," Roget allowed, lowering himself to the mauve couch and crossing his leg precisely at the knee. He straightened his trouser crease, the sharp gesture revealing his controlled agitation. "And then perhaps she'd never been caught in previous crimes."

Justin leaned against the makeup table. "Go on," he said grimly.

"As I told you six months ago, I wanted a discreet appraisal of my entire collection. I planned to dispose of the coins, but I didn't want to alert certain parties to their sale. You'll forgive me if I don't go into details as to why. It's a private matter really."

Camille was wondering if those details were worth speculating on when she realized that Roget was staring at her, his dark eyes glittering strangely. To distract his attention from the flush that she felt covering her cheeks, she sat down in a chair opposite him. She wanted to keep her back to the mirror. It was hard to produce a smile with a dry mouth, but somehow she managed one.

"Genevieve finished her appraisal quickly and efficiently," Roget went on, never taking his eyes off of Camille. "I asked her to follow through on the sale. She was in the midst of contacting prospective dealers when one of the coins disappeared. Genevieve discovered its fake twin the morning after the party." He paused significantly before asking, "You remember that party, don't you, my dear? Your close-up magic was perfection, especially the tricks with the coins."

Rubbing her damp palms on her breeches, Camille tried not to panic. Was this it, then? Would prison walls close in on her after all?

"I didn't switch the coins," she said, barely able to hear her own voice over the raucous pounding of her heart. "You have to believe me."

Roget studied her for mere seconds before saying, "I think I do. Then it must have been Richard Montgomery himself, yes?" Camille bobbed her head as he went on, "As I suspected. There'd been some talk about his having a seemingly endless supply of money without any visible business interests. So Montgomery switched the coins, passing mine to you after removing it from its case in the liɔrary sometime earlier in your performance. I hope you were very angry when you discovered his perfidy.''

"I was furious," Camille whispered.

"Had the theft been noticed immediately and your things searched, your fingerprints would have been on the coin. Who would have believed Montgomery was the thief rather than you?" When Camille gasped, Roget gave a harsh and humorless laugh. "Ah, you hadn't thought of that, had you? Clever man, that ex-husband of yours."

Is that why Richard had involved her—so that she could be his scapegoat if things went wrong? Not daring to glance at Justin, who must have been feeling quite victorious now that he had learned the truth about the stolen coin, Camille swallowed hard.

Her voice was a raspy imitation of its normal self when she weakly insisted, "I did try to make him return it. He wouldn't, because of his gambling debts—"

"Please don't go on." Roget held up a hand to stop her, then straightened his bow tie before continuing. "Montgomery's petty theft must have given Genevieve ideas. By telling me she was sure I could get a better price, and she a higher commission if I allowed her more time to pit one dealer who desired them against another, she stalled the sale of the rest of the collection. Foolishly I agreed."

"How can you be so sure Genevieve is your thief?" Justin asked indignantly. "Richard Montgomery might have committed both thefts."

"Illogical. He would have stolen all the coins at the same time if he'd so desired. But that's exactly what your sister wanted me to believe. She hinted that the three of them collaborated together in the theft of the first coin—Montgomery and Camille as well as Max, who'd been having some financial difficulties himself."

"Leave my father out of this!" Camille cried. "Ma doesn't know anything about the coin or why I left Paris."

Roget nodded in gentlemanly agreement. "One evening Genevieve told me she had made an assignation with Richard Montgomery. She planned to confront him and coerce him into giving her the coin. I didn't suspect a thing until it was too late. The scheming young woman disappeared along with the rest of my collection."

"That still isn't proof of her guilt!"

Justin practically spat the words at Roget, yet Camille recognized a doubtful edge to his tone. She glanced at him surreptitiously. His posture as he leaned harder into the makeup table was that of one who was half-convinced of his own defeat.

"Then why did she fake her own murder if not to throw me off her trail?" Roget demanded, pounding the arm of the couch with a tightened fist. "If Montgomery was the thief, he would have fenced the entire collection. As it is, my coins haven't surfaced. They're too rare to go unnoticed, you know." Using only the tips of his fingers, he smoothed the fabric he had disturbed. "I hired my own investigators to look for them, but they seem to have vanished—like magic. Genevieve must still have the entire collection safely hidden."

"Maybe," Camille said thoughtfully, "but there's something that doesn't make sense. Why would she have risked exposure by coming to New York and working for her own brother who believed her dead?"

"I think I can answer that," Justin said. He sounded resigned. Camille thought that he no longer doubted his sister's guilt. "Genevieve was always attracted to excitement, always liked to take risks. I think she enjoyed putting herself in danger so she could escape stimulated but unscathed."

"Ah, and what bigger challenge than facing her own brother to see if he recognizes her?"

"I looked right through her," Justin admitted softly. "I didn't see beyond the fake glasses and imitation Southern accent."

Roget frowned, the lines making his pinched face seem almost frightening. He was staring straight at Camille again. She shivered, sensing that the man thirsted for revenge in spite of his restrained demeanor.

"No one has ever been so successful in conning me as Montgomery and Genevieve have. It's a developing pattern that I don't at all like. She had me chasing shadows. Perhaps you'll be amused to know I thought you had the coins, Camille."

"You believed *I* was the thief?"

"Actually I thought you were in on it with Montgomery. That's why I came to New York after I received Justin's invitation. Also, one of my investigators here read that you were going to perform with Justin at Illusions. I was determined to follow you home myself, but you got away from me quite cleverly. If I hadn't known better, I would have thought you'd transposed yourself to another place."

"Then you're the one who followed me, not—"

Looking from Roget to Justin, Camille felt a great burden lifted from her. Justin hadn't followed her after all.

"Yes, it was I who followed you, and later I searched your dressing room for some clue."

So Edouard Roget had been both pursuer and invader.

"That was the day I received the threatening note," Camille exclaimed. "I thought whoever had left the note was the same person who'd searched through my things so carefully." Calling on her photographic memory, Camille saw Vivian in that very room, standing by the pile of props, while Camille tried to convince her that the place had been searched. "She planted the threat while I was in here, right under my nose!"

"What threat?" Max demanded from the doorway. "Someone has threatened my daughter? Let me at the monster!"

"I'm afraid the monster isn't here," Justin said, straightening himself to his full height. "But I'm going to find her myself."

"I'm coming with you." Camille was already stripping off her jacket. The rest of the costume and the makeup could wait until later. "I have a few things I want to say to her."

"I'll do this myself. She's my sister."

"The very reason you'll have me with you, as well," Roget said, dusting his trousers as he rose. "Not that I don't trust you, my friend."

"I didn't know that you had another sister, Justin." Max stared at Justin with a frown. "You can't mean Genevieve, because she's dead."

Camille wrapped her green coat around her, then took her father's arm. "No, she's not."

"But I was sure I read— Am I getting senile?" Max looked genuinely worried.

"No more than the three of us," Justin muttered as he led the way from the dressing room.

"I don't understand."

"I'll tell you all about it, Max."

And that's exactly what Camille did after Justin had got his own coat and they had set off for Genevieve's apartment. Luckily Camille had been there on the occasion when she and "Vivian" had gone out to dinner.

A short taxi ride took them through Soho and Greenwich Village and on to the Chelsea address Camille had given the driver. In the rush to get into the taxi Camille had found herself wedged tightly between Max and Justin in the back seat. If she was slightly distracted in telling her story, it was only because the taxi was uncomfortably crowded, she told herself, not because *he* was pressed up against her almost intimately.

Camille explained everything as quickly as she could, starting with Richard's involving her in the theft of the coin, going on to Genevieve's rigging the illusion and her own discovery of Vivian's identity and ending with Roget's theory about the cleverly planned theft.

Through it all Max silently listened, patting her hand supportively in the appropriate places.

When they arrived in front of the four-story brownstone, Roget paid the driver while Justin led the way to the lobby entrance. He rang Genevieve's doorbell again and again, but there was no response. Obviously furious with frustration, he began pounding on the glass door with his fist.

Max stayed his arm. "Continue that, my boy, and you'll rouse the neighbors to alert the local *gendarmerie*."

"If only we could find a way to get in," Roget muttered darkly.

"With three magicians working on it, that can't be too hard a task," Camille assured him.

Taking the lead silently, Justin pulled a slim tool from the lining of his coat. He picked the lock of the lobby door easily. Genevieve's apartment door took a little longer, but he was famous for his escapes. Camille knew that the lock Justin couldn't open hadn't been invented.

Her faith in him in this small thing was soon rewarded. The door to Genevieve's apartment swung inward.

Too bad Justin had destroyed the faith she'd had in him as a friend and lover, Camille thought sadly as she watched him proceed into the darkened apartment.

JUSTIN FLIPPED A LIGHT SWITCH on the wall just inside the door. A bare bulb hanging from the ceiling illuminated a shabby living room, which he stepped into reluctantly. Stopping in the middle of the room, he jammed his fists into his pockets and looked around.

He had a hard time imagining his beautiful, luxury-loving sister living in this place with its few pieces of plain, sturdy furniture, scuffed wooden floors and paint peeling off the wall in back of the radiator. But he didn't have any shock or surprise left in him. Those commodities had all been used up during the past hour.

Max wandered past him and glanced out of a grime-caked window. "Seems she's flown the coop, my boy."

"If we search carefully," Roget added from his side, "perhaps we'll find some clue as to where our little bird has flown."

Camille spoke softly from somewhere behind him. "I'll go check the bedroom."

Max and Roget volunteered to search the kitchen and bathroom.

They could search the entire building for all the good it would do them, Justin thought, instinctively knowing his sister had indeed vanished without trace.

Suddenly the numbness of the past few minutes wore off and he cursed aloud. If she'd needed money, why the hell hadn't Genevieve come to him? He would have denied her nothing . . . Even as he formulated the thought, he knew his sister would never have been satisfied with his money.

It had been the daring of taking something that belonged to someone else that had intrigued her. Merely remembering the excitement in Genevieve's voice when he'd spoken to her on the telephone a few days before she'd faked her own death made Justin's gut uneasy. He couldn't shake the feeling that he would have been able to stop her from turning nto the deceptive, dishonest woman she had become if only 1e'd faced the truth about her character years ago.

"Nothing in the bathroom," Roget said disgustedly as he ejoined Justin.

"Nor in the kitchen," Max added. "Camille, what's taking you so long?"

"I'm coming." Brow furrowed in concentration, Camille came out of the bedroom, studying the slip of paper in her hand. "I found this under the bed near the telephone. Genevieve must have dropped it."

"Well, my girl, don't keep us in suspense."

"If I could read it, I wouldn't." Her green eyes perplexed, she looked directly at Justin. "It's gibberish, like the notebook and the calendar."

"What notebook?" Roget asked.

"Genevieve kept a notebook recording speculations about who stole the coin," Justin told him. "One page was nothing more than scribbling—letters, numbers, abbreviations of words."

"Where is this notebook now?"

"Someone stole it."

"Let me see that."

Roget seized the slip of paper from Camille and studied it for a few seconds, his expression intent on his task, but he shrugged his shoulders. Reluctantly about to return it, he abruptly changed his mind and looked at the slip in his hand once more.

"I know what this means!" he shouted, stabbing his finger at the paper. "It's an Air France flight number, time of departure and gate number. And here—CDG—that's Charles de Gaulle airport, and her arrival time." Roget checked his gold Rolex watch. "Too late. Genevieve is already on her way to pick up the coins!"

"What now?" Camille asked as she took the note and checked it herself.

"Do what you want. I'm returning to Paris." Roget's face was grim as he turned to the front door. "I'll find her and recover my property. I'll hire every investigator in the city if necessary."

With Max and Camille only a few steps behind, Justin followed him out of the building, knowing Roget wouldn't be able to book a flight until the next day. The Frenchman went his own way without a backward glance.

"Odd little fellow," Max muttered. "Harmless, I guess."

"Don't underestimate him," Camille said. "He found me and the truth, didn't he? He wants his pound of flesh. I wouldn't be surprised if he gets it."

And as the three of them wearily climbed into a taxi that Justin had flagged down at the corner, there was no question in his mind that he, too, would be on his way to the City of Lights on the first flight he could book. He had to find his sister himself, before Edouard Roget got to her, so that he could persuade her to return the coins and provide whatever other restitution the Frenchman would demand.

Then he would make her inform the police that she was still alive.

Justin wasn't sure what would happen to Genevieve. If Roget had wanted the police to handle the case, he would already have told them what he knew. Undoubtedly his pride had prevented him from going to the police at the beginning. He would hate to look like a fool. Even now, Justin wasn't convinced the man would press charges.

Genevieve could easily make up a story to appease the *gendarmerie* about why she'd played dead. Perhaps she'd go free, even if she was proved guilty of stealing Roget's collection.

But could he let her get away with that?

Justin had come up against the problem of love and loyalty versus ethics, which he wasn't ready to face. How many times had he broken his own rules of morality and honesty since setting off on his quest to find a nonexistent murderer? He wondered if he had a right to make another person follow the St. Cyr rules of moral conduct that he himself had so easily ignored.

His thoughts turned from the philosophical to the practical situation at hand.

Sitting between him and Max and staring out of her father's window, Camille was a silent reminder of Justin's own guilt. His hands ached to touch her, but he clenched his fists instead. It made him sick inside to think that the woman he loved had taken the brunt of his own ethical trade-offs.

If only he could convince her of how much he had truly loved her and how shattered he had been when he'd thought her an accomplice to his sister's murder!

But he couldn't tell her any of that with Max sitting at her other side and with a ghostly Genevieve interposed between them.

He'd have to wait until he returned from Paris.

Justin didn't know how long he'd be gone, so he thought he'd better ask Kipp to set up another act for Illusions. The club would open to the public on Wednesday. Getting a replacement shouldn't be too difficult, since he'd already spoken to several magicians who had expressed interest in working at the club in the future. His thoughts were all practical when they alighted from the cab.

But when they entered Camille's apartment, Justin's reaction to Richard Montgomery's presence was strictly emotional. Richard lay sprawled the length of Camille's sofa—the sofa on which he and Camille had made love—reading a magazine and sipping a drink exactly as if he owned the place.

"What the hell do you think you're doing here?" Justin demanded.

Rising from his prone position, Richard set the drink and magazine on the coffee table.

"Actually, St. Cyr, I'm here at Camille's invitation. She wanted to protect me from you, not that I need protecting." He strolled to Camille's side and casually draped an arm over her shoulders. "Where did you get the insane idea that I killed your sister, anyway?"

Justin glanced at Camille. From her defiant expression he knew Richard was telling the truth. So she'd warned him off. Did she still have feelings for her ex-husband? Stiffly he backed away, now unsure of what he intended to tell Camille when he returned from Paris.

"You're not leaving," Max protested.

"Sorry, Max. I've got a lot of things to do before morning."

"So you're going after her." The anxious note in Camille's statement made him look back at her. She still stood sheltered under Richard's arm, not seeming at all uncomfortable or displeased. He couldn't believe her expression was vulnerable and her eyes held fear. His imagination was playing tricks on him.

"Yes. You're free of me," he told her. And then he turned away to open the door, softly adding, "For now."

With one last glare at Richard Montgomery, who had the temerity to grin at him, Justin stormed out of the apartment, wondering if he was vacating Camille Bayard's life as well.

CAMILLE FELT THE IMPACT of Justin's scathing look as though it had seared her physically. Instinctively she took a half step toward the door to go after him. Then she froze.

What was she thinking of? The man had betrayed her. She wanted nothing more to do with him.

You're free of me, he'd said.

Then why didn't she feel free?

Maybe because Richard had warpped his arm around her so possessively, she realized, stiffening. At first she'd allowed the embrace merely to spite Justin. Then she'd become indifferent to his touch when she'd focused on Justin's leaving and all that it meant to her.

She'd known Justin had been using her.

Then what was the big deal?

She still loved Justin St. Cyr. And *that* was a big deal indeed.

Turning her anger with herself on Richard, Camille snapped, "Get your arm off me!"

"Anything you say, love."

"The problem with you is that while I say a lot of things, you never take them seriously."

Richard strolled over to the coffee table and retrieved his drink. "Maybe it's because I just don't believe you."

"How did you get in here, anyway?"

"I picked the lock, of course." He held the glass up to her in a silent toast before downing its contents in a single swig.

While Camille fumed inwardly, Max cleared his throat. "Well, I guess you'll be doing your own acts for a while, eh, Camille? Look at the bright side of the situation. We can spend some time together until Justin returns."

"I'm not so sure I'll ever work with that man again." The quick statement came from her own lips, yet the thought stunned her. Some of her anger drained away, leaving in its place an inner turmoil that she hugged to herself. "One thing I do know is that I'm not waiting for Justin to return. I'll be out of here tomorrow."

"Now you're talking. We can fly to the Côte d'Azur for a little sun and fun in Monte Carlo." Richard dared to approach her again, a broad smile splitting his face. "I knew you couldn't really have a thing for that repressed rabbit-producer."

"Justin isn't repressed!" Camille stared at Richard furiously, knowing he'd continue to needle her about Justin unless she put a stop to it now. Shouldering past him, she headed for the bedroom, intending to pack. "And I'm not going anywhere with you. I'm flying to Paris to find Genevieve."

"Whatever for?" Max asked, following her into the bedroom and sounding truly appalled.

She drew a bag from her closet and threw it onto the bed, barely missing Velvet, who was curled up there. Velvet yowled indignantly and scampered to safer quarters. Realizing that she'd have to find someone to take care of the cat, Camille decided to call Leotie first thing in the morning. She was sure Leotie would agree to help her out.

Max sat on the side of the bed and assured her, "Justin will find her."

"And then what? Genevieve always knew exactly how to wind him around her little finger. What makes you think she's lost her touch?" Camille asked bitterly. "He'll probably end up helping her escape with the coins."

"You're not being fair, my girl. Justin may love his sister, but he's a man of principle."

"Really? Is that why he set me up as bait to bring you and Richard and Roget running to New York so he could determine which of us was guilty of a murder that hadn't been commited?" Her anger returning, Camille pulled clothes out of the dresser and threw them into the suitcase. "Justin twisted his ethics to suit his own needs then, because he loved Genevieve and had a storehouse of guilt he needed to assuage. What makes you think he'll act any more nobly when he finds her?''

And where had Justin's principles gone when he'd seduced her to fulfill various other needs? she silently asked herself. That had been Genevieve's fault, albeit indirectly. If Genevieve hadn't faked her own murder, Camille might never have run into Justin. She might never have been so foolish as to fall in love only to be betrayed.

''Are you willing to act as her judge, then?'' Max asked softly. ''You surprise me, my girl, especially since the coins have nothing to do with you.''

''I have my own reasons for wanting to find Genevieve, Father, the most important of which is her attempt to harm me by rigging the elevator in our pirate illusion. I could have been killed.''

''But you weren't. Please leave Genevieve to Justin,'' he begged her. ''I have a bad feeling about this. My instincts tell me you'll find her only to regret it.''

Ignoring the chill that raced down her spine at her father's words, Camille drew a few things from her closet and added them to the other clothes. When she continued defending her decision, she was speaking as much to Richard, who was lounging in the bedroom doorway, as she was to Max

''Try to understand that I have to do this for myself. I need to regain my self-respect. Besides which, finding Genevieve and returning the coins to Roget might make up for my involvement, involuntary as it was, with Richard's theft from him.''

''I should have guessed you'd feel compelled to make restitution for something you haven't even done,'' Richard muttered. ''I'm not going to let you go alone.''

''Forget it! This isn't an opportunity to get me back, so don't waste your time.''

"I want to help you. I owe you that much for involving you in the first place."

"Guilt, Richard? I don't think so. You never wore guilt well, as I remember." He didn't even cringe under Camille's suspicious glare. She tried to figure out his angle. What was in it for him? A larger bankroll, no doubt. "Hmm. Perhaps you see this as your opportunity to get your hands on the rest of Roget's collection."

"I'll ignore that, since it's not worthy of you." Richard actually sounded serious and determined to help. "I'm sure I know every possible fence Genevieve might use to get rid of the coins in Paris. I don't think she'll try to smuggle them out, considering the circumstances."

Though she didn't trust him, Camille knew he had the right contacts. "I don't know..."

"Well, I do," Max said decisively. "As little as we like to admit it, Richard does know what he's talking about. We'll all go. With the three of us working together Genevieve Gendre doesn't stand a chance of escaping."

Accepting that decision was a real relief. Camille hadn't actually looked forward to going it alone. Nor did she look forward to her next encounter with Justin St. Cyr if she succeeded in turning his sister over to the police. But now was not the time to dwell on her pseudorelationship with him.

Camille didn't doubt that she would come face-to-face with Genevieve in Paris. In the past the other woman had always been more devious than she. While Camille had created illusions, Genevieve had become one, influencing people and shaping events to suit herself.

This time, who would have the upper hand?

Chapter Eleven

April in Paris. A time for lovers, for holding hands and strolling down tree-lined quays built along the Seine, for people-watching while sampling wines at Left Bank cafés on the Boulevard Saint-Germain.

Her purpose grim in comparison, as she left her father's narrow five-story town house on the Île Saint-Louis—the smaller of the two islands in the Seine—Camille didn't want to think about springtime or lovers. Scheduled to meet with Max and Richard in a quarter of an hour, she would head for one of those very cafés she would prefer to avoid.

After a sleepless transatlantic flight, the three of them had landed at Charles de Gaulle Airport early that morning. Since then Camille had barely had time to freshen up and nap for a few minutes while her partners made some preliminary inquiries. She'd bothered to rest only because they insisted.

What good would she be if she fell asleep on her feet? Max had demanded. Genevieve would walk right by her unnoticed. And of course, he was right.

Camille had gotten some sleep in spite of her recurring dream about Justin using his powers to trap her in some dark, dank underworld. Though her eyes felt scratchy, they were open, and though her body still ached with jet lag, she moved along the quay with purpose.

As she passed the corner flower shop, Madame Lebrun called out a cheerful greeting. And old Monsieur Pillaut who was sweeping the sidewalk in front of the restaurant next door told Camille how much he'd missed her pretty face.

It was difficult to remain detached from the very pulse of the city that had won her fourteen-year-old heart when she'd first been introduced to it.

As she crossed the Pont Saint-Louis to the Île de la Cité, the larger island that had been medieval Paris, Camille couldn't help but feel she was a part of the city once more. Down below, one of the glass-topped *bâteaux mouche* allowed its passengers a romantic view while it sailed along the Seine. Ahead was the rounded apse of Notre-Dame. Camille could see the Gothic structure from her bedroom and had often curled up on the window seat to watch the setting sun cast its fiery glow around the silhouetted cathedral.

Skirting Notre-Dame, she crossed another bridge to the Left Bank and headed for Saint-Germain. She knew that only a month ago the trees that lined the famous boulevard would have seemed grotesquely gnarled by excessive pruning, but now their limbs stretched and sprouted new growth while perfuming the air with the scent of spring.

It wasn't fair, Camille thought sadly. Everything in Paris made her ache to be with Justin.

She forced herself to think of Genevieve, and the clear blue sky suddenly seemed overcast. Camille shivered in spite of the sun that beat down on her as she reviewed the plan Richard had suggested. She told herself it would work. One of them would find Genevieve and devise a way to trap her.

For once in her duel with Genevieve, Camille hoped the advantage would lie with her. To that purpose, she'd worn a sophisticated outfit that was as far removed as she could find from her more colorful New York City wardrobe. Luckily Max hadn't cleared out her closets or drawers after she'd disappeared from Paris. Her silver-gray suit with its matching silk blouse spelled haute couture, and the slender-heeled pumps and small clutch were of the finest gray Italian leather. In a disposable plastic bag she carried gray-tinted sunglasses and a chin-length black wig that would camouflage her eyes and hair.

Two could play at disguise.

As she approached the Café Belle Epoque, she saw that Max and Richard were already waiting for her. They sat at one of the tiny marble tables outside among rank upon rank of chairs facing the fast-moving traffic.

His golden hair windblown, Richard slowly lifted his eyes from the hem of Camille's calf-length skirt to the jet pin resting above the swell of her breast. He allowed his hot gaze to linger there momentarily before meeting her eyes. He reminded Camille of their first encounter at a yachting party. The difference lay in his affect on her. While she'd been flattered then, now she was merely annoyed.

"You must practice that hungry look," she criticized, sitting down in an empty chair next to Max. "But I'm neither the appetizer nor the dessert anymore." As a matter of fact, in the mood she was in, she would be tempted to hit him if he continued with his nonsense.

"Let's get on with it," Max said. His terseness made it obvious that he too was on edge. "I ordered another café au lait when I saw you coming."

"Good. I could use it. When this thing is over, I'm going to sleep for days. So what did you two find out?"

"I've narrowed the places to which Genevieve might take coins of so great a value to four," Richard told her, pulling out a list, "the most prominent and legitimate of which is

closed on Monday. Of course that doesn't mean she can*
contact the owner at home."

"Let's hope she doesn't know who he is," Camille mut
tered, glancing at his list. "So there are three left, one fo
each of us to investigate."

"I don't know if you're familiar with Cour aux Anti
quaires, but it's an arcade on the Right Bank that houses
more than two dozen dealers. Max will head there looking
for Jean-Claude Devaux, a man with a special interest in
coins.'

"He's legitimate?"

Max nodded. "As far as we can tell. But remember, the
coins haven't been reported missing. If Genevieve makes up
a believable enough story about them coming from a pri
vate family collection, Devaux might be tempted to buy, no
further questions asked."

"La Madeleine." Camille noted a Monmartre address. A
sleazy area at best. "Is that where you want me to go?"

"Too dangerous," Richard said a touch too quickly.

"The neighborhood or the proprietress?"

He grinned. "Both. I'll take her . . . uh, it. You can check
out Galerie Sorel at Place de l'Odéon."

"An art gallery?"

"A front, or rather, legitimate art in the front of the shop,
various other commodities in back," Max explained. "The
place is owned by the Sorel brothers. Ask for Guy, but be
careful, my girl."

Richard seemed as concerned for her safety as her fa
ther. "Pretend you're interested in buying then stall him if
he seems overeager. Max and I will handle him from there."

Camille had a difficult time acknowledging his attitude as
anything but patronizing. Still, knowing Richard was
thinking of her welfare, she remained silent while vowing to
use her own judgment, no matter what the situation.

The waiter finally brought her French coffee. It was another of the small things she'd missed during the past few months. She added two lumps of sugar—not the pristine white ones that were served in the U.S., but uneven brown chunks—to the thick espresso and foaming cream.

She savored the rich brew while they discussed their plans further.

If she didn't get an immediate lead, she'd keep an eye on Galerie Sorel for the remainder of the day. So would Richard and Max with their assignments.

They hoped that Genevieve would show up at one of the three places. Whoever spotted her would follow her wherever she went. Richard handed Camille and Max the phone number of a message service so that they could call in every hour or so to coordinate their activities in case of a breakthrough.

Camille was eager to get started.

Wishing the two men good luck, she kissed Max, who was taking care of the check, and headed for the ladies' room. There she brushed her long hair up off her neck and back from her forehead. After clipping it in place at the crown, she pulled on the sleekly styled black wig, which she'd once used for performances. The transformation was amazing. With the sunglasses in place, her own father wouldn't recognize her.

If he'd still been around when she left, she might have tested him.

Her thoughts were not quite so frivolous a few minutes later when her taxi dropped her off at the Left Bank address of the Galerie Sorel. The enormity of the task she'd set for herself had finally hit her. This was no game she was playing. It was reality, and one that could prove to be frightening and even dangerous at that.

Her stomach knotted alarmingly as she passed throug[h] huge wooden doors that led to a courtyard. Following t[he] directions lettered on a beautifully crafted sign, she climbe[d] a set of steps that led to the art gallery. Camille hesitated [a] moment before opening the door. A small bell tinkled, a[n]nouncing her arrival.

"Good morning." A youngish man, in his twenties pe[r]haps, greeted her before she had a chance to close the do[or] behind her. "Is there something special you'd like to see?["]

Guy Sorel, she thought, but what she said was, "I haven['t] been here before. I'd like to look around, if that's all rig[ht] with you."

"Of course," the pleasant young man said with a charm[]ing, very Parisian smile. "There are almost a dozen rooms[,] so take your time. If you need assistance with your selec[]tion, my name is Alain "

"I'll remember."

It was a surprisingly large place, though not very bus[y,] perhaps because of the early hour. Customers could hav[e] gotten lost wandering through the maze of paintings, prints[,] sculptures and textiles. That was exactly what she was tryin[g] to do. Camille realized as she strolled from one room to an[]other. She was putting off talking to the man she'd come t[o] see—but only until the knot in her stomach dissolved

What if that never happened?'

Taking a deep breath, Camille headed back toward th[e] gallery entrance, intending to find Alain. The bell signale[d] the opening of the front door. When she spotted Alain, h[e] was greeting another customer.

Camille stopped abruptly a room away from where the[y] stood. There was something about the young woman with[] orange-red hair that made Camille slip behind a wall hang[]ing as though she wanted to inspect its other side. Her view[] was slightly distorted, but she could see Alain and his cur[]

ent customer through the various holes in the finely crafted
macramé work.

"I'm here to see Guy Sorel," the woman said in French.
"He's expecting me."

"Your name?"

"Jeanne Dubois."

Catching her breath, Camille stared at the woman, who
was garishly dressed in skintight black stirrup pants and a
multicolored baggy sweater. Her ankle socks gleamed white
against her purple shoes, and her mismatched dangling
earrings accentuated the stiffly gelled red hair.

Jeanne Dubois or Genevieve Gendre? At this distance
Camille couldn't tell for sure.

"Yes, I think I remember him mentioning you," Alain
said. "Please come with me."

Looking straight ahead, the woman silently obeyed.

When the two passed on the other side of the hanging,
Camille got a better if brief look at the delicate profile,
which flickered at her through the holes in the macramé like
the frames of a silent movie. In spite of the layers of makeup plastered on the lovely face, Camille would have known
those features anywhere.

They belonged to Genevieve.

Wanting nothing more than to dash after the traitorous
woman and wrest the coins from her, Camille held herself
back. Caution was the keyword in enemy territory. Slowly
she followed through room after room, pretending to view
the artwork while heading inexorably toward the unknown. Her pulse seemed to pick up with every footstep,
while each breath seemed shorter than her last.

It was when she arrived at the fifth room that she realized the salesman hadn't taken Genevieve any farther into
the gallery complex. To one side a door stood ajar, allow-

ing Camille to hear the conversation of an inner chamber occupants.

"Mademoiselle Dubois, a pleasure." The voice was dee and slightly gruff. "It's been some time since you'v brought me business."

"I can assure you the wait will be worthwhile."

"Alain, if you will see to our other customers?"

"Of course."

Camille pretended to inspect a shelf of kiln-fired potter until Alain bustled by her, already alerted to another ar rival by the tinkling bell. When she was sure he was out o sight, she angled closer to the door, which still stood open a crack.

"Now what is it you have for me?"

"Some very valuable coins." Genevieve paused slightly before adding, "I appraised them at more than fourteer million francs."

"Fourteen...!" The gruff voice smoothed, now silk "You were right, my dear. A very worthwhile wait."

"Well, you needn't wait any longer, Sorel. I can deliver the merchandise today, assuming you can raise the necessary funds, that is."

"I could have—say a million francs—in an hour or two."

"Don't be ridiculous. I want ten."

"You always were a greedy one." Sorel sounded disapproving, as though chastising a naughty child. "You know very well I couldn't sell the coins for anywhere near their worth. Three million."

"Eight."

"Four, and that's my final offer." His tone turned hard, that of a shrewd businessman who knows when he has the upper hand. "I don't think you're in a position to bargain, or you wouldn't be so anxious to unload those coins today. Is the law breathing down your neck?"

"Law?" To Camille's utter disgust, Genevieve played the innocent to the hilt. "Why, these coins are part of my family's legacy, just as were the other things I brought you. It breaks my heart to part with them. But obviously you don't appreciate my business, so I think I'll offer the collection to someone more amenable."

Hearing Genevieve push back her chair as if to leave, Camille quietly moved in the direction from which she had come, pretending interest in various pieces of art so as not to arouse suspicion in case anyone saw her. Ears attuned to the two still sequestered in the inner room, she stopped when she heard Sorel ask Genevieve to wait.

Sorel accepted her offer, and they agreed to make the exchange several hours later.

Camille continued on, hurrying this time, anxious to be out of the shop and waiting on the street when Genevieve left. Planning to follow her straight to the cache before confronting her, she didn't want to rouse Genevieve's suspicions. Camille thought she'd be delayed for a moment when Alain spotted her, but another customer demanded the salesman's immediate attention and Alain turned regretfully away.

Hearing Genevieve's low laugh mingling with Sorel's—they were gaining on her!—Camille slipped out the front door. Without pausing to close it fully, she ran down the steps and out of the courtyard, her quick pace keeping up with her pumping adrenaline. Her stride didn't slow until she hit the noontime pedestrian crowd strolling along the sidewalk.

She was staring calmly into a storefront window a few doors to the south when Genevieve passed her.

Confident of her disguise, Camille waited only a minute before heading south also, knowing that even if Genevieve saw her, she couldn't possibly know she was being followed. When Genevieve passed through the gates of Luxembourg Gardens, Camille swore silently. Then she hurried to catch up so that she wouldn't lose her prey on one of the paths crisscrossing the formal gardens.

Camille was so busy watching Genevieve and trying to figure out where in a public park a coin collection could be hidden that she didn't notice a child chasing his ball across the path until she almost tripped over him. The little boy went sprawling, and a woman began screaming at her. Ignoring the hysterical adult, she righted the child, then looked around for Genevieve. She had a moment of panic before spotting the other woman on a crosswalk leading to the Boulevard Saint-Michel.

She ran in earnest now, cursing the expensive shoes that hindered her, and rushed through the park gate just as Genevieve commandeered a taxi. Looking around wildly, Camille spotted another empty cab and signaled its driver. He screeched to a halt, his rear tire mere inches from her toes.

"Follow that silver taxi up ahead!" she ordered in French as she climbed in.

Eyeing her suspiciously, the driver muttered, "I think you've seen too many spy movies."

"Please! They're getting away! I'll make it worth your while."

If he had serious reservations that money wouldn't overcome, he didn't voice them. The driver simply plunged his vehicle fearlessly into the traffic like a true Parisian cabbie. Camille was thrown from side to side as the taxi wove in and out of the dense noonday stream of cars, but the silver vehicle ahead was never out of sight. Finally it pulled over to a curb at Place Denfert-Rochereau, and Genevieve stepped out.

"Stop here," Camille told her driver. He did so with alacrity, and she handed him double the amount on the meter.

Obviously impressed with her largesse, he leaned out of the window and asked, "Would you like me to wait for you? I've always liked spy movies myself."

Camille smiled absently, focused as she was on Genevieve, who was walking up to an old, official-looking building made of gray stone blocks. But as the driver sped away, Camille suddenly became aware that she'd left her purse on the back seat of his taxi. Since she didn't dare draw attention to herself by shouting and waving at him, she'd have to put up with the loss of some money and credit cards. No matter. At least she'd left her passport at Max's.

Genevieve was lingering by a green metal enclosure attached to the building—an entrance of sorts—and furtively glancing around her. Camille, who was barely a dozen yards away, stopped an old man and asked for directions to the Louvre as a cover. The ruse worked.

From the corner of her eye she saw an unsuspecting Genevieve slip something out of a pocket before huddling close to the green metal door. Since the door didn't open at once, Camille was positive that Genevieve wasn't trying to use a key.

The thief was picking the lock!

A little trick her brother had taught her? Camille wondered, then was angry with herself for conjuring an image of Justin in her mind's eye. The man was out of her life for good. After all, she wouldn't want a personal relationship with him after what he'd done to her, and he certainly wouldn't want any part, personal or professional, of the woman who'd put his sister behind bars. Still, she couldn't help the yearning she felt for him, even now.

Waiting only a few seconds after Genevieve had swung open the green door and disappeared inside, Camille cut off the long-winded old man as politely as she could and headed for the building herself. Chest tightening at the thought of the coming confrontation, she tried the doorknob. It gave without a hitch. She opened the door carefully and scrutinized the unlit entrance area before her, hearing only the distinct sound of leisurely retreating footsteps.

Why should Genevieve hurry when she believed herself to be alone?

Not wanting to wander around in total darkness, Camille left the door open a crack and took off her sunglasses, setting them on a small table. The faint light filtering in illuminated a couple of darkened ticket windows, as well as crude handprinted signs announcing a modest entrance fee, limited hours of attendance and the sale of a guidebook in various languages. The place had to be a tourist attraction of some kind, but there was nothing to indicate exactly what it was. About to slip out onto the street to check for the identifying sign she must have missed, Camille heard two men arguing outside. From the sound of their voices they seemed to be standing right by the door.

Not daring to go out now, she hurried in the only other direction possible, toward the very thing she was avoiding—a winding staircase that sank downward into total darkness. Noting the shift in tempo of her heartbeat, she hesitated only a few seconds, long enough to prepare herself mentally as she did before entering closed places for her more complex illusions.

It was Genevieve's fault that she was frightened of dark, closed places, Camille reminded herself, using the memory to give herself courage.

Because she could still hear Genevieve's echoing footsteps, Camille took off her own shoes so she wouldn't alert the other woman to her presence. Descending the tight circle in the dark brought with it a dizzy sensation she couldn't control by sheer will. She hugged the wall, uncaring of the wear on her suit. She was more worried about the fear that was boiling in her stomach and looking for release.

She wouldn't let it!

This time, she would not give Genevieve the upper hand.

Her nylon-clad feet hit the cold slabs with increasing rapidity until she began to see glimmers of light regularly washing the walls just below her. At this point she realized that the footsteps she was following were louder, closer. She was rapidly gaining on an unsuspecting Genevieve.

Then the light was gone, and the footfalls changed tempo. Camille suspected that Genevieve was off the stairs, walking in a straight line. Even so, she wasn't prepared for the jar to her body when her foot met level ground instead of a lower step. She almost cried out, but the sound died in an expulsion of breath that she managed to control.

Pausing to steady herself, she fastened her gaze on a thin beam of light that now flickered ahead. She had a feeling that she was entering a narrow, never-ending tunnel.

Camille started forward with purpose, but it wasn't long before she had to stop to put on her shoes. The path beneath her feet had changed from concrete to gravel-coated earth.

What kind of tourist attraction could be down here, so far below the city streets? Camille had heard about the guided tours of the famous Paris sewers. If she wasn't careful about where she stepped, maybe she'd find herself drowning in the sewage.

She wished she could laugh, could share the humor of the situation with Max and Richard. But she hadn't had time to call the phone number Richard had given her and leave a message. She was alone in this. And she was afraid.

If only she could see. She'd give anything for one of her magic flashpots, even if the light did warn her prey. No, she didn't mean that. She couldn't fail now. She was just spooked by the dark and the close atmosphere, which reminded her of her recurring nightmare.

As she literally felt her way along the damp wall, Camille fought against the feeling of being trapped, of imagining the dank tunnel closing in on her until all the air was squeezed out of her lungs.

She wished her imagination wasn't quite so vivid.

The air was humid and impossible to breathe properly, but Camille sucked it up in large drafts. Moisture dripped from the ceiling in spots; she hoped that what chilled her when it hit her face and slid down the back of her neck was only water. Sheer determination kept her going, kept her putting one foot in front of the other, when every nerve in her body begged her to give up and go back.

But then, who knew what waited behind her?

Stop it! Don't start imagining terrors that don't exist! Camille warned herself.

She had enough to worry about, as it was.

It was becoming more and more difficult to follow the flickers of light, and they disappeared altogether at times. Genevieve was getting too far ahead.

The fact was brought home to Camille physically when she failed to turn a corner that she didn't see and ran straight into an iron grating in the wall. Her hand shot through an opening in the grating and her body whacked into the iron bars so hard that she could hardly bite back a cry of pain. She fell hard onto the gravel path, mangling her left arm in the grating in the process.

Rising carefully and nursing her injuries, Camille could only hope that Genevieve hadn't heard the rush of gravel spewing from under her leather soles and the sound of her skirt ripping when she went sprawling.

When she started off again, it was by feeling her way with both hands, one on each wall, ignoring the pain caused by the movement of her left shoulder and arm, and forcing herself to move faster than was probably wise.

She found other such iron-barred gratings along the way, blocking openings of some kind. Other tunnels? There were also places in the tunnel so wide that she could keep contact only with one wall, all the while hoping that the tunnel didn't branch off in several directions. At times she felt fresh air mingle with the thick, humid stuff she'd been trying to breathe for at least a quarter of an hour.

What kind of underground network could be so extensive?

Puzzling over this problem, Camille remembered reading about the centuries-old stone quarries that tunneled below much of Paris. That's where she must be, she decided with some relief. At least an abandoned quarry seemed more welcoming than a city sewer.

After an abrupt left turn, the ground sloped downward, rapidly taking her farther into the bowels of the earth. Camille ignored caution and rushed along, only hoping she was moving in the correct direction.

Suddenly she was almost upon the light, which now seemed fixed in one place. She hid behind a pillar so that she wouldn't come directly up to Genevieve, who was just a few yards away, her body clearly outlined by the light.

Still, Camille was close enough to read when, before passing through an open portal, Genevieve directed her flashlight at some lettering above it.

Camille's gaze followed. She translated the sentence carved in French on the door's stone lintel: *Stop! Here is death's empire.*

The skin crawled along Camille's arms and legs, yet when Genevieve passed under with a low, mocking laugh, Camille followed, albeit reluctantly and with renewed apprehension. She refused to consider the significance of the chiseled warning, ignored the knot in her stomach. It was only after she'd crossed the threshold herself that she realized she was immersed in total darkness once more.

She stood stock-still, trying to get her bearings, to make her eyes adjust. Listening.

But there was nothing. No light. No sound. Nothing but her own heartbeat and the involuntary ragged breathing she couldn't control.

The light had melted into the darkness, and the footsteps had faded away.

Genevieve must have turned another corner.

Fighting the sudden spate of fear that threatened to engulf her and leave her powerless, Camille reached out, searching for the security of the wall. Finding nothing at first, she moved farther into the blackness.

Finally she touched it.

Strangely enough, the wall's texture seemed to have changed. It felt lumpy, like small stones cemented together. Moving forward, Camille ran her hand a little lower. More lumps. Higher. Here the surface smoothed out somewhat.

A larger rock?

Frowning, Camille ran her entire hand over the surface. It felt brittle and hollow rather than solid. Suddenly her questing fingers went through a set of large, round holes, and she pulled her hand away, shocked.

It almost felt like...

Heart pounding, she hesitated before touching it again. But she couldn't help herself. She traced its outline to be sure. Two large round holes, a third oval between, ragged hollows below. Recognizing her own morbid curiosity, she moved her hand along the wall, feeling the ghastly pattern repeating itself. Stomach churning with the knowledge of where she was, Camille swayed as the smell of death and decay closed in on her.

Her nightmare was coming true!

She had to get out of there. But in which direction? Which way was out? She was dizzy with fear. Not wanting to believe she was truly trapped, she denied it, her words a mere whisper.

"Oh, God, no!"

"Ah, but yes, Clever Cammi!" came a gleeful reply as a beam of light split the darkness in two. "I'm so glad I didn't lose you after all."

Horrified, Camille stared at the now-illuminated wall of centuries-old human remains and knew the imbedded skulls were grinning blindly at her egocentric foolishness in thinking she could outsmart Genevieve Gendre.

Chapter Twelve

Trapped like a doe fixed by the headlights of an oncoming car, Camille remained frozen, her skin crawling at the sound of chilling laughter.

"You knew..."

"That someone was following me," Genevieve finished for her. "Though I wasn't sure that someone was you until I got a good look at you talking to the old man outside. I had no trouble seeing through those clothes and that wig." She clucked regretfully, the sound echoing through the tunnel. "And I thought you, as a magician, knew how to create a proper illusion."

Chagrined at her victorious tone, Camille moved with purpose toward the light but stopped abruptly when she saw the gun in Genevieve's hand.

"We have some distance to go yet. That way." Genevieve indicated the direction with her flashlight while waving the gun menacingly to punctuate the command. "Don't try anything foolish, unless you want to become a permanent resident of the Catacombs."

Genevieve would probably enjoy that, Camille thought as she obeyed.

They passed an uncountable number of bones stacked in precise piles, ends out, like so much firewood; and rows of skulls, which made a macabre design. Camille shivered even while she stared, as morbidly fascinated as those who chose to visit this unorthodox tourist attraction.

Though she'd vaguely known of the Catacombs, the dumping ground for several cemeteries that had been obliterated two centuries before because they'd become a health hazard, she'd never seen them for herself, nor had anyone ever described them to her. And even if some attempt at a description had been made, she would never have been able to imagine the manner in which this ossuary displayed the remains of six million people.

When they got to an open area containing an altar of sorts, Camille stopped. Was this where the priests had prayed over the millions of nameless lost souls? Who would pray for hers if she didn't figure out a way to overpower Genevieve?

Facing her tormentor, she asked, "Could you so easily add murder to your list of crimes?"

"Only if you tempt me, Clever Cammi. You know, I've often thought that name is quite inaccurate." Genevieve waved Camille on, down another tunnel, following closer this time. "You haven't been very clever at all these past few weeks, have you?"

"I don't know. I think I've done fairly well, considering I've never had to deal with anyone as devious and dishonest as you, Genevieve."

"I'll take that as a compliment, especially considering it comes from someone who married a professional thief."

"Don't consider yourself flattered."

"But why shouldn't I? I put on the performance of my life in New York City. I made you believe I was your friend. I even fooled my own brother."

"What was the point of that?" Camille asked, glancing over her shoulder but unable to see the other woman's face clearly because of the bright light. "An ego trip?"

"Not completely. Justin had something that belonged to me. You see, the day after I faked my murder, I realized I'd left a very important notebook in my apartment. It contained some vital information I needed, so I returned for it."

"But Justin got there and found it first," Camille guessed.

"I saw him go into my building, so I waited across the street. He was stuffing something into his pocket as he left. I went in to check, even though I was sure he'd found the notebook." Genevieve chuckled again, making the hairs rise on the back of Camille's neck. "Aren't you going to ask me what it contained that was so important that I came to New York and took the chance of his recognizing me while I was trying to get it back?"

As they entered another of the galleries of death, Camille thought quickly. Remembering the page of notations combining abbreviations and numbers, she stopped and turned to Genevieve.

"The code—directions about how to find the coins?" Camille had noticed that in some places there was nearly a foot of empty space between the top of the stacked bones and the ceiling. "Up there, perhaps?"

"Not quite accurate, but close." Sounding miffed that her guessing game had been cut short, Genevieve grudgingly admitted, "Maybe you're more clever than I thought."

"You're the clever one to hide the coins in a place of the dead, just where you pretended to be."

"It did amuse me. Of course, I meant to retrieve them once the heat was off and I could fence them without getting caught. I merely had to wait longer than I'd originally planned. Do yourself a favor and don't move."

Keeping the gun steady in her hand, Genevieve tucked the end of the flashlight under her arm and produced a small object from her sweater pocket. The notebook. She checked its contents carefully while keeping an eye on Camille.

For the moment Camille had no intentions of moving, but she figured that Genevieve would let down her guard sometime. Then she'd make an attempt to wrest the weapon from her. In the meantime, she'd keep her talking and look for a way to distract her.

"Your brother thought I stole that damn thing."

"You led me to the notebook yourself the day you came rushing out of Justin's dressing room, trying to pretend there was nothing wrong. Your emotions were so transparent that I decided to take a look in there myself. It didn't take me very long to find you'd left this on a shelf. I guess I should thank you for that," Genevieve said thoughtfully, "but I find it so difficult to be grateful to you for anything."

"What did I ever do to make you hate me?"

Checking the inscriptions on some plaques imbedded in the wall of human remains, Genevieve sounded almost indifferent when she spoke. "You replaced me in Justin's heart."

"What? He's your brother."

"Yes, and fifteen years ago I begged him to come home with me to where he belonged. He wouldn't because of you and your father," Genevieve said, her voice betraying her bitterness now. "Justin adopted the two of you as his family while he willingly abandoned me."

"Your logic is incredible."

"Everything about me is incredible, but then you should know that by now." Genevieve checked the notebook again, never allowing the gun to waver. Backing up, she seemed to have found the inscribed plaque she was looking for, because she began counting vertical rows of bones. "You were the one person I never could fool. I guess that makes you fairly clever after all."

"Not enough to figure out why you stuck around the club once you got what you wanted."

"I saw no reason to leave immediately, since no one had the slightest idea of who I really was. Why shouldn't I have stayed to see the opening? Magic has always fascinated me. You should remember that."

"I remember a lot of things about you," Camille said heatedly, "especially your locking me into Max's cabinet."

"But you never told, because you knew no one would believe that I could do such a thing."

Genevieve counted skulls, her hand stopping at one that looked no different from all the others. Without taking her eyes from her prisoner, she reached so deep into the gaping mouth that Camille suspected there had to be a hiding place in the wall behind the skull. A second later Genevieve pulled out a small leather pouch with a triumphant cry.

Camille's pulse picked up in tempo as she tried to distract Genevieve while inching her way closer. "I can understand why you got a job at Illusions and created Vivian, but why did you have to fool me into thinking we were friends?"

Genevieve's tone returned to indifference. She said, "Justin should have let me join his act, as I asked him to do. He refused me, but he didn't refuse you, did he?"

"That's why you tried to hurt me by rigging the elevator in the robbery illusion?"

Only a few more steps.

Camille heard the clink of coin on coin when Genevieve juggled the leather pouch and slipped it into her sweater pocket. Before she could take a bold step forward, Genevieve blinded her by aiming the flashlight beam directly into her eyes.

"I did it because I couldn't help myself," Genevieve said, sending a shiver along Camille's skin. She could tell that Genevieve was really enjoying the situation, relishing the fear that suddenly crawled up Camille's spine and befuddled her senses. "Not then. Not now. The whole thing gave me a certain pleasure it would be difficult to explain. All you need to know is that you're not going to walk away from *this* illusion, Clever Cammi. I hope you like the setting you've chosen for yourself."

Camille's mouth went dry and her heart began to thud. She had to find a way to get that gun! Now! Playing up the weakness she really did feel, she swayed, allowing her legs to take her a step closer to the other woman.

"Stop right there!"

Pretending distressed innocence, Camille clutched at the wall, hoping the skull she clung to would come loose in her hand so that she could use it as a weapon. It didn't. It was wedged in solid. If only she hadn't forgotten her purse in the taxi, she could have used it!

Even while trying to figure out what she could do to protect herself, she allowed her voice to tremble when she cried, "I thought you weren't going to kill me if I didn't do anything foolish."

Genevieve backed up, putting a safe distance between them. "And I thought you were familiar with all of my faults. In addition to everything else, I'm a terrible liar. I've gone too far to quit now."

"But murder..." Camille's horrified words echoed through the ossuary and along the rows of grinning skulls.

"The world thinks I'm dead. How can a dead person be accused of murder? Too bad you caught on while my own brother didn't."

"But he did. He knows."

"I don't believe you." Genevieve's laugh was chilling. 'You're trying to—"

Her words were cut off by a male voice, which came from the direction of the doorway. "Believe it, Genevieve!"

Justin!

As he stepped into the circle of light, Camille realized that she'd never been so glad to see anyone in her life. She wanted to run to him, to feel his arms around her. But unable to interpret his expression as he stared at his sister, she couldn't move.

Did his arrival mean she would be safe—or sorry?

JUSTIN DIDN'T WANT to believe the exchange he'd heard a moment before. That his sister had faked her own murder was bad enough. Now she'd threatened Camille and had talked about the pleasure murder would give her. But she couldn't be serious.

"Oh, Justin!" Genevieve exclaimed. "Thank God you found me. You have no idea—"

"I think I have," he said grimly.

"No! Nothing is what it seems. Really." Genevieve's voice took on a familiar heartbroken tone, which she'd perfected when she was a child. It had worked on him then, but he recognized the artifice for what it was now. Her pleading left him cold when she said, "I can explain if you'll only give me the chance."

"You have an excuse for stealing two million dollars in coins and then pretending to be dead?"

"Yes! It wasn't even my idea. *He* forced me into it."

"And who is this mysterious person?" Camille demanded, her tone ripe with skepticism. "Or is *he* someone who lives in your warped mind?"

But Genevieve ignored her, concentrating on Justin. "I'll tell you everything later. But now you have to help me." If his eyes hadn't been opened to his sister's treachery and practiced deceit, he might have believed her when she made her voice tremble. "Your partner came after me and threatened me with this gun. I got it away from her. I'm only protecting myself."

"Don't try to lie your way out of this, Genevieve," Camille cried, her voice unnaturally harsh. "You can't fool Justin anymore."

"Don't listen to that woman! I'm your sister, your flesh and blood. You've got to protect me from her. She's dangerous. You have to believe me."

Genevieve had lying down to such an art that Justin doubted whether she even knew what the truth was. But he had to try to save her in spite of herself. As she'd said, she was his sister. He'd walked away from his responsibility to her once, but he couldn't do so again.

"All right," Justin said, hardly looking Camille's way. "You can give me the gun, Genevieve. I know how to use it if I have to."

He could feel Camille stiffen next to him. Damn the woman! Didn't she trust him enough to know that he'd never hurt her? He loved her and was trying to protect her, for God's sake!

If Camille believed his ruse, Genevieve wasn't buying. He could tell she was trying to play for time while pretending to be the injured innocent party. "You could overpower her with your strength, but I couldn't. I think I'd rather keep the gun myself."

Justin realized the time for pretense was long gone. "Give me the gun."

Instead of handing it over, his sister trained the weapon on him. "I said no."

"Are you going to shoot me then? Your own brother, your flesh and blood?"

"I'd hate myself for it, but I will if I have to. It's obvious you won't believe a word of my story."

He couldn't believe anything she told him anymore. He knew it, should have known it long ago. This wasn't the Genevieve of his heart. The woman with the gun was a stranger. Perhaps the sister he'd loved had never existed, except in his own imagination. Staring at the gun in her hand, he felt something in him die, yet he couldn't give up yet.

"Listen to me, Genevieve. It's not too late to start over. Let Edouard Roget have his damn coins," Justin pleaded. "Chances are he wouldn't prosecute. The only thing you'll have to worry about is explaining to the police why you faked your own murder. If you're lucky, they'll let you go with nothing more than a severe reprimand."

"You must be dreaming if you think I'll hand over more than fourteen million francs to that pompous fool. I *would* rather kill you first."

"She'll do it, Justin," Camille told him. "She'll kill us without blinking an eye."

"Actually, the thought of all the money I'll get for the coins in my pocket is making me feel rather generous toward you both. I have something more stimulating in mind than shooting you. I have no doubt you'll come out of this alive. Eventually." Genevieve stepped back, waving the gun. "This way."

Justin would have tried to grab his sister as he passed her, but he couldn't take the chance. He'd never forgive himself if Camille got shot in the process. They didn't have far to go before reaching one of the iron-grated gates that barred the way to a side tunnel. Genevieve ordered Justin to stop and undo the thick twisted wire that held the gate shut.

As they made their way along the tunnel, she said, "I'll bet you're wondering how I know the Catacombs so well.

One of my lovers was an important city official who had access to this place. He gave me a very interesting and very private tour late one night. Did you know there's an area called the Crypt of Passion?'' Her low laugh was wicked. ''An appropriate name, as he showed me.''

An unwelcome image of his sister, surrounded by skeletal remains and locked in a passionate embrace with her lover made Justin shudder. ''Is that where you're taking us?''

''No. I plan on leaving you right in here.'' Her flashlight illuminated a rough-hewn wooden door set into the stone wall facing them. ''Open it and go in. Carefully, now.''

Justin obeyed. He pushed Camille in first, thinking to protect her while he overpowered his sister. But before he had a chance to try anything, he felt metal pressed into his back. Controlling the urge to do something foolish—or deadly—he entered the chamber.

''Toward the end of World War II, the Catacombs were the headquarters of the French underground in Paris,'' Genevieve went on informatively. ''Charles told me that the Resistance set up this room as a holding tank for German prisoners. He pointed out that the means the French used to keep the Germans subdued is still in working condition.''

She swept the opposite wall with light so that Justin could see sets of chains, each set attached to a spike pounded into the mortar.

''You can't really mean to leave us locked in here.''

Though Camille whispered the words calmly, Justin could sense her fear. He reached to comfort her, but when she went rigid at his touch, he withdrew his hand.

''Think of it as a challenge to your skills,'' Genevieve said. ''But then, you never did like escapes much, did you, Camille? I guess you'll have to trust my brother to get you out of here—if he can,'' she added with relish. ''Even though he's a first-class escape artist, he might have some trouble with rusty old locks like the ones on these chains, since he can't possibly have a key. And of course, they aren't rigged with false rivets, are they? It'll be a real test of your true talent, won't it, Justin, dear?''

"I've always been very good at meeting challenges," he told his sister dryly.

Genevieve ignored Justin's sarcastic reply and pinned him in the beam of the flashlight. "Justin, get over there to the spike farthest to the left. Hold out your hands where I can see them. Cross your wrists. Camille, you can do the honors and lock my brother up. I'll be watching closely, so don't try to get away with anything, either of you. I will shoot if I must."

Camille slowly followed the beam of the flashlight.

Knowing this would be his only chance to get a good look at the thing, Justin studied the thick chain hanging from the spike and the thinner chain linked to it. Two small loops had been made in the thinner chain, and an open padlock sagged from the free end. He realized that the looped chain was similar to the German transport chain, which the German police had once used exclusively for transporting their prisoners—and which Houdini had used in some of his escapes.

Justin stared at Camille's shadowed face as, reluctantly obeying Genevieve's orders, she forced a loop of chain over each of his hands and pulled the rest over his crossed wrists. Furtively she tested first the chain and then the padlock for weaknesses before locking the twisted chain in position.

She glanced directly at him, her expression questioning. Her nostrils flared and she took a deep, trembling breath. Recognizing her growing fear, Justin kept his own face blank. He hoped that she didn't realize there was no way he'd be able to get at the lock with the chain tightly entwining his crossed wrists.

He wasn't at all sure he'd be able to accomplish the escape.

"Now move away from him carefully," Genevieve ordered Camille. "Over to the right."

Realizing that Camille had stiffened and fearing that she was going to make a desperate try for the gun, Justin quickly snapped, "Do as she says," and with more certainty than he felt, added, "Trust me. I'll get us out of here."

With a sharp nod of acknowledgment, Camille moved to the right, never taking her eyes off Genevieve. "You won't get away with this, you know."

"Who is there to stop me? By the time you two get loose, I'll be long gone. Camille, stop there at that spike. Get your hand in that first loop and hold out the other."

Justin watched his sister put the end of the flashlight under her arm so that she had one hand free. Then she shoved the gun directly into Camille's stomach and moved in to push the second loop of her chain into place. His mouth went dry as he prayed the woman he loved wouldn't do something brave and stupid. Then Genevieve twisted the rest of the chain over Camille's crossed wrists, snapped the padlock shut and stepped away, and Justin realized he could breathe normally again.

"I'll find you, if it's the last thing I do," Camille promised Genevieve. "And when I do, you won't have the upper hand."

"You don't have what it takes to defeat someone like me. If we ever meet again, you won't know it, because I'll be a new person. Literally. I don't merely don different colored wigs like this one and expect to fool the world," Genevieve said, snatching the black wig from Camille's head, "though this might come in handy at the moment. If I were you, I wouldn't try to make any new friends in the future."

"Tell me something. If Justin hadn't come along, would you really have killed me?"

As she backed toward the exit, Genevieve laughed, the sound bouncing creepily through the small room. "You'll never know, will you?"

With that she left, slamming the wooden door. A metal clunk followed by a scraping sound told Justin that she'd locked it from the outside and taken the key with her. He didn't mind when the blackness closed in on him, but then unlike Camille, he'd never been afraid of dark, enclosed spaces.

Worried, he asked, "You okay?"

"Yes."

She didn't sound okay. The single syllable came out low and strained.

He gave the chain attached to the spike a series of sharp jerks. Nothing. Though he'd hoped some of the individual links might be rusted enough to split, they continued to hold fast. And no matter how he angled his hands, he couldn't get his fingers near the padlock—not that getting to the lock would be much use without one of his tools.

He could hear Camille testing her own chains, but mixed with the chink of metal was the sound of her uneven breathing. Justin decided she might feel better if he kept her talking while he continued to work on the chain around his wrists.

But before he could say a word, she asked, "Do you think you can do it, Justin?"

"Have you ever known me to fail one of my escapes?"

"But you told me that you retired because your heart wasn't in your escapes anymore, and you knew that it would be suicide to continue."

Justin stopped working on the chains and stared into the endless dark. Then, taking a steadying breath, he admitted, "I lied. My retirement was part of the plan."

"Oh." Camille was silent for a moment before asking, "Then you *can* do it?"

Avoiding a direct answer, he said, "If someone asked you who was the best at escapes, what would you tell him?"

"You," she admitted, sounding hopeful.

Not wanting her to know how worried he truly was, Justin tried to distract her from thinking about it. "How did you find my sister, anyway?"

"Luck. Richard and Max figured out the businesses where she might fence the coins. I guess you could say I was at the right place at the right time."

Justin held his arms akimbo, forcing one hand to lie lengthwise over the other. "If you asked me, I'd say Sorel's was the wrong place for *you* to be." But what he was doing seemed right. With his elbows straight out, there was a little slack in the transport chain.

"Yes, I guess you would think that since it means you've ended up a prisoner here with me," Camille said bitterly. "What did you plan to do before I interfered? Help her escape?"

"Damn it, Camille! Don't put words into my mouth. I was thinking of your welfare. Sorel can be dangerous."

"I—I'm sorry that I find it difficult to trust your motives. But you can hardly blame me after everything that's happened between us." Justin thought she'd finished, but she softly added, "And maybe the dark is getting to me. I can almost feel the walls closing in...."

"Hang in there." He tried working one hand free, but to no avail. He needed more slack. "You're not alone."

"You wouldn't understand. You're not afraid of the dark."

"Maybe we're simply afraid of different things."

"St. Cyr afraid?"

"No, not St. Cyr. Justin, the man."

He didn't explain that he was afraid he'd lost everyone who ever meant something to him. His mother and father, who had died. His sister, who'd been as fake as one of his own illusions. Camille, who'd mistakenly trusted him. And the man who had been a second father to him—Max would never forgive him for what he'd done to Camille.

He didn't say anything, because he was too busy trying to give himself the slack he needed by pulling on the chain with his teeth. Compacting his left hand as best he could, he tugged on it, using sheer strength to inch it through the narrow loop.

"Justin?"

Not wanting to lose his slight advantage, he didn't reply, merely grunting at her while continuing his painful task.

"Justin, is something wrong?"

He grunted once more. With his teeth he was pulling the chain on his right wrist tighter while forcing the widest part of his left hand through the loop. The way his flesh was feeling, he wasn't too sure if he'd ever be able to use the abused hand again.

"Justin, answer me, please!" Camille demanded.

Finally he wrenched his entire hand through the loop and let the chain drop from his mouth. Getting the right amount of slack to pull his right hand through was a far simpler task.

"I've got it!"

"Thank God! I thought . . ."

"That I couldn't do it?" He let the chain drop against the wall. In his relief, he couldn't help teasing her while he felt his way across the room to where Camille was trapped. "If you were any kind of magician, you'd be able to free yourself too.''

If he'd expected her to laugh, he was sadly disappointed. Her sudden renewal of fear was a tangible thing. Hearing her indrawn breath, he found her shoulder and knew her trembling was due to his words.

''Damn it, Camille!'' he swore under his breath as he felt his way down her arm to her hands. ''I know what I did to you in New York was rotten, but can't you find it in your heart to trust me a little?''

''I trust you as much as you trust me.''

''I guess I deserve that.'' Justin tested the transport chain. He could tell that it was looser on her. ''Getting the chain off you will be easier than it was for me.''

Justin explained what she needed to do with her hands while he worked the chain for her. Though the process was somewhat easier for her, as he'd predicted, he still heard a muffled moan. But when she was freed, Camille didn't complain.

Instead she murmured, ''Now all we have to do is get through that door.''

''It'll be a piece of cake, but only if you have some kind of tool on you. I'm afraid I didn't come prepared.''

''I did, but I lost my purse.''

''Great. Have you got anything on you I might use? A piece of jewelry?''

''The clip in my hair!'' He heard the *plink* as she undid it. ''Here.''

His hand closed over hers, trapping the makeshift tool within her fist. ''I'll do my best, Camille.''

''I know you will. If anyone can do it, you can.''

She allowed him to grasp her wrist and lead her across the room to the opposite wall. He found the thread of her pulse and noted its jagged surge—because he was touching her or because she was still frightened? He'd reached for and found the door with his free hand, yet he was reluctant to let her know. He didn't want to stop touching her.

"If only we had some kind of light," Camille said, as he continued to shift around as though he were still looking for the right place. "Don't you have matches for those cigarettes of yours?"

"Some, but I think we'd better save them in case we need light to find our way once we get out of here." He stopped and felt for the metal plate at the door's edge. "I'm used to opening locks in the dark anyway."

"Locks you've worked on before," she murmured, trying to pull her hand away.

Justin wouldn't let go, yet. Her wrist tensed under his firm grip, and he could feel her pulse speed up. Knowing he might never again have another chance to be this close to the woman he loved, he could barely restrain himself from wrapping Camille in his arms and kissing her; knowing his embrace wouldn't be welcomed, he didn't make the move.

"If it means anything to you, Cammi, I'm sorry."

"You said that before."

"But you didn't believe it."

"Should I have?"

"Yes, though I can understand why you didn't. For what it's worth, I want you to know that I care about—" Justin swallowed hard. If it was confession time, then he might as well go all the way. "That I love you."

She jerked her arm away. This time he let her.

"And of course you expect me to believe whatever you choose to tell me," she accused, her voice breaking. "Just as I believed all your other lies."

"It's the truth."

"Stop it! I don't want to hear any more. Actions speak louder than words, Justin, and you used me very badly. Do you think I can forget so easily?"

"Forget? No. Forgive? I hope so."

Justin turned to the door. He didn't say another word while he worked on the lock with Camille's metal hair clip. He could feel the anger and resentment pouring from her, though she too remained silent. Nothing he could say would convince her of the truth.

It wouldn't matter if he told her he'd been devastated when he'd thought her a partner in murder, or that he'd felt as guilty as hell for using her when he'd known she was innocent, or that he'd been both elated and worried when he'd spotted her outside the Galerie Sorel, where he'd gone to buy information about his sister's activities. He was sure Camille wouldn't believe any of that, any more than she'd believe he'd been furious while following her through the tunnels leading to the Catacombs, inwardly cursing himself, because he knew it was his fault that she was putting herself in danger.

Even as he heard the snap of metal indicating that he'd mastered the lock, Justin St. Cyr felt helpless. For once in his life all the magic in the world couldn't help him. Camille Bayard would never believe him, would never love him in return.

He was forever trapped in a lonely, loveless illusion of his own making.

FOR ONCE IN HER LIFE Camille was glad to be trapped in the dark. At least she could hide the tears that were swimming in her eyes from the man who'd put them there.

Why did Justin choose to tell her he loved her when she could never believe it? Why did he try to give her hope when she knew it would go unfulfilled?

Suddenly the sharp clunk of metal pierced through her silent thoughts, and she forced emotion back. She had to remain calm and collected. She had to get out of there before the walls started closing in on her once more.

"Come on!" Justin ordered, finding her wrist.

Camille didn't fight him this time. She had no desire to wander alone through her living nightmare. She knew Justin would do his part to get them out of this hellhole even if she couldn't trust him to do anything else. Whether she wanted to admit it or not, she felt safe with him.

They walked together toward the death and decay of the Catacombs. Camille sensed the place as they neared it.

"Which way do you think is out?" she asked.

"Since the tunnels leading off the path we came by are barred by iron gratings, I'd say there's only one route that goes all the way through. Whether we go back the way we came or continue in the same direction probably doesn't matter."

"Let's go on, then, and hope it's a shorter path."

Justin found his matches and lit one so that they could get their bearings. Ignoring the sightless eyes that seemed to stare at her, Camille moved on, telling herself that the dead couldn't hurt her as the living Genevieve had threatened to do. Careful to use the remaining matches only when necessary, they found their way through the ossuary quickly and, Camille noted with relief, silently. Justin didn't try to convince her of his feelings, and she didn't want a renewal of her emotional turmoil. Not now. Not until this thing was ended.

Only then would she think about what he'd told her.

Either the path they had decided to take was shorter or circumstances made it seem so; the winding stairway that would take them up to the surface was a welcome discovery. Leading the way, Camille rushed up the stairs, pausing only once to catch her breath. They emerged into a silent lobby, the door of which stood open to the street. She ran out to a deserted side street to breathe in the fresh spring air.

"It's so good to be out of that place."

"Come on," Justin said, already heading for the nearest busy street. "Let's find a taxi. I'm going back to the Galerie Sorel, and you can go on to Max's."

"There's no rush, Justin."

Turning to face her, he inched his way back. "Cammi, we don't have time to argue about this. I want to get there before she closes the deal with Guy Sorel."

"She can't." Camille slipped her hand into her skirt and pulled out a small pouch. She shook it, making the coins within jingle. "I picked her pocket with one hand while she was putting the chain over the other."

Justin's face turned red and he shouted, "Are you crazy? She had a gun in your stomach, for God's sake! She could have killed you!"

"I told Genevieve when next we met I would have the upper hand," Camille said, managing a weak grin. "And *I* don't lie. Besides, she might have killed us both anyway."

Justin turned his back on her and stalked off. From the stiff set of his shoulders, she could tell he was furious with her—an encouraging sign. He hadn't wanted her to be hurt. Maybe he could make her believe he cared. Sliding the pouch back into her pocket, she caught up with him. But he didn't pay any attention to her.

At the busy intersection, he flagged down a taxi and ordered the driver to take them to Place de l'Odéon, then subsided into angry silence. Unsure whether he was angry with her or with himself, Camille left him alone. They'd have plenty of time to argue later. He stared out the window, ignoring her completely, until they were barely a block away from their destination. And then when he spoke, it was to the driver rather than to her.

"The lady is going on to the Île Saint-Louis—"

"No, I'm not," Camille interrupted. The driver glanced back at her curiously. "I'm going with the gentleman."

"Don't be foolish," Justin growled, his face closed. "It might be dangerous."

"I've faced greater danger before and I'm still alive." She was unable to stop herself from adding, "No thanks to you," even though she knew that gibe wasn't completely true. He'd gotten her out of the holding tank.

Justin didn't retort angrily, as she thought he might. He merely fished inside his blue corduroy sports jacket for his wallet. He counted out French francs in silence.

The driver suddenly pulled over to the curb. "I can't go any farther," he told them. "Traffic's jammed up. The police have blocked off the area. But your address is right over there."

As she alighted, Camille stared at the large crowd gathered outside the gates of the Galerie Sorel. Cars were stacked back into the intersection, the drivers blowing their horns or getting out to curse the police, who were trying to clear the street. And in the distance, the wail of an ambulance pierced the air. The sound cut through her.

"What in the world is going on?" she asked, mesmerized by the confusion ahead.

"Let's find out."

Camille and Justin crossed the street quickly, running between the cars. Camille's instincts were humming, but she didn't try to analyze their message. Knowing only that she absolutely had to force her way to the front of the crowd, she squeezed through a knot of stalled pedestrians, who yelled at her angrily. She didn't bother to apologize. One last line of people was blocking her view. Suddenly she stopped trying to get through, and her gaze focused on the only thing she could see—a black wig splayed across the sidewalk next to a woman's hand, which was covered with bright red blood.

"Justin!" she cried, stretching out her hands to him as he burst through the front rank of the crowd and shoved a policeman out of the way. She followed him, clawing her way out into a small open ring. Two other policemen were about to help the first to seize Justin, who was kneeling beside a body. "No, leave him be!" Camille shouted. "She's his sister!"

In spite of her hatred for Genevieve, Camille felt tears well in her eyes as she stood over her. There was no mistaking the grief and guilt registered on Justin's face as he pulled his sister's limp body into his arms. Camille crouched down across from him, and from this viewpoint saw fresh blood still seeping from the hole in Genevieve's side.

"She's alive!" Camille told Justin, picking up a compress someone had made from a thin jacket.

Justin took the blood-soaked cloth from her and positioned it over the wound to stop the flow of blood. As though she recognized his touch, Genevieve stirred, and her pain-filled eyes fluttered open.

"Justin?"

The word was so soft it was almost drowned by the ambulance siren as the vehicle pulled up a few yards away.

"Don't try to talk."

But Genevieve ignored his order, and Camille strained to hear her. "Couldn't kill you. Or her... Knew you'd get free. Just couldn't resist the challenge of the coins..." Licking her lips, she paused before going on. "Cammi has them. Warn her..."

Her voice trailed off as she stiffened with pain. Hear
pounding wildly, Camille hovered closer, wondering why sh
should be warned.

But Justin demanded, "Forget the coins. Tell me who di
this to you."

Genevieve gripped his sleeve with bloody fingers. "He'
a master..." Her face a mask of pain, her voice a wea
thread, she slowly forced out the words. "...of illu
sion... will kill her for coins."

Then, eyes fluttering closed, Genevieve sank into uncon
sciousness. Justin was pushed out of the way, and Camille
could only stare as two men in white carefully lifted his sis
ter onto a stretcher. A renewed dose of fear pressed in o
her, threatening to choke her, as Genevieve's words echoec
through her head. Someone would kill her for the pouch i
her pocket.

Camille shivered as Justin helped her to her feet and she
was faced with the awful truth: the illusion had not ye
played itself out.

Chapter Thirteen

Camille stared out of the window, wondering how she was managing to stay on her feet. It was a little after dawn, yet the sun still had not broken through the early morning gloom. In contrast with the antiseptic cleanliness of the waiting room, the buildings surrounding the hospital seemed as grime-covered as she knew herself to be.

Though she'd scrubbed her hands and face in the ladies' room, her haute couture suit was filthy and torn, her Italian shoes were scraped and stained and her hair was a tangled mess. Turning from the uninspiring view outside, she sat down, thinking she should make another attempt to sleep.

The empty corridors of the quiet hospital reminded her of exactly how alone she really felt. She was exhausted, filthy, depressed and...yes, more than a little afraid, but not only for herself.

Hoping Genevieve would regain consciousness, she'd waited there with Justin all night. His sister had survived surgery in spite of the seriousness of her wound. The doctors predicted she'd live, but as far as Camille knew, Genevieve had not yet awakened to name her assailant. Justin was keeping vigil over her.

Master of illusion, Genevieve had whispered. Camill
tried to blank the words from her memory, but she faile
They echoed through her mind every time she tried to res
She refused to interpret them, refused to give credence to th
unacceptable fear that threatened to consume her.

Distracted from her thoughts by the sound of footsteps
she looked out to the corridor, hoping to see Justin. An
other nurse was making her rounds.

Longing and loneliness and the growing fear welled in
side her, threatening to spill out through her eyes. Sh
couldn't remember the last time she'd actually cried; sh
hated the burning feeling behind her lids. She lowered then
wearily. Exhaustion was making her imagine things, mak
ing her feel weepy again, Camille told herself, even as sh
knew she was telling herself a lie.

Lies. Everyone had lied to her. Richard. Genevieve. Jus
tin. Why should the rules be different for her? And ye
Camille knew she couldn't lie to herself—not about some
things, anyway.

At the moment only one truth gave her hope. She loved
Justin St. Cyr and with all her heart wanted to believe he
loved her in return. But as she'd told him in the Catacombs, actions spoke louder than words. To make her believe he cared, he'd have to show rather than tell, and
Camille wasn't at all sure she was willing to give him the
opportunity to do so.

Though she had to admit that Justin had protected her
first from his sister and then from the police who'd questioned him—he'd chosen not to turn in her or the coins—she
didn't trust him totally. Considering the way he'd used her,
was he any better a person than Richard? Even as she made
the comparison, Camille knew there was a big difference in
the motives of the two men. But there was very little difference in how their actions had affected her.

Fleetingly she thought about Richard. He and Max were waiting for another call from her. Earlier in the day she'd given them an abbreviated version of what had happened, but had gotten out of telling them the name of the hospital to which Genevieve had been taken. She hadn't been able to face either of them at the time in her shattered state.

A gentle hand nudged her shoulder. "Camille?"

Her eyes flew open to meet Justin's, which were pools of emotion in his drawn, stubbled face. "Is Genevieve . . . ?"

"Still unconscious. The doctor assured me she'd be all right, though he couldn't say when she'd waken. I decided I had more important things to do than sit around until she did. You might as well come with me."

He had already stalked out of the waiting room and into the corridor before Camille could even get to her feet.

"Wait a minute!" she shouted after him, making a passing nurse shush her. Camille was so tired that she could hardly keep up. "Where are you going?"

"To Max's. Your ex-husband should still be there."

She forced herself to go faster. "You want to see Richard?" She caught up with Justin near the nurses' station and grabbed on to the bloodstained sleeve of his jacket. "Why?"

Stopping suddenly, he gripped her shoulders. "Because he tried to kill my sister. Because he'll try to kill you if I don't stop him."

Releasing her, he strode to the elevator and punched the down button. Camille trailed after him, more slowly this time, trying to digest his accusation. Trying not to draw conclusions of her own. Trying not to feel relieved.

"Justin, you're not making any sense," she said finally. "You just told me Genevieve hasn't regained consciousness."

"She doesn't have to. Don't you see? She said to warn you. That he'd kill you for the coins." He was staring at her as if she were dense. "It's obvious the man is someone you know, someone who knew she might take the coins to Galerie Sorel. Richard knew."

Camille shook her head in denial. The elevator doors opened and they stepped in. "Richard couldn't kill anyone," she said, not caring that she had the attention of both the other people in the elevator. "He may be a thief, but he doesn't have a violent bone in his body. Not that I expect you to believe me, even though I was married to the man."

"He fooled you once. He could do so again. Besides which, those coins are worth a fortune. A man desperate for money might do anything to get his hands on them."

Desperate for money. Someone who knew about the Galerie Sorel. *A master of illusion.* Another magician. No, it couldn't be. She'd never believe it.

Then why did uncontrollable tears spring to her eyes and roll down her cheeks even as she denied the possibility to herself?

Swallowing the lump that tried to choke her, Camille whispered, "Justin, please promise me that whatever you find out, you won't do anything rash."

DID SHE CARE SO MUCH, then? Justin wondered bitterly as he took a last drag on his cigarette. He didn't even know why he was smoking the damn thing. It didn't make him feel any better. Crushing the Gauloises under his heel, he followed Camille into Max's town house. She'd gotten her tears under control before they'd even left the hospital, but since then she'd been silent and tense.

Richard Montgomery—con man, thief, possibly murderer. And she was worried about the bastard!

With one part of his mind Justin told himself he was a fool for loving Camille, while with another he only wished she could love him with the same intensity she seemed to feel for her ex-husband. Taking the stairs two at a time, he caught up with her as she stepped into the living room. Max turned from the window, looking only mildly surprised to see them.

"I thought I spotted you on the street, my boy. Why didn't you telephone? We've all three been waiting and wondering about your sister."

But Justin wasn't paying any attention to the old magician or to Edouard Roget, who rose from the couch. Vaguely aware of Camille stirring nervously beside him, he focused on the blond man in front of the fireplace, drink in hand. Richard stared back, acting as though he hadn't a care in the world.

"You're a thief and you intended to be a murderer, Montgomery, but you won't get away with it!"

"What the hell are you talking about?" Richard asked, seeming to be truly startled. "This is the second time you've tried to make me out to be a murderer, and all because of your scheming bitch of a sister."

Not needing more incentive than those words, Justin flew across the room, planning to choke the truth—if not the life—from the villain.

"Justin, stop!" Camille screamed from behind him.

Richard's glass crashed to the floor as he swung a punch. His fist barely skimmed Justin's cheek. The blow wasn't powerful enough to stop Justin from latching on to Richard's throat, but he felt himself grabbed from behind. Why was Max trying to stop him?

"Let me go!"

"He couldn't have tried to kill your sister," Max said. His voice was calm, but his grip was fierce. "Richard was with me when Genevieve was shot. We'd been here for more than an hour by then, worrying our heads off about Camille.''

Justin continued to strain against his mentor for a few seconds more, then allowed himself to sag backward. Justin obviously believed him, so Max let his hands drop. Looking around, Justin noted Camille's expression of relief. Had she been afraid that he would kill Richard Montgomery?

"Then I don't understand why Genevieve warned Camille as she did," Justin said. "I was so sure . . .''

"Your sister is not dead, I take it?" Roget asked.

Justin shook his head. "They say she'll live.''

"And my coins? Do either of you know where they are?''

Camille reached into her skirt pocket and pulled out the pouch. "I have them right here.''

Roget held out his hand. "Good. I'll take them.''

"Wait, Edouard," Justin said. "I want you to know I tried to persuade Genevieve to give the collection back to you herself, but of course she wouldn't agree. Her determination almost got her killed. That changed everything. Now the coins are evidence in her attempted murder, and they have to be turned over to the police.''

Before Roget could say a thing, Camille asked, "Why didn't you do that before, when the police questioned you at the hospital?''

"Because I had no intention of letting the man who shot my sister get away. I thought I could use the coins as bait to catch him.''

"I told you that you were wrong about Richard." Justin could almost feel the relief in her voice. "At least you can give the police the coins.''

Pouch in hand, Camille started across the room to Justin, but Roget grabbed her roughly and pulled her hard against his body. "I'll take those coins. *Now*.'' He snatched the pouch away from her before she could protest, then slipped them into his pocket. When his hand reappeared, it held a gun.

Justin's heartbeat accelerated. The barrel of the gun was pressed into Camille's right side exactly where Genevieve had been shot. His gut twisted as he realized his mistake, and he tried to play for time by pretending he didn't know what was going on.

"I don't understand the point of this." Justin walked toward him until Roget dug the gun hard into Camille, making her wince. "We're not trying to steal your coins," he continued. "The police will return them."

"I can't allow you to involve the police," Roget announced in a deadly tone, dispelling the image he had always projected of a fussy little man. Dangerous was more like it. "The coins have, shall we say, a clouded past."

"That's why you didn't involve the police when my sister stole them."

"When she double-crossed me, you mean. We plotted the switch together after Montgomery gave us the idea. Genevieve must have figured she could get away with the theft as long as I thought she was dead."

"Why would you want to pull a switch on your own coins?" Max demanded.

Max looked more helpless than Justin had ever seen him. The magician's terror for his daughter's safety was written not only on his face but also in his defeated posture, which made him look truly old as nothing else could.

"It was a matter of simple economics," Roget replied. "My business was failing and I needed millions of francs to keep it from going under. How I've kept it afloat this long is a testimony to my double set of books and my ability to juggle funds back and forth."

From the corner of his eye Justin saw a movement. Richard was going to try to overpower Roget. His first impulse was to stop Richard, but that might endanger Camille. Justin knew he had to do the next best thing—keep the Frenchman distracted.

Forcing himself to ignore Richard's furtive movements, Justin said, "You could have sold the coins."

"Selling them wouldn't have brought in enough money to save my business. I decided to have the coins insured, since they can't be traced back to an owner. These coins can't be identified. None of them are one of a kind, and of course coins don't have serial numbers. The plan was to sell the originals underground then sometime in the near future claim they were stolen—switched, if you will—and collect the insurance."

"Genevieve may have talked to the police by now," Justin told him, knowing Richard was about to make his move. He felt the sweat bead his body as though he were the one stalking Roget. "You still have time to get away with those coins. I swear no one will try to stop you if only you let Camille go."

"I certainly plan to take them, since they're my only liquid assets." Justin heard the coins jingle when Roget edged around a chair. Then the Frenchman backed toward the door, dragging Camille with him. "Paris is not the only cosmopolitan city in the world. This young woman will be insurance that you won't interfere with my getting to another of them."

It was then that Richard tried to jump him from the side. Roget was faster and whipped the gun around. It went off like a deadly firecracker.

In a second the muzzle of the gun was again pressed against Camille's side, and Roget was already dragging her out of the room when Richard sank to the floor.

"Richard!" Camille screamed.

Justin barely paused to check on Richard, who grunted, "Go after them!"

"Don't let him kill my daughter," Max pleaded from where he knelt beside Richard.

"I won't let anything happen to Cammi," Justin vowed with more fervor than certainty.

As he left the town house, Justin couldn't rid himself of the picture of a bleeding Genevieve looking up at him in pain. Then the face changed to Camille's....

By the time his feet had hit the pavement, Roget and Camille were halfway across the bridge that would take them across to the Île de la Cité. If the bastard so much as hurt Camille, he'd kill him, Justin vowed as he ran after them. The image of her panic-stricken face when she saw Richard fall stayed with him, but he decided it didn't matter how she felt about her ex-husband.

Maybe he was a fool, but he was going to save the woman he loved for another man.

WHILE ROGET FORCED HER along the walkway past Notre-Dame, Camille tried to figure out how she could get away from him. But thinking clearly was nearly impossible with his hand cruelly gripping her left arm, which was still sore from her misadventure in the Catacombs, not to mention the deadly weapon he was pressing into her side. She had no doubt that the man would shoot her as he had Genevieve.

Glancing over her shoulder as they passed the open square in front of the cathedral, where tourists gathered in groups to take pictures, Camille thought she caught sight of a familiar blue sports jacket. Sensing that Justin was following behind, she prayed he had a plan.

"I'm going to put the gun in my pocket," Roget informed her when they were near the police station, which stood opposite the cathedral on the other side of the square. "But don't think I won't shoot if you give me any trouble."

"Why don't you let me go now, before anyone else gets hurt?" she begged him, surreptitiously noting the uniformed policemen in the area. Two stood in the open entryway, another was coming through a doorway in the courtyard beyond and a fourth was stepping out of an official car at the curb. Surely they would help her, Camille thought as she asked, "Isn't it enough that you almost killed Genevieve over those damn coins?"

"I meant to kill her." The coldness in Roget's voice so chilled Camille that she abandoned her idea of signaling the policemen. "I'm only sorry I didn't succeed. None of this would be necessary if I had. She knew too much. I couldn't take the risk of her talking."

"And what about Richard?" Camille demanded, remembering how bravely he'd tried to rescue her.

"Undoubtedly Montgomery will survive. But if he doesn't . . ."

Roget's uncaring shrug was more eloquent than words. The man was horrifying.

When he'd found her in her dressing room at Illusions, Richard had told her he loved her enough to give his life to save hers. Then Camille had thought he was making nothing more than an idle boast, another attempt to win her back, but perhaps he had indeed seen his promise through, she thought sadly.

Roget rounded a corner and headed toward the flower market, which was on the other side of the police station. He pretended to fondle her shoulder rather than grip it. Then he dipped his head to the hollow of her neck. Camille shuddered when his wet lips touched her, even though she knew he meant nothing personal by the intimate gesture. She realized that if any of the uniformed men looked their way, they would think she and Roget were lovers, perhaps on their way to work after a long night together.

He certainly was making her heart pound—in fright!

Unable to tolerate her untenable situation any longer, she croaked out the thought uppermost on her mind. "And what about me? What do you plan to do with me, Monsieur Roget?"

"Your life is in your own hands." He sounded matter-of-fact, as though he had no feelings about the subject one way or the other. "I no longer hold anything against you, since you were so kind as to retrieve my coins for me. If you behave, you will live to see another day."

And if she didn't behave . . .

His unspoken threat was clear enough.

Genevieve had been correct in calling the man a master of illusion. Camille had never once suspected his duplicity in the theft of the coins. She'd thought Roget a fussy businessman, peevish at being thwarted but harmless, only to learn his was the most dangerous illusion of all.

She had to admit that this chilling discovery actually had come as a relief. When she'd assumed that Genevieve was trying to warn her about another magician, Camille hadn't really believed that her father could turn to crime merely because he was down on his luck, but Max had inevitably come into her mind. She'd been wrong about so many things since this misadventure began.

Maybe she'd even been wrong in judging Justin too harshly. Actions spoke louder than words, she'd told him. Well, he was taking action now, and on her behalf. If only he didn't lose them, Camille was sure he'd figure out a way to render Roget harmless. She had to slow her captor down in order to give Justin time to catch up with them.

"Oh!" she cried, stumbling slightly and letting her shoe slide off her foot as she stepped off the curb. "The heel must be loose, from my adventures in the Catacombs, I expect."

Feeling the gun jab her in the ribs through Roget's jacket pocket, Camille froze, the breath caught in her throat. Was she about to die a mere hundred yards from a police station?

"Hurry, then," Roget growled. "Get it back on."

Though he tightened his grip as she felt for the shoe with her foot, he didn't seem to see through her ruse. He didn't give her time to stall further, either. Once the shoe was back where it belonged, he forced her to cross the street to the flower market. Camille could only hope she'd given Justin enough time to spot her before she disappeared between the stalls.

Surreptitiously she looked around the market, searching for Justin. Catching sight of a blue jacket rounding the corner across from the police station, she sighed in relief and couldn't resist asking, "Planning on buying some flowers?"

"Your humor is not appreciated in this situation. Unless you want me to buy flowers for your funeral."

Camille decided it would be wisest to keep her mouth shut, however much she was wondering where the man was taking her. She figured she'd find out soon enough.

The Métro. She realized he was planning to take her into the subway as soon as she saw the Art Deco facade of an entrance a little way ahead. Wildly looking around for Justin as Roget pulled her down the stairs, she couldn't sight him. Despair clouded her mind for a moment, long enough for her captor to pull two of his *carnet* tickets from his pocket and insert them into the automatic turnstiles. It wasn't until she'd gone through the turnstile and Roget had caught up with her that she knew she'd missed a chance to escape.

"Can't you let me go now, Monsieur Roget?" she asked him. "You can get away. I won't try to stop you."

"And I won't give up my insurance."

Until he didn't need it anymore.

And then they were caught up in the melee of Parisians on their way to work. Camille's stomach lurched. She realized that it was up to her to figure out how to get away—and quickly! She might not have much time. Suddenly queasy, she figured her face must be as green as the metal stairway that led down to the bowels of the Cité station.

She was so exhausted that she could barely think. Roget pushed her aboard a train already waiting at the platform. But a minute later Camille realized that she wasn't alone after all. From her first-class car she could see through the windowed doors connecting it to a second-class car. There, in the middle of the passengers crowding into it, she sighted a familiar blue sports jacket pushing its way in and an even more familiar mustached visage above it.

Camille's heart soared. Justin hadn't lost them, after all! Her stomach calmed and her pulse quickened with renewed determination to outsmart the devious Frenchman. How could she keep Roget distracted so that he wouldn't see Justin? She had barely had a chance to consider the problem when Roget pulled her out of her seat at the very next stop, Châtelet.

She decided to try the shoe routine as soon as they stepped off the train. "Monsieur Roget, wait. My heel." But though she tried to get the shoe to fly off her foot, the Frenchman pulled her on, making her twist her ankle instead. Hot pain sizzled through her leg.

"If the damn shoe is so much of a problem, get rid of it," Roget growled.

Rejecting that idea, and gritting her teeth against the twinges in her ankle that attacked her with each step, Camille limped on. "How far am I going to have to walk?"

"As far as I tell you to. Now hurry."

"I'm trying."

Instead of going faster, however, she leaned her weight into Roget, purposely making the limp more pronounced. They were jostled by the hurrying Parisians, some of whom were rushing up to the street, others taking one of the *correspondances*, tunnels to other lines.

Just as Camille spotted Justin being pushed by the crowd in the opposite direction, Roget led her into a tunnel posted with a sign indicating the platform for the Pont de Neuilly train. It was a vast corridor of white tile, its starkness broken only by a disheveled bum sleeping on the ground, an empty wine bottle clutched in his hand. They were almost half the way along its length when several tawny-skinned, raggedly dressed children and teenagers suddenly appeared out of nowhere to surround them.

Gypsies. Thieves. Camille had heard that bands of them roamed some of the larger Métro stations.

"Get away from me, you filthy little beggars," Roget muttered as a girl kissed her fingertips, then touched him almost reverently.

He pushed the girl aside so roughly that she almost fell, but another took her place, then another. Before Camille knew how it had happened, she was separated from Roget. While two small children herded her to one side, a half-dozen older ones concentrated on touching and stroking him, deaf to his curses. Not wasting any time, Camille backed away up the tunnel, heading for the platform, but not before one of the teenage girls had picked Roget's pocket and relieved him of his coins.

As she tried to run in spite of the pain biting into her ankle, she heard Roget roar, "Camille!" His voice echoed off the tile walls.

Hobbling on, she glanced over her shoulder just as the edge of Roget's hand made contact with the thief's throat. He retrieved his pouch, and Camille faced forward again. Only a few more yards to the platform. She hoped Justin would be able to find her. She looked back to see Roget coming after her. He tossed aside a young boy who stood in his way. The Gypsies screeched in rage but didn't follow.

"Come back, or I'll shoot!" Roget threatened.

Her accelerated heartbeat filled her head with an inner noise that competed with both the explosion behind her and the ricochet off the wall to her right that immediately followed. Swallowing the fear that told her to obey him, she ran faster—straight into a solid body.

"Justin!" Wanting nothing more than to huddle against him and feel his safe arms around her, Camille frantically pushed at his chest instead. Justin didn't budge. His expression was hard; his eyes were narrowed at a fixed point behind her. "We've got to run," she yelled at him, bunching his lapels in her fists to stop him even as he seemed ready to push forward to get at Roget. "He'll shoot us both."

As if to confirm her statement, Roget fired. The bullet whined mere inches from Camille's ear this time, its closeness making her heart leap. Without saying a word, Justin grabbed her left arm and jumped back around the corner and onto the platform, whipping her with him. She moaned as her sore arm and injured ankle protested. Justin paid no attention. He was pressed against the tile wall, his dark head mere inches from the mouth of the tunnel.

"Stay back," he ordered tersely.

The echoing slap-slap of leather on concrete told her that Roget was almost upon them. "Justin . . ."

"Quiet."

She felt the tenseness in his grip before he let her go to ready himself for the enemy. The people on the platform were frozen in horrified shock at what they were seeing. No one uttered a sound.

Roget rounded the corner and Justin leaped. Both men went sprawling, throwing wild punches, rolling over and over. Roget finally landed on top. Using his gun, he savagely backhanded Justin in the face. Even from where she stood, Camille saw the blood spurting from Justin's nose and swore she heard the crack of his skull as his head flew back to hit the pavement.

Desperate to help him, she searched the platform for a makeshift weapon and found a discarded beer bottle lying under a bench. The crowds had melded together, but Camille was oblivious to them. When she turned to protect Justin, however, Roget was coming for her. She threw the bottle into his face just before Justin tackled him at the knees. The two men flew forward this time, and so did the gun.

Camille stepped on Roget's hand to get it. He screeched shrilly while continuing the fight by kicking sideways. His foot landed square in the middle of Justin's stomach.

Picking up the gun, Camille pointed it at Roget, yet she couldn't bring herself to use it in case she accidentally shot the man she loved. Justin was pinning him down. But a second later Roget freed himself and stood up. He was about to kick Justin again.

"Stop it!" Camille cried, her voice competing with the warning blare of an oncoming train.

Justin grabbed Roget's raised foot and twisted it. The man fell sideways and rolled half off the platform. His hands gripped the edge and he caught himself from falling the rest of the way, but obviously he was stunned and didn't have the strength necessary to pull himself up.

Unless Camille and Justin helped him, he'd be killed by the train, which was approaching the station at full speed.

Hesitating only a second, Camille stepped forward, and at the same time Justin rose to his feet and reached out his hand. He snatched Roget's wrist, and with a steady heave, pulled the panicking man to safety. He was slightly off balance when Roget leaped up. Tense and determined, Roget seemed ready to push Justin onto the tracks in his place.

Before he could do so, Camille's automatic reflexes brought the gun in her hand snugly against the hollow at his temple. "I can't miss at this range," she promised, just before the rubber wheels of the train shushed over the tracks next to them.

Brakes screeched and the train slowed. Edouard Roget folded in defeat, his dangerous illusion finished. Without lowering the weapon, Camille looked past him to Justin, whose gray-blue eyes told her of his thanks and more.

And without words, she let her own eyes tell him that his actions had indeed allowed her to believe in his love.

Chapter Fourteen

"What in the world were you thinking of to hide all of this from me, Monsieur St. Cyr?"

Antoine Fouchet drummed his fingers on the uncluttered surface of the utilitarian government-issue desk at which he was sitting. Justin, his face swollen and blood-streaked, stood with his back to the only window in the office Fouchet had borrowed. They were in the police station above the Châtelet Métro stop. Fouchet was the man who had been in charge of the investigation into Genevieve's supposed murder.

"You should have turned over the notebook when you found it, or at least when I questioned you at the hospital." Fouchet shook his balding head. "Hmm, suppressing evidence ... obstructing justice ... I could bring some serious charges against you."

"But you won't."

Justin thought he spotted a glimmer of admiration in the sharp brown eyes behind the wire-rimmed glasses before Fouchet echoed, "No, I won't. I don't approve, but I do understand. I'm merely thankful that neither of you was killed during this unfortunate episode. I do expect you to act as witnesses at your sister's and Roget's trials."

"We're both aware of that and are willing to testify," Justin responded.

Since he was the logical choice to handle the increasingly complex case, Justin had demanded that Fouchet be present when he and Camille made their statements to the police. Until Fouchet arrived, Justin had refused to answer any questions. While waiting for him, he'd called the hospital to learn that Genevieve had regained consciousness and was sleeping naturally. So she'd recover only to spend time in prison. After that Justin would offer her a new start, but he was realistic about his chances of getting her straightened out.

Relaxing for the first time since they'd been brought to the police station, he wished Camille would relax, too. She'd tensed up when she called Max and the phone hadn't been answered, and since then she had done nothing but worry about whether Richard was alive. Even now she sat uncompromisingly straight in her chair, absently running her finger along a rip in her skirt, concentrating on the tear instead of Fouchet's comments.

Justin had to give her credit. She hadn't tried to whitewash her guilt in protecting Richard from the police when he'd involved her in the coin theft. While the uniformed policeman had taken down their statements on a noisy manual typewriter, Fouchet had listened in relative silence and so far had not commented on that part of Camille's story.

Aware of footsteps on the stairs, Justin glanced away from Camille as Richard appeared in the doorway. His arm was in a sling, and this gave him what Justin feared would be an appealingly rakish look.

"Camille, love, thank God you're safe!" Richard said.

She whipped around at the sound of his voice, and her lips parted in a smile. "Richard, you really are alive!" The tenseness eased from her as he walked toward her. She rose and hugged him awkwardly, avoiding his wounded arm. "That was such a foolish thing you did, trying to save me. I'll never forget it, though."

Justin tried focusing on the view from the window, but hearing her concerned tone affected him as much as seeing her touch Richard. It was obvious that Camille still cared about her ex-husband. What a fool he'd been, Justin chided himself, for misinterpreting the look she'd given him in the Métro after pulling the gun on Roget! It had made him believe that he could still hope for a future with Camille.

"I called home to see if you were all right," Camille was saying. "When there was no answer, I thought Roget had killed you."

"Just a flesh wound," Max assured her, coming from behind. He stopped next to Richard and Camille. Justin noted that the old magician was a little out of breath from the climb to the second-floor office. "He'll live."

"How did you know where to find us?" Justin asked.

"*I* had them brought here." Fouchet drummed the desktop, as if to punctuate his words. "Before taking Monsieur Montgomery to the hospital, Monsieur Bayard called the police for assistance in rescuing you. In spite of what you might think, Monsieur St. Cyr, at least some members of the Paris police force can put two and two together and come up with four."

Justin felt properly chastised for taking the law into his own hands, if not repentant. Fouchet turned his attention to Richard.

"Now, there's a little matter of a stolen coin not currently part of the collection given to me as evidence. This young lady was kind enough to tell me all about it."

"Let me assure you, Camille is innocent," Richard said, facing Fouchet. "I stole the coin and used her as a pawn. She knew nothing until it was too late to stop me."

"I could arrest you for the theft," Fouchet informed him, though Justin was sure that, because of the strange nature of the case, not to mention the lack of hard evidence, Richard might never go to trial. "Or we could discuss a deal. I could use your assistance in a very important investigation I'm working on."

"I've always been good at making deals."

"Then perhaps we can negotiate." Fouchet turned his attention back to Justin and Camille. "The two of you can go. I want to take both their statements and then talk to Monsieur Montgomery alone."

Justin moved away from the window, but Camille stayed put, saying, "I'll wait with you, Max."

"No, Camille. You go home and get some rest. I insist."

She nodded. "I promise I'll get some sleep after I clean up," she agreed, kissing her father's cheek. "The way I look, I wonder that I didn't scare off those Gypsies."

From his view at the doorway, Justin couldn't see a thing wrong with her. He found Camille infinitely appealing in spite of her dishevelment, but then he'd take her any way he could get her. He didn't think he stood much of a chance to have her at all, however, when Richard placed a hand on her arm to stop her from leaving and she didn't object. As a matter of fact, there was a disturbing air of expectancy about her, as though she were suddenly charged with new energy. Did Richard have that great an effect on her, then?

"I know I've blown it twice with you now," Richard said, "and I regret it deeply."

Frowning, Justin backed away from the scene uneasily. The soft smile on Camille's lips couldn't have been meant to discourage Richard.

"Let's not rehash the past now," she said.

"Then let's look to the future. Since you were so concerned about me, I thought you might want to give me one more chance." Richard grinned at her. "They say three's the charm. If you love me half as much as I do you, we can make it work this time."

Not wanting to hear her reply, Justin decided it was time for the magician to make himself vanish.

GLANCING AT THE DOORWAY, Camille realized that Justin had left without her. Though she hadn't had an opportunity to tell him so in words, she thought he understood she loved him. At least they *seemed* to have been on the same wavelength during the shared moment in the Métro.

Throughout the past hour or so, however, she'd sensed his growing doubt about her personal feelings. Unfortunately, she hadn't been able to do anything about reassuring him. She'd been too worried about Richard and the awesome responsibility that went with thinking he might have forfeited his life for hers. But once assured Richard was alive, she'd felt her spirits soar and her energy renew itself.

Now all she had to do was convince one know-it-all magician that she was his for the asking.

Kissing her ex-husband on the cheek, she said, "I'll always care about you as a friend, Richard, but that's not a good enough reason for making a life together."

The corners of his perfectly sculpted lips turned down, and the expression made him seem less charming. "It's the ultimately ethical escape artist, isn't it?"

"I'm afraid so."

"I knew it all along," he muttered. His brown eyes held a hint of genuine sadness. "I was trying to fool myself into thinking you might come back to me. Well, you'd better go after him before he gets away."

Camille laughed. "He'll never get away from me. I'm a magician, remember?"

"Why don't you do a disappearing act *now*, so that I can get on with my work?" Fouchet suggested dryly.

"I'm gone." She hurried toward the door, but paused on the threshold. "Oh, Max, if I'm not home tonight, do me a favor. Don't call the police for reinforcements. I can handle this one myself."

"Good luck," her father replied warmly, his green eyes sparkling with humor. "I hope I won't see you till tomorrow."

She smiled at Max's not-so-subtle way of giving her and Justin his approval.

Feeling as though she'd just shed the weight of the world, Camille had to restrain herself from skipping down the steps of the police station, since her ankle still gave her a twinge now and then. Even so, she hurried, knowing that Justin had quite a lead on her. Once outside, locating him wasn't difficult. She'd had plenty of practice lately, and she could have spotted the blue sports jacket a mile away. Luckily it was only half a block ahead, moving in the general direction of the Seine.

Camille followed, hurrying, trying to narrow the gap between them. She pushed her exhausted body to new limits, even while wondering how in the world she managed to do so. An overdose of adrenaline was the only answer; she could feel the stuff now, whizzing through her veins, as she almost ran to catch up with Justin. She'd had enough shocks and scares in the previous few days to last her a lifetime. From now on, if she was lucky, all her excitement would be on stage—or better yet, in the arms of the man she loved!

While she was momentarily distracted by thoughts of the wonders that renewing their relationship would bring, Justin had managed to get away from her. Looking around, she realized he'd disappeared. Bewildered, Camille wondered how she'd lost him so easily. The street was lined with stores, but surely he hadn't decided to go shopping after all they'd been through. He had to be as tired as she was.

She slowed down, her adrenaline level draining to zero. She couldn't even rouse the energy to stare back at a passing woman who was sneering at her battered appearance.

All she could think about was that she'd have to wait until she got back to New York to tell Justin she forgave him and loved him in spite of the way he'd used her. The prospect seemed anticlimactic. Sighing in disappointment, Camille figured she'd better go back to Max's after all.

To that end, she turned around—and for the second time that morning ran smack into Justin St. Cyr.

Camille's spontaneous smile faded as she realized that Justin wasn't returning it. As a matter of fact, he didn't look at all welcoming. His body was tense, his stance aggressive. And yet, studying his tired, stubbled face, Camille concluded that his expression held a mixture of suspicion and longing, disbelief and hope. Her heart responded to his uncertainty.

"Why were you following me?" he demanded.

How dense could one man be? Unable to help herself from teasing him, she widened her eyes and pretended innocence. "Following you? I was merely taking a walk. Good cardiovascular exercise, you know."

Justin's mustache twitched an encouraging tad, yet he didn't allow himself to laugh or otherwise loosen up. He simply took her arm and steered her in their original direction, heading toward the Seine, which lay directly ahead. Camille neither protested nor tried to strike up a conversation, but waited for him to tell her what was on his mind.

They took the nearest bridge to the Île de la Cité. Stopping about halfway across, Justin turned her toward the railing facing west. As they watched the river drift by, he seemed to relax a little.

And yet his voice was rough and the words sounded final when he said, "It's appropriate that the illusion ends here at the river, since this is where it all began with Genevieve's supposed death." He was staring into the distance at the Pont Neuf, the bridge below which his sister's car had been found.

"The illusion ended in the Métro." Camille felt her throat tighten at the thought of saying goodbye to the man she'd hoped would be her partner not only in work but also in life itself. "But what about the magic between you and me, Justin? Must that end too?"

His expression remained wary, as though he couldn't trust himself to interpret the meaning of her words correctly. "You don't hate me for the way I used you?"

"No," Camille said honestly. "I hated what you did, even while I couldn't stop loving you. As I said, actions speak louder than words." She paused and touched the sides of his face gently, frowning at the ugly discolorations and puffiness that Roget had inflicted on him with the gun. "Does that feel as bad as it looks?"

He caught her wrist, and though his grip was firm, he didn't hurt her. "Forget about it. Go on."

"All right." He let go of her hand and she dropped it to the rail, then looked out across the Seine. Instead of focusing on the Pont Neuf and all the terrible memories it represented, she looked to her left, to the Eiffel Tower, the symbol of the city of love. "You did use me badly, but then you put your own life in jeopardy to save mine. Maybe I'm being foolish, but I guess that evened things out in my mind and made me realize you do love me. I can't say I approve of the way you went about trying to find your sister's supposed murderer, yet I know you never meant to hurt me."

"I didn't like what I was doing. I didn't like it from the beginning." Justin's tone was low and urgent and, to Camille's willing mind, believable. "It was something I was compelled to start, in spite of my conscience. Something I had to finish, even after I fell in love with you. Can you ever forgive me?"

"I already have."

She turned to him, allowing her eyes to meet his. Camille felt a welcome heat creep through her as Justin's hypnotic gaze seemed to enter her, searching for the truth.

Finding it, he took her in his arms, murmuring, "Oh, Cammi, you can't imagine how much I love you."

"I think I can, because I feel the same way."

She clung to him, never wanting to let go. He inclined his head, filling her with expectancy. Then their mouths met in a kiss that was at once tender and passionate and full of enchanted promises.

April in Paris. A time for lovers.

Love was in the air and in her life. Camille could taste it and smell it and feel it bloom inside her. This was what real magic was all about.

When Justin pulled away, she felt that he took part of her with him. "Shall I flag a taxi, or do you think you can handle walking a few more blocks," he asked, smoothing the tangle of her hair from her forehead.

"Walk to where?"

"My apartment."

Adrenaline frothed through her at the words. "What are we waiting for? I could run all the way."

In the end they walked, two battered, bruised lovers who clung to each other for physical as well as emotional support. Though she might be sore and weary, Camille felt more lighthearted and certain of her future than she had in years.

Somehow they made it to the Left Bank and to the building with the rococo facade that Justin called home when he was in Paris. With his arm still around her, he led her up the stairs to his third-floor flat. The last rays of sunlight shone through the huge living room, softly illuminating the gray dust covers on the couches and chairs.

"I didn't bother to uncover the furniture, except for the pieces in the bedroom, of course."

"You don't have to apologize." Facing him, Camille trailed her fingers up his chest and smiled mischievously. "Are you really interested in spending time in any other room than the bedroom?"

"Actually, yes." When her smile became a frown, he added, "The bathroom. We're both filthy."

"But we're in Paris. We could set a new fashion trend."

"I don't care about fashions or trends. I like my women naked and clean."

Bristling, she echoed, "Women?"

"Stop trying to pick a fight." Justin turned her around and pushed her toward a doorway. "Save it for later—if you have any energy left by then."

Since the energy she had now was purely fabricated, Camille decided to let him have the last word, but only until she spotted his large canopied bed. "That looks good enough to sleep in," she said with a sigh.

"First things first." Justin walked to another doorway and snapped on a light. "Strip and shower. I'll find you a robe."

"What kind of wily wizard are you, anyway?" Even as she complained, she began to undress on the way to the bathroom, leaving clothes where they dropped. "Can't you get rid of this filth with a simple abracadabra or something?"

He didn't bother answering, so she stepped into the shower and turned on the water, groaning as it pelted her sore muscles. She took her time shampooing and soaping herself, but when she was squeaky clean, Justin hadn' joined her. Disappointed, she stepped out of the shower. He was waiting for her with a fluffy maroon robe and a kiss that conjured up almost enough heat to dry her without help from a towel.

"My turn. Go wait for me in bed."

She took a towel anyway, and wrapped it around her wet head before doing as he'd asked. The bed was so comfortable that it felt like heaven. Still she couldn't help grumbling just a little, even if he couldn't hear her over the water.

"Haven't you ever tried saving energy by showering with a friend?"

Did she imagine it, or did he really say that when they showered together, they would be creating energy rather than saving it? She removed the towel from her head and threw it to one side.

Snuggling down into the huge pillows, she cocooned herself with covers and let her mind drift to warm, hazy places that sparkled with love...

Warmth was slowly transformed into blazing heat, and Camille wasn't sure if she was awake or asleep, aware of reality or caught in some illusion of her own creation. Opening her eyes, she looked out into the room beyond the canopied bed, now darkened but for candles shedding a light that shivered up the walls in sensual waves.

She turned toward that which created her inner fire.

Justin. Her dark sorcerer. Mesmerizing her with his molten eyes. Seducing her with his deft hands. Possessing her with his provocative manhood.

She must be spellbound.

For surely the ecstasy he stirred in her as he first stroked, then suckled at her breasts was part of some enchanted illusion. And yet as he labored over and within her, he felt as real and solid as any mortal man. Her man. Pulling him deeper inside her, she absorbed his flesh with her own so that they were as truly one as two could ever be.

Only twenty-four hours ago, she would never have believed they could be so close.

She stroked his chest, moving her hands around to his sides and down his thighs, wanting to give pleasure as well as take. He groaned and rolled onto his back, bringing her up over him, relinquishing his power and yet reinforcing it by running his hands up her belly to her breasts.

Camille moved in ancient rhythms of his choosing, powerless to resist the magic he conjured from deep within her.

How could she resist anything about him when she was in love with the man?

Justin St. Cyr was the first love of her life, and now Camille knew he'd be the last. It was as if destiny had chosen them to be together.

As the room seemed to spin and reality and illusion melded together, she could hold back no longer. Her cry of pleasure split the silence, drawing from him an equally joyous sound. He shuddered against her. Leaning over him, she pressed her forehead to his face and her breasts to his chest delighting in the slick sweat gathering between them.

They lay bonded together like that for what seemed eternity. She couldn't get enough of touching him, taking in the texture of his face through her sensitive fingertips. Watching his expression grow more contented with each passing second, she rimmed the cleft in his chin, letting her finger trail up to his mustache.

Then Camille frowned, for even in the semidarkness she could see the bruises on his face, an awful reminder of what they'd gone through before the fates had allowed them to be together.

Not wanting to indulge in morbid memories, she rolled over to lie at his side. The maroon robe twisted around her uncomfortably. Pulling the thing off and tossing it from the bed, Camille couldn't resist teasing Justin about it.

"The least you could have done was make that thing vanish."

"I wanted to save my powers for more important tasks," he said, flicking his eyebrow at her.

"More important—like what?"

Justin laughed at her faked innocence and she joined him. She needed laughter in her life again.

"I'll get you for that one," he promised.

"Any time. After all, St. Cyr and Camille are a team, right?" When he didn't agree immediately, she looked at him suspiciously. "Right?"

"You know, I've been thinking about that."

The gravity with which he spoke made her heart skip a beat. Was he about to tell her he didn't want them to work together any longer? "Thinking about what?" she asked.

"That it might be good for publicity if we could call ourselves St. Cyr and St. Cyr. What do you think?"

Camille sat straight up in bed. Unless this was an illusion, he was asking her to marry him! She was sure her heart skipped two more beats, but she kept her voice as casual as she could.

"I don't know. That's a terribly unromantic way to put it. You'd think a master showman would do things with a little more flair."

"Flair, huh?" Justin practically leaped out of bed, and Camille had trouble keeping her eyes above his waist, where his hands were sweeping the air. "The lady wants a little romance.'' Reaching behind her ear, he plucked a camellia from thin air. ''How's this for a start?''

Taking it from him, Camille realized it was a real flower, not some stage prop. ''Where did this come from?''

Ignoring her question, Justin was already pulling something out of a dresser drawer.

''Notice,'' he said, coming back to the bed, ''this is a perfectly blank piece of paper.''

''It's so dark in here that I can hardly see a thing.''

He moved a candle closer. Holding the paper for her inspection, he flipped it from one side to the other so that she could see it was indeed blank. Then he folded it into a small bundle.

''Now I'll say some magic words: Camille, I love you, and I want to marry you.''

With a flourish he presented the paper to her. Her hands shook as she unfolded it, even though she knew what she would find. She held the paper nearer the candle.

''Camille, I love you,'' she read, ''and I want to marry you.'' Frowning, she looked up at him. ''I accept on one condition.''

''What's that?''

''You tell me how you did this. A fresh flower—from where? And the note...'' She gave his nude form a significant once over. ''You don't have any secret pockets on you that I don't know about, do you?''

''Nope, I used magic, pure and simple.''

Not really wanting to spoil his illusion, she relented. ''All right. I'll marry you. But if you want our marriage to last, you'd better make sure you keep it full of magic.''

''That goes both ways, Clever Cammi.''

''Come here, and I'll show you some now.''

As Justin slipped into her waiting arms, Camille knew all her future illusions would be enticing ones.

Take 4 best-selling love stories FREE
Plus get a FREE surprise gift!